REDEEMED

Sharon Torbett

ISBN 978-1-0980-6094-7 (paperback)
ISBN 978-1-0980-6095-4 (digital)

Christian Faith Publishing, Inc.
832 Park Avenue
Meadville, PA 16335
www.christianfaithpublishing.com

Printed in the United States of America

CHAPTER 1
His View

There was something about that last town I didn't like. I felt so uneasy there that I didn't even stay long enough to eat supper. And I certainly didn't intend to sleep there. I'd rather sleep under the stars with my saddle for a pillow. But with any luck at all, I'd find a ranch that would put me up in exchange for some work. The sun was still quite high in the sky, so I had some time.

As I traveled along, my mind kept returning to the town I'd left behind and rehearsing possible reasons for my extreme loathing of the place.

My peace of mind increased with every *thunk* of my horse's hooves. It was like an actual physical presence was settling down over me and calming me. I marveled at the sudden rush of good feelings as I headed for a place I'd never been and never heard of.

"Well, I don't know where I'm going, but I sure feel good about going there," I said to myself.

My horse pricked up his ears and whinnied at the sound of my voice. He even seemed happy to be heading out again before he'd been fed or rested. It sure was strange.

I was still savoring my good feelings when we topped a rise and a ranch came into view. It seemed to be just waiting for us. Old Jack quickened his pace without being told. The place looked a little run-down the closer I got.

The man who lives there is either sick or lazy, I thought to myself as I surveyed the uncut wood, a shutter hanging from one hinge, poorly patched fences, and a gate that would be a real challenge to open and close.

"Either way, he needs some help," I muttered, "and that's where I come in."

I was tying my reins to the porch railing when I heard the sound of a struggle. I reached for my whip and very reluctantly allowed myself to be drawn toward the sound. All my good feelings of a few minutes ago drained out of me. I sure didn't want to get involved in family trouble. I'd had enough of my own. I leaned against the fence and watched a woman struggling in the arms of a man. He was obviously enjoying himself—she was not. Neither of them spoke, but he was chuckling to himself while she exerted all her strength trying to break his grip. I watched, trying to discern if this was a lovers' quarrel that I should stay out of. As I watched, blood began to trickle from the woman's nose.

"Oh, God, help me," she cried out.

Her words went through me with a hot, tingling sensation that spurred me to action before I even thought about it. I unfurled my whip and cracked it, just nipping the back of the man's neck. He jumped like he'd been shot and released the woman, who fell to the ground and bounced right back up and ran to the far side of the corral.

"Is this your husband?" I asked before she could disappear from view and leave me with a sticky situation.

"Certainly *not*!" she exclaimed in horror.

"Well then, you'll have to move along," I said, turning to the man, "and don't even think about going for your gun." But I could see that he wasn't going to heed my warning, so I was forced to use the whip again. It tore the gun from his hand and cut the flesh in the process.

"You're meddlin' in somthin' ain't none of your business," he growled as he headed for his horse, holding his wounded hand with his good one.

I walked over and picked up his gun and started to toss it to him, but thought better of it. He might try to catch it left-handed and shoot somebody. I held it for a few seconds, then I walked over and put it in his saddlebags. I didn't want him to have an excuse to come back real soon.

"I wouldn't want to leave a man without a gun," I said. I could tell his feelings were mollified a little bit. "I stopped by here to get a meal and some rest and you were sure preventing that from happening," I offered by way of explanation.

The man made a grunting sound as he mounted his horse and rode away.

I watched him out of sight then turned toward the sound of the well being pumped. The woman was trying to stop her nosebleed. When she saw me coming, she headed for the house.

"I'll do some work around here for a meal and a night's lodging for myself and my horse," I offered before she could disappear. She turned to face me before she went through the door.

"I owe you that much—you don't have to work for it. But you'll have to eat and sleep in the barn."

"You don't owe me anything. I chased him off because he was interfering with my plans. I figure that women who flirt and carry on get what they deserve." I could have bit my tongue out as soon as the words were out of my mouth. She stiffened her back and raised her head. Bruises were beginning to appear on her face and blood was still oozing from her nose and one eye was beginning to swell.

"When your supper is ready, I'll put it on that stump and ring this bell. Don't try to come to the house before you hear the bell or I'll shoot you."

Her voice was as cold as ice and I knew she meant it. There was a battle going on inside me. One part wanted to help and comfort her. The other part was angry at her.

"Why didn't you shoot that other guy?" There was a tinge of sarcasm in my voice. My angry part kept winning out, but I didn't really want it to. Down inside, I knew this woman did not deserve this treatment, but I couldn't seem to shut my mouth.

She looked at me a full minute through half-closed lids.

"It's none of your business," she answered, "but just by way of warning, I'll tell you. He got me off guard by acting like he wanted to help me. He drug that tree in here for firewood and I came out of the house to thank him—without my shotgun. Then he grabbed me. I won't be so foolish again."

That last she threw over her shoulder as she went inside and closed and locked the door behind her.

I stood there for a while before I went after my horse. I led him to the barn. There was a mare in the barn and precious little to feed her. She made a terrible racket when I came in and I could tell she was good and hungry. I fed both horses and went in search of more food. I finally found some under some old boxes and boards. It seemed to be hidden there. That puzzled me. But I left it there. Something strange was going on. When I heard the bell, I jumped and made a beeline for the door, but was treated to the sight of the woman's back as she went back into her house. I don't know why I felt a twinge of disappointment. I certainly had no hankering for female company. I'd had enough of that to last me a lifetime.

I went to bed, fully intending to ride out of there in the morning. But then, in the middle of the night, I was awakened by intruders. I lay still and listened. It sounded like two men. They were searching the barn for something. One of them lit a lamp and I was able to see them clearly through the cracks in the wall of the stall where I was sleeping. I was amazed to see two teenaged boys. One was obviously more nervous than the other.

"Put that light out. She'll see it from the house and come out here with her shotgun," he hissed.

"Don't worry," the other answered. "I've done this many times. She'd never dare to come out here in the dark. Not and leave her daughter alone." He wasn't even whispering. "I know there's hay here somewhere. She was in town yesterday and bought some. We just gotta find where she hid it this time."

"I got a creepy feeling that we are being watched and I want to get out of here. Besides, we have no right to take her hay."

"You are a sissy. I'll bring someone else next time. I thought you wanted adventure."

"Not this kind. You said we were going to have fun and get paid for it."

"My Pa'll pay you."

"And just who might your Pa be?" I asked as I cocked my gun.

Both boys froze. Then they instantly changed roles. It was amazing to see. The brave one became timid and the timid one became bold. He closed his eyes and said wearily, "I told you we were being watched." The other one was shaking until his knees were literally hitting together and he began to stammer.

"We-we-we d-d-don't m-m-mean any ha-ha-harm." He turned to run.

"Don't move if you value your life," I warned.

A wet spot appeared on the front of his pants.

"I expect an answer to my question."

The other boy spoke up. "His Pa is Mr. Tate that owns the store in town. If you'll let us go, I promise we'll never come here again. At least, *I* never will. I had no idea what I was getting into tonight."

"What's your name?" I asked.

The young man sighed. "My name is Zedekiah Black. My Pa is dead and it will break my mother's heart if she hears of this."

"What's young Mr. Tate's name?"

"William Tate Jr."

"How much hay have you stolen from this woman, William?" I asked. He was starting to recover and beginning to get sullen and refused to answer. So I reached for my whip and raised it up above the stall and cracked it right beside his head. The trembling began again.

"I d-don't remember," he stammered.

I flicked the whip lightly across his back—just enough to raise a welt and help his memory.

"This is the fifth time I been here," he spat out.

"And did you bring a friend each time?"

"Yes."

"Did you carry the hay away on horseback or in a wagon?"

"Horseback."

His friend's head whipped around and I knew the kid was lying. So I gave him another taste of the whip.

"We got a wagon over the hill tonight, but I usually just use the horses," he whined.

I thought for a while. There was something about this lopsided situation that I was seeing that just made me want to interfere and try to even the score a little bit.

"I believe we're gonna pay your Pa a visit," I finally said. "You boys hitch that wagon there up to those two horses." They complied and I watched from the shadows.

"Now drive it out the backside of the barn, but don't think about taking off, because I have a gun besides this whip and one of you will be dead." The boys weren't inclined to test me out. They drove the wagon out and waited while I put out the lantern and shut the door. I climbed in the back of the wagon and headed for town. When we got to Tate's store, I sent the other boy in to call the elder Tate outside. I had my reasons for wanting to stay in the shadows. When the boy saw his father, he started whining.

"Pa, he used a whip on me!"

"Who did?" he demanded.

"I did."

"How dare you touch my boy. I'll have you horsewhipped."

"Your boy is a thief who steals from widows. I caught him red-handed. He's lucky to be alive. That's dangerous business to be sending a kid on."

"Now you know—boys will be boys. They didn't mean any harm." His belligerence had turned to a whine. "Anything they damaged, I'll be glad to replace."

"Well, now, that's exactly what I had in mind. Since your son has admitted to at least five trips out to that widow lady's barn in the middle of the night to rob her blind, I figured you could just fill this wagon full of hay to make restitution," I said as I got out of the wagon and moved further into the shadows, dragging his son with me.

"Let my son go first."

"You fill the wagon first, and don't try to scrimp on the hay. I mean—fill it full."

Old Mr. Tate's expression got worse with every bale of hay he brought out. I wouldn't let either boy help him. I didn't dare let him get his hands on either of them till I got what I wanted. Finally, I figured the wagon wouldn't hold any more hay.

"Now, I think you owe the lady for all the mental suffering you've put her through. So you just bring out a bag of beans, cornmeal, flour, a ham or two and some bacon."

"This is robbery."

"No, what you had your son doing was robbery. This is restitution—with interest. While you're at it, bring a jug of molasses and try to be cheerful about it. You know the Lord loveth a cheerful giver."

That last remark seemed to sting the man like a whiplash. He jumped and almost ran back into his store. He brought the things I demanded as fast as he could. When I had released his son and started to drive away, he called after me.

"All we're tryin' to do is get that woman to move into town where we could take better care of her."

By the time I'd taken the other young man home and returned to the barn where I was staying, I was very tired. I just put the wagon back in the barn and went to bed. But that last remark of Tate's kept running through my mind like the tune to an old song. I even dreamed about it. By morning, I had myself reset to blame this woman for her troubles.

CHAPTER 2
Her View

I got up early in spite of the lack of a rooster. It made me mad every morning that they couldn't even leave me my old scrawny rooster. I had thought that when the hens were all gone, that would be the end of it where the chickens were concerned. That old rooster was too tough to cook. But no, they had to clean me out. They just killed it and left it out there. Just like the dog. Just left it there with its throat cut for us to find. That rooster seemed to be the last straw for me. I hadn't wanted to be the one to start shooting. But they were pushing me into it. Maybe that was what they wanted—an excuse to shoot me. The thought came like turning a light on. Then they could take my daughter for their evil schemes. Of course! That was it. And I almost fell into their trap. I got trembly all over and had to sit down. I needed to pray. I was getting bitter. I couldn't get bitter or I'd lose the Lord's direction. I wouldn't hear His voice like I just had.

"Without You, I'm a goner," I whispered. "Don't leave me, God. Forgive me and help me to forgive them—whoever they are."

Suddenly I realized that except for that drifter in the barn, someone would have died last night. I would have shot someone last night. I was ready for it after my session with that two-faced x-preacher yesterday. I could feel the hardness again, but suddenly I began to weep quietly so as not to awaken my daughter. Memories of the good times flooded over me. The church services. The quilting bees. The days when this was a good place to live. How everyone had pitched in to help me after Jed had died.

"Don't worry. We'll take care of you and the little girl."

The words were so clear, it seemed I could actually hear them, and I saw the warm, smiling faces of Mr. and Mrs. Tate, the storekeepers. The pain it produced in me was almost unbearable. But after I'd cried it all out, I felt better. I put it all once again in God's hands.

"Thanks for sending that drifter. Not only to rescue me, but to keep me from killing somebody. Is this what You mean by the 'manifold' grace of God? Everything You do seems to have many reasons and many results."

As I prayed, I felt my peace returning and with it, my confidence that God was with us and would see us through this somehow. I stepped outside to better appreciate the sunrise and felt the chill of fall in the air. Little stabs of worry tried to penetrate my peace, but I refused them entry. Thoughts of winter and the need for food and firewood could wait. I wanted to savor this wonderful feeling—like God was all around me.

"I wish I could keep this awareness of Your presence always," I said as I pumped the water to make coffee.

"Who you talkin' to?"

The voice startled me and I spilled the icy water over my feet. I'd forgotten about the drifter. I moved quickly to widen the distance between us. It alarmed me that I'd let him get so close. I should have learned my lesson yesterday.

"God," I answered. I couldn't read his expression to see what his response was.

"I'll fix you a breakfast before you leave," I offered. "It'll have to be more fried potatoes and coffee. That's all I have."

"Who said I was leaving? Aren't I welcome?"

"Not really. I can't afford another mouth to feed. I thank God for sending you in the nick of time, but now you should probably keep moving."

"What makes you so determined to stay out here by yourself? Why don't you move into town so people could take care of you?"

I looked at him for a minute while I contemplated his question. Was he an emissary of the ones in town who were trying to rob me of my property and my self-respect, or was he just curious?

"Why didn't you stay in town so they could take care of you?" I asked.

Now it was his turn to stare at me. I could tell he was doing a lot of thinking.

Finally he answered.

"The whole place made me very uncomfortable and I felt like I needed to get out—like I was being led out of there—to here."

"Well," I said, "there's your answer," as I turned toward the house. "I'll start that breakfast."

His voice stopped me in my tracks.

"There's plenty of food in the barn."

I turned slowly to face him, waiting for further explanation.

"Some of the local thieves decided to make restitution last night."

I wanted to run and see, but I was afraid to make myself vulnerable. So I stood rooted to the ground, my heart pounding so hard that I thought surely it must show.

"Go get your shotgun and come out to the barn. I'll wait right here without gun or whip."

I dashed into the house and returned, gun in hand, following a safe distance behind him. I stood right by the door until my eyes had adjusted to the gloom, then looked carefully around to be sure there was no one else in the barn. I stared in amazement at the loaded wagon.

"Who did this?" I finally managed.

"This came from Tate's Store. Their son and another young man were in here last night trying to steal hay. So I just escorted them home and encouraged Mr. Tate to reimburse you for what's been stolen."

I could feel myself going pale. I had to sit down to keep from falling. To think I might have killed one or both of those boys last night.

"The young Mr. Black was definitely an unwilling participant. The other one sucked him into it against his will."

"Zedekiah."

"Yeah, that was it. Nice kid."

"What if I'd killed Mary Black's son..." I began to feel sick to my stomach. He and Jennie Lu had played together as young children. She called him Zeddie. Or Bill Tate for that matter. I didn't like him as well, but I...I'd never have forgiven myself.

"I guess I should go into town and thank the Tates," I began, but was interrupted by the drifter.

"I wouldn't do that if I were you. They weren't exactly cordial about it."

"You mean you forced them to send this stuff?"

"You might say that."

I sat there, looking at that wagon-load of food, and felt helpless. We needed it so badly, but my pride wanted to refuse it. I thought about all the nights I had sat helplessly in the house, watching lights in my barn, knowing I was being robbed, but being afraid to confront men who would force me to shoot. Was this God's way of returning it to me, or was I condoning theft? I knew from experience that there was no help from the law. The sheriff seemed powerless. He only made excuses. After a while, the drifter spoke.

"You want this food or not?"

"I want it, but I'm not sure if I should keep it. I wonder if this will give them an excuse to come in here shooting or send the sheriff to have me arrested."

"If the sheriff comes, it'll be for me, not you. And if they come shooting, we can hold them off. That is, if you know how to use that gun, or is it just a bluff?"

"Don't try me. I can use it. But I can't hold them all off alone."

"I'm not going anywhere for a while. I've got my curiosity up and I've decided to stay. And I don't intend to starve or live on potatoes either. So you might as well put this stuff in your cellar. I'll carry it over—keeping my distance, of course." He spoke as he threw a bag of flour over his shoulder and headed for the house with just the hint of a smile. I grabbed the jug of molasses and followed him.

"And just where do you think you're going to sleep when it gets cold?" I continued the conversation.

"Right there in the barn. Animals keep a barn quite cozy."

"There aren't any more animals, but that old horse."

"Where's your cows?"

"The same place my sheep and goats and chickens are. Either dead or stolen."

"I'll get them back."

"How?"

"Same way I got your hay back."

"I can't pay you."

"All I ask is food."

By this time, we were in the house and poor Jennie Lu was plastered against the wall in shock. She looked like she'd seen a ghost.

"Don't worry, little girl. I'm just bringing you some food and your mother's got me well covered with that shotgun."

When he came back up the cellar stairs, he said, "Now, you stand right there and guard me while I carry the rest of the stuff over. I don't need your help."

I couldn't help but smile a little.

"Bring that bacon next time and I'll start frying some." I had to get the last word in.

When he came back the next time carrying a bag on one shoulder, he plopped the bacon on the table as he passed through. I had set the shotgun in the corner and had the coffee boiling and Jennie Lu busy peeling potatoes. The prospect of a real meal was kind of exciting. But I couldn't forget that he might just be getting my guard down, so I kept my gun within easy reach. By the time the food was in the cellar, I had breakfast ready. I invited the man to sit at the table and eat, but I sent Jennie Lu to eat in my rocking chair by the window. I still didn't trust this guy close to my daughter. I stood by the stove, watching every move he made. He looked from Jennie Lu to me and started to say something, then just shrugged his shoulders and sat down and ate. When he was through, I started to refill his plate, but he waved me away. When he moved his hand, I jumped back. He looked at me for a minute and I saw just a flicker of something like sympathy pass through his eyes. But he blinked it away.

"I'll work on firewood today," he said, "in case we have any reprisals from town, but I'd like to leave early in the morning to round up those cattle if you could make me something to take along to eat…just some cornbread or biscuits with some of that bacon grease on them."

I nodded. I was happy at the prospect of being able to cook. My mind was already planning meals for the whole week. I couldn't wait for him to leave so I could go see what I had. When he went out, I locked all the doors and Jennie Lu and I ran down into the cellar. We were like two children at Christmas. We put beans to soak for tomorrow. Then we started on corn bread. I decided to start some yeast bread. I couldn't believe that man had shopped so thoroughly. I had everything I needed. We were set for several months. Maybe it would last all winter with the potatoes, onions, and squash I had managed to grow.

By the time the sun was high in the sky, I had the bread rising and I had made some gravy with the bacon grease to eat over fresh biscuits. I had baked a squash to go with it. The only thing I was missing was butter and eggs. I thought of my cow and nanny goat and felt a lump in my throat. My cow was stolen in the night and I found my nanny with her throat cut one morning. I put it all from my mind and thanked God for what I now had. I went out the front door and around the porch, looking for the drifter so I could give him some lunch. I came up behind him where he was splitting firewood. I was surprised at the size of the pile he'd made. I stood and watched him for a few minutes. I was fascinated. He was obviously very experienced. The way he split that wood reminded me of cutting a cake. He cut it right where he wanted and never seemed to miss. A thought came to me unbidden.

"For a drifter, he's very good at splitting wood."

"Are you ready to eat?" I asked.

He jumped and dropped the ax.

"Do you have to sneak up on a man like that?" he asked, irritated.

I couldn't help laughing. "I wasn't sneaking," I defended myself.

He grumbled all the way to the watering trough, where he washed thoroughly. I appreciated that thorough washing. I went on toward the house.

"Where's your gun?" he called after me.

"I forgot it," I confessed.

"Well, don't get careless. Your troubles aren't over," he said, motioning toward town.

I looked up to see several riders cresting the hill. I went immediately into the house and told Jennie Lu to go to her room.

"Take your lunch if you want to," I added.

She did.

I got my gun and set it by the front door. My heart was beating in my throat—slow and hard. I saw that it was the sheriff with Mr. Tate and a few others. They stopped at the gate, which I noticed had been repaired since yesterday.

"Mrs. Stone," the sheriff called.

I stepped out onto the porch just as he put his hand on my gate. I reached behind me and swung that big gun up and rested it on my arm.

"If you step into this yard, I will shoot you," I said. And I meant it. They all became very still. "If you go for your guns, you'll probably get me, but not until I've killed most of you," I added.

"And I'll get whoever she misses," the drifter spoke from the corner of the house.

"Now, I have reason to believe that you have stolen property in your house, so I need to search. If you have nothing to hide, you shouldn't object."

"I object to thieves and rapists and kidnappers setting foot in my house and I will not be preached at by them."

The sheriff's back stiffened. "Are you accusing me of those things?" he asked.

"You keep real bad company, Mr. Sloane. You're usually known by the company you keep."

He snorted.

"That man with the purple necktie tried to kidnap and rape me yesterday. I was rescued by this cowboy who just happened to be passing by. He took a whip to him and that's what's wrong with his hand. Mr. Tate has been stealing from me continually until I and my daughter were facing starvation. This same cowboy caught his son in the act last night and he admitted that he'd been stealing from me continually and this man demanded restitution."

"He confessed that because he was being tortured," Tate interrupted me.

The drifter spoke up. "I'd like to speak to the sheriff in private."

"Don't do it, Sloane. He'll use that whip on you."

"With all you guys out here? I'm not that stupid."

Sloane turned toward the gate that would enter into the barnyard.

"Come to the barn and talk to me," he said. "You men sit still."

When Sheriff Sloane returned, he mounted his horse and turned it back toward town.

"I have some investigation to do on my own," he explained. "I'll settle this later."

"We'll be back," Tate threatened.

I went inside and sat in a chair, waiting for my heart to calm down. The drifter came through the back door. Jennie Lu came out of the bedroom.

"That sure was a good lunch!" she exclaimed. "I haven't had anything that good in years!"

"Well, dish me up some. I'm starved," the drifter said.

Jennie Lu obliged, then she went and sat in my rocking chair, remembering that she was supposed to keep her distance.

Suddenly, I was so hungry that I couldn't wait until the man left. He was taking his time. He went to the stove for seconds so I got myself a plate and filled it, leaving the gun against the cupboard, then moving it over across my lap when I sat down. It was awkward, but the food was delicious. I offered him cornbread and molasses for dessert. He helped himself to it and another cup of coffee. When he was through, he unbuttoned his shirt and revealed a gun strapped to his chest. I leaned forward, lifting the shotgun. Jennie Lu stopped in mid-rock, catching her breath.

"Relax," he said quickly. "I'm giving this to you. That big gun is too cumbersome. You won't keep it with you always. Put it back on the pegs above the door, but leave it loaded. It was very impressive out there today. But if you get caught again like you did yesterday, you'll have this always handy."

He laid the gun in its holster on the table. Then he took a pouch of ammunition from around his waist and laid it beside the gun.

"Strap this on you wherever you feel most comfortable. Be careful, it's loaded. Maybe you should put it on your leg just as a precaution. A leg wound is less serious than a chest wound." With that, he turned and left the house.

I sat there, unable to move I was so shocked. My chest still ached from the combination of the shock of the men at the gate, then seeing the cowboy baring his chest to reveal a gun. My extreme fear was turning to anger as I was trying to collect my wits.

"I'd like to use a horsewhip on him," I muttered, "scaring me like that! I about had a heart attack."

"Me too," Jennie Lu gasped.

"You wait, I'll find a way to pay him back for that," I promised.

"Good," Jennie Lu said. "I'll help you. That was awful! Nice gun, though!"

"Ummm," I murmured as I picked it up and headed toward the bedroom so I could try it on.

The next morning, the cowboy was nowhere to be seen when I went to the well. I looked in the barn just to be sure. It was nice to be able to go into my own barn. I checked everything over. He'd taken both horses. That puzzled me. I hoped he hadn't stolen my horse. That was all I had left. It sure looked like he planned to come back. He'd made himself a nice little room in an empty stall. The whole barn was neat as a pin. He'd found the old stove I had hidden up in the hayloft and had it set up with the pipe going out between the boards on the backside of the barn.

I hope he doesn't burn my barn down, I thought to myself. But when I saw all the wood he'd cut and all the repairs he'd already made to the place, I had to grudgingly admit that it was nice to have a man's help.

Jennie Lu and I spent a wonderful day cooking. But I kept an eye on the road to town. I could never truly relax. I missed that old dog. I used to rely on him to warn me when anyone was around.

"I wish I'd kept that dog inside at night," I spoke my thoughts aloud.

"Mother, do you realize how many times you've said that?" Jennie Lu asked.

I laughed.

"Just thinking out loud," I tried to explain. I didn't know why I couldn't get over my sense of loss over that dog. Suddenly I looked at my daughter with gratitude. If I missed that dog this much, how hard would it be to lose her? I gave her a hug.

"I'm glad I still have you," I said.

"I'm glad we have each other," she responded.

Toward evening, I got out our sewing project. When it got dark, I lit the lamps, but it wasn't long before I got that creepy feeling that we were being watched. After a while, I mentioned it to Jennie Lu.

"I'm going to act like I'm going to the bedroom. You just keep acting normal, like you're talking to me. If that cowboy's out there, I'm going to teach him a lesson. If it's someone else....I'll know."

Jennie Lu threw back her head and laughed, but I could see the fear in her eyes. She was such a tough girl.

"You be careful," she said quietly.

"I will," I said just as quietly, then I began to laugh as if I'd heard something humorous as I put my sewing down in my chair. I picked up a candle and lit it before I headed toward the bedroom.

"Where did you put that box of lace?" I asked.

Jennie Lu threw her head toward the bedroom door.

"I think it's under your bed," she answered and bent her head over her sewing.

As soon as I was out of sight of the windows, I set the candle down and reached for my shotgun as I slipped out the door, opening it as little as possible. I stood there, waiting for my eyes to adjust, with my heart beating hard and slow. I moved in the deep shadow to the far end of the porch. I put some of my skirt over the railing to see if I'd get any reaction. Nothing. Then I carefully looked around the side of the house. The moon shone full here and showed plainly a bare wall. It wouldn't be a good place to go. I would make a clear target in that moonlight. I went to the other side of the porch and repeated the process. It was dark there, but I could see well enough to be sure no one was there. I went back to the front steps, went down them and ran quickly into the shadow of the trees in front of the house. This was risky and my heart was pounding. I moved quickly to the end of the row of trees from where I could get a clear view of the yard between the house and barn. Sure enough, there was a man sitting on the well curbing, watching us through the window. I made a dash for the barn.

CHAPTER 3
His View

I sat on the well curbing, feeling pretty good about myself. By moving quickly, I'd managed to round up about fifty head of cattle. Just like I'd thought, they were so confident, they hadn't even bothered to change the brands on her cattle. Taking that boy with me was a smart move, also. They'd all been hesitant to act too ugly in front of him. Most of them were stammering and making excuses. I was able to repair some fences and get those cattle into the closest pasture without too much trouble. That boy was a big help. He was certainly worth the coin I'd given him. I told him to keep that money between him and me. I didn't want this woman wondering where I got the money.

I concentrated my attention upon her and her daughter framed in the window. It was a peaceful looking picture. They were talking and laughing together and were obviously carefree. The woman got up and lit a candle and headed for the other room, obviously searching for something. The girl called instructions after her. Pretty soon, the girl laughed and called out something else. She kept talking to her and laughing as she worked on her sewing. I smiled to myself, thinking about this poor woman thinking she was holding me at bay with that shotgun. As if I couldn't take it away from her anytime I wanted to. I guess she saw that when I'd exposed my body gun in front of her. I smiled again, thinking of it. Of course, a shotgun was a formidable weapon. I certainly wouldn't take it lightly. Just then, I felt a gun barrel between my shoulder blades and heard a low voice say, "You are a dead man!"

My hands flew up and my heart constricted in my chest. I'd been too confident and gotten careless. Someone had followed me. My whole life flashed before my mind and it wasn't a very pretty picture. I tried to swallow, but my mouth was dry.

"Get up—slowly," that low voice growled. "Move away from the well—slowly. I don't want to contaminate it."

By this time, I was sweating profusely and my mind was racing. I had to think of something. When I moved into the moonlight, a feminine voice said, "Oh, it's you. What, pray tell, are you doing out here? Spying on us?"

I started to put my hands down.

"Oh, no! Not until you explain yourself."

I put my hands back up, but I couldn't manage to speak.

"Well, sir. Cat got your tongue?"

"You scared me to death." My voice squeaked like an adolescent boy.

The woman broke into peals of laughter. That brought her daughter to the door.

"We did it!" she called. "We scared the liver out of him!"

"Good!" the daughter exclaimed.

I felt like a trapped animal. I wanted to be angry, but I was too relieved. I moved into the shadows as I became aware that my clothes were wet. I remembered my disdain for the terrified boy in the barn when he wet his pants.

"You can put your hands down. But I'd like to know why you were out here watching us."

"I came to get a drink and was trying to decide if the sound of the pump would scare you ladies." I lied in my best wounded friend voice. I didn't actually know why I was watching them.

"Not nearly as much as that horrible feeling that you're being watched."

"Good Lord!" I burst out. "You two are like a couple of Indians."

"Well, remember that the next time you want to come skulking around. There's coffee and food if you want it."

"I'll wash up first," I said, turning to look at her for the first time, but there was no sign of her. She had disappeared into the darkness.

I pumped a bucket of water to take into the barn with me. When I looked up from the well, she was back in the picture, framed by the window, laughing and talking with her daughter as they sewed, looking the picture of feminine defenselessness. I shivered in spite of myself. I was trying to work up a fury, but all I could muster was amazement and the beginning of something I think might have been respect. I decided it might be wisdom to call a truce in the battle of the sexes that had started between her and me. There was no doubt that she desperately needed my help, but she'd made it quite clear she was not to be trifled with.

"This will get us nowhere," I muttered as I changed my soiled clothing in the privacy of my stall. A mouse scurried and I jumped and whirled around. I had to laugh.

"She really got your goat," I muttered, as I headed for the house. I hated to go in. I could hear feminine laughter before I even left the barn. But I was so hungry that I put my pride aside and knocked on the door. I could smell the coffee. "She must be making a fresh pot," I thought. That calmed my feelings a little. A fresh pot of coffee was exactly what I wanted. When I opened the door, the warmth and the smell of good home-cooked food washed what was left of anger and resentment right out of me. I was almost ready to laugh at myself. But instead, I sat down at the table and concentrated on eating. I was famished.

"We rounded up fifty head for you today," I managed to say between bites. I hoped to make her ashamed of herself.

"Who's 'we'?" she responded without expression.

"Zed Black and me."

"I can't pay him," she reminded me.

"He's just making amends," I explained.

"Where are they now?"

"In the near pasture."

"Well, I hope somebody don't cut the fence tonight."

I shrugged as I was drinking my coffee.

"There's plenty of grass in there. I think they'd have to be driven out and I'd probably hear that. What you need is a good dog or two."

Her face tightened and her jaw was clenched and unclenched several times. I knew I had touched a sore spot. The daughter finally spoke up.

"We used to have a really good dog. They slit his throat one night. Mother has never forgiven herself for not keeping him inside at night."

I couldn't think of anything to say, so I got up and went to the stove for seconds. I was thinking about how I could come up with another dog. I was going to need a dog when it came time to move those cattle again. I couldn't take advantage of that boy's guilty conscience indefinitely.

"Well, we'll be all right for a while," I said as I pushed back from the table. "There's a lot of grass in that pasture."

I turned my attention to the dress the two women had been working on. It was hanging on something like a statue of a woman with no head. It was obviously a wedding dress. My curiosity had been thoroughly aroused and I had to satisfy it before I left the house. Even though my better sense told me to keep my mouth shut, I plowed ahead, knowing I was headed for trouble. I looked at the dress and back at the woman.

"Are you getting married?" I asked bluntly.

"No," she answered.

"Sure looks like a wedding dress to me." I motioned toward the dress.

"It is."

"Makin' it for someone else?"

"Yes."

"Who?"

There was a long pause.

"My daughter."

I looked from the dress to the young girl beside her mother, then back at the dress.

"Don't think it'll fit her, and she's too young to get married," I said.

"It's not for now!" the child exclaimed.

The mother gave me a disgusted look and turned away. So I felt like I had to defend myself. I shouldn't have, but I couldn't seem to stop myself.

"You can't know what size she'll be when she gets married. You should just wait until the time comes. You'll probably have to make the whole thing over again."

"We're making it to fit Mother," the daughter spoke up before her mother could shush her, "because I'll probably be her size when I grow up."

I couldn't maintain my adversary stand with the daughter. Her obvious excitement over the dress threw water on my critical fire. I smiled in spite of myself.

"It's sure a nice dress. But I don't see why you don't make one you can wear right now. There's a lot of money in that dress."

"Most of the material came from my grandmother. She used to have a dress and hat shop. And my mother says she might not be around to make my dress when I get married. She wants to make sure I'll have a nice wedding."

This last was said in a slower and quieter tone of voice, and it affected me like a slap in the face. I suddenly felt like the stupid fool that I was. The mother, who had been standing with her rigid back to me, turned slowly to face me with her head held high and a face like stone.

"I really don't see that it's any of your business how I educate my daughter," she said.

I looked into her eyes for a minute, feeling like I was about to cry. The enormity of her situation was finally getting through to me, I guess. I fought for composure before I could respond to her.

"You're right," I said as I headed for the door. "It's none of my business."

Back in the barn, I berated myself for stupidity and wondered why I couldn't keep a civil tongue in my head toward that woman. The next day, I kept to myself except for meal times, which I ate in silence. I needed time to puzzle over this situation.

Sometime in the night, I made up my mind it was time for me to move along. When the lady came out to the well in the morning, I was packed up and ready to move along. When I told her, she gave a little nod, showing no emotion, not even surprise.

"I'll pack you a little food," she said, turning back into the house.

When she returned with the neatly wrapped package, she also handed me the gun I had given her.

"No, you keep that gun," I responded. "That was a gift."

As I rode out the gate, I never looked back, but I couldn't resist a glance over toward the front of the house as I rode by. The girl's face was framed in the window for just a second before the curtain was dropped. I realized with a shock that there were tears glistening on her cheeks.

That night as I slept under the stars, I was still trying to shake the picture of that girl's face from my mind. I had an awful feeling upon me that I couldn't seem to get rid of. It was like a vice was being tightened on my head with every mile I traveled. I found myself talking to that unseen presence that was with me again. But this time, it was for ill instead of good.

"She was taking care of herself just fine before I came along," I burst out as I threw my coffee grounds out on the ground.

"They are not my responsibility," I mumbled as I fell into a fitful sleep. I saw that tear-stained face all night long. In the morning, I was so miserable, I ate very little from the package of food. When I opened it, the aroma of the ladies' kitchen almost brought tears to my eyes.

"What in the world is going on?!" I exclaimed as I put the food away and prepared to move on. The urge to go back was almost overpowering.

"I can't even get along with that woman," I argued, not knowing with whom I was arguing. My horse whinnied a sympathetic response, only to be kicked in the ribs and told to shut up. He bolted forward and almost unseated me.

"Good enough for you, you idiot," I muttered as I righted myself and got the horse slowed down. "You can't even get along with yourself!"

I continued this way for nearly a week, which is testimony to my great stubbornness. However, I have to say in my own defense that I had not really traveled very far in that week's time. This was due to two amazing things. First of all, every step I took away from that place caused me great misery of a kind which I could never explain. It was like a terrible black cloud of terrible foreboding would settle over me and cause me tremendous anxiety. If I would for any reason change my direction and head back the way I had come, this terrible condition would instantly and completely lift off of me. I found this out completely by accident. As I stubbornly continued on in my misery, a deer crossed my path and reminded me that I would soon be out of food and I'd better do some hunting. So I decided to give chase. That animal led me back exactly the way I'd come and I found to my amazement that I had a wonderful day following that deer, though I never succeeded in shooting it. The next day, I gave up and resumed my journey, only to find myself tormented by the same gloominess as I'd experienced before. I'd traveled all day and made very little progress and hadn't succeeded in bagging anything for my supper either. By my campfire that night, I admitted to myself that I was not cut out to be a hunter.

"I'd probably starve before I mastered the art," I muttered to myself as I drank my coffee and ate the last piece of cornbread. The next day, following another miserable, nearly sleepless night, I spied another deer to which I again gave chase. This animal did exactly what the other one had done and led me in the way I had come. Again, I experienced the miraculous lifting of the darkness I had been experiencing. By nightfall, I had finally succeeded in killing the deer. I drug it up onto a ridge to make my camp for the night. To my amazement, in the distance, I could see the little ranch house I had left nearly a week before. The slanting rays of the sun illuminated it so clearly that I thought I could make out a figure moving from the well to the house. The smoke was curling up from the chimney. As I studied these signs of peacefulness, such a sense of relief swept over me that it brought tears to my eyes.

"All right! All right!" I muttered angrily. "Give me some kind of sign tonight and I'll go back tomorrow."

Just then, I heard a noise and someone called a greeting from the darkness.

"Come on in," I responded. Soon, he appeared in the dusk as I prepared to light a fire.

"Need some help with that deer?" he offered. "I'd be glad to help in return for a good piece of it." He was obviously a trapper. He had hobbled his pack animals near the bushes so they could graze a little before sundown. I was glad for his help because I knew very little about deer. As we worked, he talked.

"See that little ranch down there? There's a woman lives there alone—'ceptin' for her daughter. I heard tell how she's been rustlin' cattle and sech and she's holed up there with a shotgun—nobody can get near."

I said nothing.

"They's plannin' to burn her out, I guess."

I froze inside.

"I couldn't figure how one woman and a little girl could be so all-fired dangerous, but when I said as much, them men got real hot under the collar, so I decided it were best I just cleared out of there real fast like...so here I am, and good luck for me, too. I get a good piece of venison."

He continued to ramble on while I stood transfixed on the ridge, staring at the ladies' house as though looking at it could somehow protect it.

"Did they say when?" I finally asked.

"What?" he responded. He was on an entirely different subject and didn't know what I was asking about.

"The ladies' house," I explained impatiently. "Did they say when they were going to burn it?"

"I didn't stay around to find out. But they seemed to be anxious to get on with it. Why? You know her?"

"We've met," I muttered as I paced the ground. All thoughts of hunger had left me. It was useless to think of traveling at night. Or was it? This was familiar ground to this horse. If I gave him his head, he'd probably take me right where I wanted to go. There was a full moon and it was a clear night. I looked at the trapper's dog. He seemed well trained and alert.

"How'd you like this whole deer—hide and all?" I asked.

"What's the deal?" he asked warily.

"I need that dog," I responded.

"No deal."

"Look, I've got a better chance of saving that lady and her daughter with a dog around," I explained.

"Risky business!" he said, shaking his head.

I picked up the carcass and threw it over my horse's flank.

"What ya doin'?"

"I'm leaving!"

"Tonight—now?"

"Yes."

"You're crazy!" he sputtered as he watched his venison disappearing.

"Probably," I agreed as I continued to break camp.

"Wait," he said. "I guess I could do sumthin' to help a lady in distress."

"She's not a rustler." I pressed my advantage. "They're the ones stealing from her."

"You been there?"

"Just came from there and I just decided I'm going back. You have any ammunition you could sell me?"

"Guess I could sell you what I just bought there in that town. I can always go back and buy more. I ain't made no enemies there yet."

The ammunition he had was just what I needed, of course. The dog took to me right away and willingly allowed herself to be led away from her former master and fresh meat.

"If that don't beat all!" the trapper exclaimed.

I tied a rope to her collar and she trotted right beside me and never looked back.

"What's her name?" I called over my shoulder.

"Lady!" he called back.

"Lady!" I muttered. "That'll have to change, I think." The dog pricked up her ears and whined.

"I'm glad you got some of that deer before we left. We've got a long hard ride ahead of us."

I went through the alphabet, putting one letter after another in the place of the 'L' in Lady to come up with a name that this dog could easily learn. I only had a few hours to teach her. I settled on

Sadie. I worked with the dog while the horse took us home. It was a good diversion, but I was still tormented by thoughts of what might be happening back there. I called myself Don Quixote all night and finally at one watering stop, I prayed for the first time in many years.

"God, if that's You out there that I've been feeling, I'm sorry for being so stubborn. If You're really real, please let me get back there in time. Amen."

When I got back on my horse, I began to feel that same sense of well-being I had when I first approached this place. "Maybe there really is a God out there somewhere," I thought. "Someone seems to be looking out for that lady and her daughter."

Before dawn, I was skirting the farmyard on foot. I had tied my horse to a little tree behind the barn, but out of sight to anyone approaching from town. I could detect nothing unusual in the yard, so I let myself quietly into the barn from the back. All seemed to be in order in the barn. I was just beginning to relax when I heard the well being pumped. I peered out the window into the dim light of an early dawn. What I saw made me feel stiff and cold and like a hand had gripped my heart so tight that I couldn't get my breath. It was a man behind that pump handle! I took my gun out of its holster as I slid quietly through the partially opened back barn door. Sadie was right at my heels. She never made a sound. I was almost within arm's length before the guy at the well sensed my presence. He straightened up and had started to turn when he felt my gun and froze in mid-motion.

"Where's the lady who lives here?" I growled.

"I am the lady who lives here!" she said with a smile in her voice as she lowered her arms and finished her turn.

Sure enough! It was her, dressed in men's clothes. I gasped for breath and stifled the urge to hug her. I was so relieved, I wanted to cry and so mad, I wanted to spank her.

"You've got a dog!" she exclaimed, kneeling with a hand outstretched.

I was glad for the distraction because I probably couldn't keep my rushing emotions out of my face. I didn't trust my voice, so I didn't say a word. I watched her make friends with Sadie while I made a production out of getting my gun back into its holster. Finally, she seemed to remember me and looked up.

"What are you doing back here? Did you forget something?" she asked.

I was prepared for this question. I gave my rehearsed answer.

"I decided it's too cold to be heading out across the country. I guess I'll spend the winter here."

She sat back on her heels and looked me in the face while continuing to scratch the dog behind the ears.

"You take a lot for granted," she finally said.

I was not prepared for that response. It took me a while to think of what to say. Before I thought of something, she spoke again.

"But I guess you can stay since I could use a hand and I especially could use a dog. When you leave, the dog stays here."

I hesitated, but she cut me short.

"That's the deal! Take it or leave it!"

I shrugged and headed for the barn.

"Easy come, easy go!"

"Where'd you get this dog?" she called after me.

"I got her from a trapper I ran into while I was gone." I turned back and saw that the dog had stood up to follow me, but she wasn't sure what to do, so she stood there, wagging her tail just slightly and let out a little whine.

"I'm surprised he would part with her," the lady continued. "She's going to have pups. Maybe that's why."

"She is!? He never mentioned it. I don't think he knew."

"Well, she is, and better here than out there somewhere. Isn't that right, girl?" she said, turning back to the dog. Sadie swished her tail a little more vigorously and whined again, never taking her eyes from my face. I slapped my leg and she jumped and ran after me.

"Hey, I thought she was going to be my dog!"

"Not till I leave," I answered. I needed that dog in the barn with me for a while.

I went and got my horse into the barn while I waited for breakfast. Then I sat on a bale of hay and leaned against a post. The next thing I knew, I was being jerked awake by the sound of the dog whining at the door. I jumped up and looked out the window. Someone was approaching from the direction of the ridge. I soon recognized the trapper from last night. Sadie was getting beside herself, but I shushed her and kept her in the barn. I didn't want her barking heard by the wrong people. When he was well into the yard, I opened the door and motioned him toward the barn.

"Get the animals out of sight," I said.

"Thought you might need some help," he said after he was in the barn.

"I might. There's been no sign of anyone yet. The Lady doesn't know about anything." I noticed she was standing in the door of the house, watching us and looking very uncertain, so I headed over to explain and also hoping to keep her from ringing that bell.

"The trapper that I mentioned to you earlier decided to come visit," I explained. "Do you think there'll be enough food for him?"

The Lady hesitated. "There's enough food," she finally said, "but make sure he leaves his guns in the barn."

"He'll eat in the barn. I don't want anyone to know he's here."

I headed back to the barn. I couldn't figure why these people seemed to be after this woman. Her property wasn't really valuable enough to be the sole cause. I kept trying to believe that she herself was somehow responsible, but last night that thought was somehow put to rest within my mind. There was absolutely no possibility that this woman had done anything to merit the treatment she was receiving. I don't know what I saw in her eyes that convinced me, but now I knew that I was going to get to the bottom of this situation or die trying. It felt good to have it settled. Suddenly, my life had a purpose again.

"Now I know why those men took off on those foolish Crusades," I muttered between swings of the ax as I chopped wood. "Now I've got my own. I feel like I was sent here. I guess I'll call it 'The Wedding Dress Crusade.' Never thought I'd be playing Sir Galahad for some woman in distress."

The next few days, I went about my job of restoring the place with a new peacefulness inside. I went to the house only to eat and that mainly in silence. The wedding dress had been removed from my sight, but sometimes at night, I saw them working on it. I experimented with watching them through the window to see if I'd get the same reaction as before, but their wariness seemed to be subsiding. I knew this was because of my presence. They were beginning to depend on me, although she would never have admitted it. I was glad to see them relaxing a little, but at the same time, it worried me. It would only make it harder for them after I left. Indeed! How could I ever leave after they were depending on me? I *had* to resolve this situation one way or another. I was trapped already! Could this be why I was so irritable around her? No, I actually kind of liked the idea of being needed and having a job that needed doing. But why in the world did she irritate me so much? It was a mystery! I could sit on that well curbing and watch them for hours, but when I was in their presence, I didn't dare open my mouth for fear I'd start an argument. I always had to criticize. It wasn't even like me.

I'd been there about a week when I got a little insight into my problem. I was watching the progress on the wedding dress as usual, when I realized it was on the real woman instead of the dummy. I couldn't resist going closer to get a better look. The daughter was insisting on taking her mother's hair down and fixing it fancy to go with the dress. The change was amazing—and disturbing. Suddenly, I realized why.

"She looks like Syble!" I gasped. "That's probably why I get irritated." I just gazed at her in amazement for a while.

"She may look like Syble, but she's a lady. It's not her fault who she looks like," I thought. "So stop harassing her."

I got so close to the window that I could hear the conversation from within. Just then, the Lady walked over to the window to use it for a mirror. I held my breath but I didn't move. I didn't dare. Would she see me? It was the closest I'd over been to her. I studied her carefully. I was surprised that she looked so beautiful. I hadn't realized it before. Then I began to see that she was deliberately making herself look bad most of the time. I didn't dare to move, so I stood there, looking into her face and eavesdropping on her conversation.

"Well, it fits me perfectly. But who knows if it'll fit you? Like our cowboy said, 'There's no way to know for sure.'"

"You look so beautiful in it, Mother. I wish you could get married and wear it first before me."

"It takes more than a dress to get married."

"Well, all the men in town seem to be after you."

"They don't want me for a wife. They're all married men."

"What do they want, Mother?"

She closed her eyes and the tears ran down her face. I took the opportunity to move further into the darkness. But I could still see her clearly.

"They want to make me as dirty as they are, and I don't really know why. Don't ask me any more questions about it, because you're too young to understand. When you're older, I'll try to explain it more. For now, just remember that if anything happens to me, you are to get to Mary Black and ask to live with her and help her with her children until you're eighteen. Then, if you're not married, you can find a way out of here and go back east where you can work as a dressmaker and make a decent life for yourself."

"Do you think they might try to kill you, Mother?"

"Yes."

"Why, Mother, why? What did you ever do to them?"

"I don't know. I really don't know. I've tried to figure it out. We used to all be friends."

"Maybe you could marry that cowboy."

The lady's laughter rang out into the night and startled me.

"I don't want to spend my life with a grouch who finds fault with every move I make. He's probably got a wife somewhere who kicked him out."

The little girl laughed at that. "Just the same, I'm glad he came back," she said.

"Yes, but don't you forget, he could change sides at any time. Every time he goes to town, I wonder if he'll come back on their side. He never talks, so we don't know where he really stands. So don't you get too friendly with him. You keep your distance."

The child grew quiet and thoughtful and I slipped away into the darkness. I lay awake far into the night, thinking about the things I'd overheard. The next morning, I awoke feeling irritable.

I was only halfway through my breakfast when I pushed my chair back and looked at the lady. Her back was turned toward me, but the grating of my chair caused her to freeze and look over her shoulder. She was wearing those old men's clothes that hung on her like a bag. Her hair looked greasy and was slicked back on her head and into a tight knot in the back. After what I'd seen in the window last night, I was certain that her poor appearance this morning was deliberate and it irritated me. Characteristically, I couldn't keep it to myself.

"Why in the world don't you fix yourself up a little?" I blurted out.

She turned slowly to face me. Spots of color were appearing on her cheeks. They were becoming.

"What is it to you?" she asked slowly and deliberately. She didn't even sound angry—just curious.

"I have to look at you. It's depressing."

We both just looked at each other for a very long time. I kept thinking of things to say and rejecting them. I figured she was doing the same thing. I noticed her mouth move slightly a few times. I'd just made up my mind to apologize and leave when she spoke.

"I don't want to be accused of bringing any of my troubles upon myself."

"Lady, that's foolish. Nobody in their right mind is going to blame you for this mess!" I exclaimed.

There was another long pause.

"You seem to forget, sir, that you already did."

I was fishing around in my memories, trying to figure out what she was talking about, when the scene of our first encounter popped into my head. I made a mental note that whenever she called me 'sir,' I should probably be prepared for a checkmate. I started to smile a little in spite of all my efforts to refrain.

"'Lady,' forget I ever said that. I didn't know what I was talking about. I guess I wasn't in my right mind that day."

CHAPTER 4
Her View

When he spoke apologetically and smiled at me that way, I was taken by surprise. I hadn't seen that boyishness in him before. I was confused and fighting back tears, and I began to back up. He got up and moved toward me like he wanted to help me and I was suddenly so terrified, I felt like I was going to faint.

"Child!" he called to my daughter. "Come help your mother!" She was immediately by my side.

He turned abruptly and went toward the door. Before he went out, he turned and spoke to me.

"Lie down and rest for a while and you'll be all right."

"Bathe her face and neck and arms with cool water," he said to my daughter.

It was then that I realized I was suddenly burning hot. He spoke in such a confident manner that I immediately began to do what he said. He stood in the door and watched to make sure I did.

"What happened to you?" my daughter asked after the man was gone. I was lying down and she was bathing my face with cool water.

"I don't know. I just got so confused and upset when he started talking nice to me that I felt like I was going to faint and then I was really terrified. This is an awful way to live! I think it's getting to me. I'm terrified of everyone."

"Maybe it's because the last time that man was nice to you, he tricked you and he almost got you."

"I think you're right, Jennie Lu. That's probably it. I felt safer with his grouchiness."

Jennie Lu started to laugh. "His Grouchiness sounds like a title...you know...like 'His Majesty.'"

We both laughed then and I thought I'd choke before I could stop. When I finally pulled myself together, Jennie Lu was at the window.

"His Grouchiness is leaving with our horse and wagon," she said.

"I wish he'd let me know when he's going to town," I complained. "Not that it matters. I've got nothing to trade anymore and I certainly don't have any money."

"He must have heard you. He stopped the wagon in the gate and he's walking back."

Soon, there was a knock on the door. He stepped inside and looked at me for a few seconds. Then he smiled.

"Good, you're lying down and you're looking better. I'm going to be gone for a couple of days, so don't let anyone in the gate till I get back. I thought I'd better let you know so you wouldn't think I skipped out with your horse and wagon."

He walked over and took my shotgun down. My heart started thumping in my head again and I put my hand on the gun on my thigh. He broke it down and checked that it was loaded.

"Where's your ammunition?" he asked as he turned toward me. Then he stopped and took a second look at me. My fear must have shown on my face and I was sitting up with my hand on my gun. He walked over to the table, which was halfway between us.

"Lady," he said. "It's time for you to lighten up a little bit. I've been here for two months. You should know by now that I'm not dangerous. If I wanted to hurt you or your daughter or steal from you, I would have done it by now. Those kind of people are usually not very patient about waiting for what they want."

He didn't sound angry. In fact, there was a gentle quality in his voice that made it sound like he was asking me a favor.

"The trapper is still in the barn. He's staying out of sight. He's got his own food out there. I just want to make sure you'll be safe while I'm gone. I've brought this bag over to put more ammunition in and you can hang it on one of the pegs. When I get back, I'll make a shelf up there for the ammunition. Just in case we get into a full scale war here."

I sighed and lay back down. "Jennie Lu, get him what's left of the ammunition," I said. "I don't have enough for a war. That's all I have right there."

"I'm glad you told me that. Now I'll get some more so we'll be more secure here. I don't mind risking my neck if all the cards are on the table and I know what I'm working with. I'm not going into town, so hopefully they won't know I'm gone. There's another town on the other side of that mountain. I'm headed there. It's about a day away."

"I know. I used to live there."

"I'll buy supplies there for the winter. Is there anything you really need? How's the food holding out?"

"It won't last through the winter at the rate we're eating now. But if we start skimping, I could make it last. I wish I could get something for the outhouse to keep the odor down. Of course, winter is coming. That will help."

"I've already got it on my list. One of the first things I noticed here was how clean you kept your toilet. So when it started stinking, I knew you had to be out of whatever you were using. So I made a note of it."

"Am I actually getting a compliment? I can hardly believe it. It must be a hallucination of the ears," I muttered to myself. "By the way, how do you plan to pay for these supplies? I have nothing to trade."

"Have you forgotten the cattle I rounded up for you? We can trade one of those for winter supplies or maybe two."

I sat up—suddenly more interested. I *had* forgotten about the cattle.

"Do you suppose you could trade one for a milk cow?" I asked.

"I think so," he responded. "I'll definitely take two head with me. In fact, I'll take that one with the calf. We'll have a hard time keeping that calf alive through the winter anyway. I was planning to butcher it, but this will be better. I should be able to get us pretty well situated with two cows and a calf."

After he left, I didn't do too much but pace the floor and watch the road to town. I couldn't settle down to anything. We went to bed when the sun went down because we didn't dare to light the lanterns. But we couldn't sleep either.

"What will we ever do when he leaves?" Jennie Lu finally put both of our thoughts into words.

"I don't know," I whispered. "God will help us."

I arose at dawn the next day and read the Bible. I was seeking comfort and peace. I began reading The Psalms and had gotten as far as the ninety-first one when Jennie Lu woke up. I read it to her and we prayed together, committing ourselves to God's care according to that Psalm. It worked wonders. We were able to go about the business of living without fear.

"What is 'the secret place of the Most High'?" Jennie Lu asked me later in the day.

"I think it's Jesus," I replied. "He's our hiding place. In another place it says 'a man shall be a covert from the storm.'"

CHAPTER 5
His View

When I arrived back at my own ranch, I went straight to the barn. My brother was surprised to see me. When I left and turned the ranch over to him, we thought we would never see each other again. I had planned to get as far as I could from this place and the woman in the house. So I had to tell him the whole story of the Lady and her daughter.

"The amazing thing is that she looks like Syble. She looks so much like her that I have a hard time being civil to her."

My younger brother looked thoughtful.

"You know Syble had a cousin that looked like her twin. Her parents raised both of them. They looked alike, but they were very different. She was just as respectable and religious as Syble was wild. Her mother had a dress and hat shop in town. She didn't live long after Syble went bad. Her daughter married a guy named Stone from over in Tateville. She was nice. Without her, I never would have made it in school. She took over mother's place and spent a lot of time with me. She was ahead of me in school and used to help me. I didn't know she had a daughter or any of this other stuff you told me. I'm glad you're helping her. She's nothing like Syble."

At the mention of that name, my mind was brought back to the present.

"Well, how is she, anyway?" I asked.

"Not good," my brother replied. "The doctor says she doesn't have long. She's gone completely crazy. I don't know if there'll be much left of the house when she dies."

At that, I just sat and remembered my foolishness. This younger brother of mine had tried to warn me about Syble and I hadn't listened. I had come home after my father's death to help run the ranch and finish raising my brother. Our mother had died years before. I met Syble at the tavern in town. She was beautiful and really took a liking to me.

"She's a whore!" my brother had warned.

I had threatened him and accused him of being judgmental.

"She's not a whore just because she works in a tavern!" I'd insisted.

After a short time, I married her and brought her out to the ranch. The first night, there was an emergency in the pasture. So I told her I'd be back later that night. I got back after midnight and found another man in our bed. Syble was yelling and beating on him, so I took out my gun. He started pleading with me not to shoot him because she had set him up.

"She got me drunk, then enticed me in here," he said.

Those were his last words before I shot him. As he was dying, I glanced at Syble in time to catch the look of satisfaction on her face before she could hide it and I realized in that moment that he had told me the truth.

My brother, Jimmy, had warned me that she'd been responsible for the death of several men. And now, all of a sudden, I knew it was true.

I walked out of that bedroom and could never bring myself to go in there again or to touch my wife. Now, she had some disease from having sex with many men and was dying.

All of this was the reason I had left—looking for a way to find peace of mind, only to run into Syble's cousin. It was unbelievable! Maybe there really was a God. Maybe He was showing me a way to regain my peace of mind. I couldn't bring the man back that I had killed. I couldn't do anything for Syble, but maybe I could save her cousin and her daughter. I realized I didn't even know The Lady's name, but things were going to change when I got back there. This was my purpose in life. It even gave meaning to the mess I'd made of my life up to now. Suddenly, I saw it all in a new way. There was a God who could redeem anything and anyone. I looked at the cross my parents had left over the barn door. Tears came to my eyes.

"What?" Jimmy asked.

"I feel like I've been redeemed," I answered.

"Does that mean you're not leaving?" Jimmy asked hopefully.

"I'm going to save that lady and her daughter if it kills me and I'll be close enough to see this mess through, also. I'm not leaving it all on you. I've got to face the music myself. I was a coward to run."

"But if you hadn't, you never would have known about Syble's cousin and her problems."

"I know. That's what I mean. I've been redeemed."

"I want to help you over there, too. I can bring all our hands over to fight with you. I owe that lady."

"Well, for right now, I need to take her a milk cow and some chickens and a lot of other supplies. Help me get this wagon loaded and then I need to hurry back. Is there someone to look after Syble if you come?"

"I've hired a nurse."

"Good. Tell the men we won't be long. We'll travel all night to get back over there."

All the ranch hands were relieved to hear that the older brother was back and wouldn't be far away. They had all been uneasy about the ranch being run by a twenty year old boy, no matter how good of a boy he was. When Jimmy had explained the situation over at the Stone place, they were all ready for a showdown right then.

"Not yet," Jimmy cautioned. "John wants to get to the bottom of it first. He and I are going to take a load of supplies over there, then I'll be back." He talked as he was packing ammunition out of their supplies in the barn.

"You guys can go into town and get more," he explained. "She can't go anywhere."

They all nodded.

"Now, keep this all under your hats. John doesn't want to scare them off till he can find out what they're really after." Jimmy threw these words over his shoulder as he went out the door.

CHAPTER 6
Her View

I didn't sleep much that night. It comforted me a little to know that trapper was in the barn, but I didn't really trust him either. I didn't trust anybody. I knew that anyone could turn on me. My friends had turned on me.

So I was standing on my porch, watching the sun come up and casting all my cares on Him, when I saw a wagon coming over the hill. It was that cowboy. I couldn't believe he was back already. Such a sense of relief swept over me that my knees almost buckled under me. I caught myself on the porch railing, only to have all my tension return when I saw that he had brought another man with him.

They stopped the wagon by the back door and began to carry its contents into the house and down the cellar stairs. I stood watching, with my gun in my hand. The second man was very young and looked very familiar to me. He kept glancing at me and smiling. Finally, he just stopped with a tin on his shoulder and looked straight at me.

"Mrs. Stone, do you remember me?" he asked. "I'm the boy you helped through school over in Titustown."

"Jimmy?" I asked, tentatively. "Jimmy McLane?"

"Yes!" he said, coming toward me with his hand extended. "This here is my big brother, John. The one that's been over here harassing you," he said, just as the cowboy came through the door with the last armload.

"He wasn't at home when you lived in Titustown."

I felt confused and overwhelmed. I sat down in a chair, still holding my gun.

"How did you men get back here so fast with all of this?" I asked.

"We traveled all night, taking turns sleeping," Jimmy answered. "John didn't want to be gone very long. He felt you were in danger."

I felt that confused feeling again. Could it be that he was really concerned about me? There had to be something else behind it. But when they went out again, I followed and left my gun behind. Jennie Lu was already out there, getting all excited about the animals.

"Look, Mother!" she exclaimed. "They brought a cow and chickens and two little goats. Aren't they cute? And there's an extra horse. They said I could ride her. And look, Mother! A kitten! Can I have her in the house, please!"

"They probably want her for a barn cat," I replied.

"They brought a grown cat for the barn. This kitten is for me."

I glanced at the cowboy and he nodded.

"Well, I guess you can have it, then," I replied.

The trapper came out of the barn just then and said, "I reckon I'll just go into town and see what's going on there since you boys are back here with the ladies. See you in a few hours."

We watched him disappear over the hill with his horse and mule. After a little pause, the cowboy spoke.

"Lady, I need to have a talk with you. Jimmy can keep an eye on your daughter, if it's all right with you."

I hesitated, but gave in as I watched Jimmy leading the goats and the cow and Jennie Lu toward the barn. He seemed to be the same sincere boy I had known so many years ago.

"There's no way you got all this for two cows and a calf," I accused.

"I didn't want to take the time to go to town, so I just brought everything from my ranch. We can settle up later," he explained, as he held the door for me and then pulled out a chair for me to sit at the table.

"How did you know about me?" I asked.

"I didn't. This was all a God-ordained accident. I was running away from the mess I'd made of my own life and happened to come by here. I tried to run away from this, too, but God wouldn't let me. And I didn't even know if there was a God."

We were both silent for a while. I had the strangest feeling like I was waking up from a nightmare into the real world again. I said as much to the cowboy.

"That is my determined purpose now," he said, "to put an end to your nightmare, and to do it, I've got to get to the bottom of it.

"Do you have a cousin named Syble?" he asked suddenly.

It was like a slap in the face.

I looked down at the floor and finally whispered, "Yes."

"Well, you don't need to be ashamed. It's not your fault.

"When I came home from my wanderings and found that both of my parents were dead, I started hanging out at the tavern in town and met her there. She took a liking to me and I ended up marrying her. Jimmy warned me not to, but I wouldn't listen until I found another man in bed with her on our wedding night. I had been called away on an emergency. I returned after midnight. I killed that man while he was begging me not to. He said she got him drunk and enticed him into her bed. After I shot him, I glanced at her and saw a look of great satisfaction on her face and I knew the man had told me the truth and that I was a fool and a murderer. From that time until now, I have never entered that bedroom. I went out to sleep with the ranch hands, then I finally tried to run from it and leave the whole mess in poor Jimmy's hands.

"Syble is dying now from some disease she got from living like that. Jimmy says she's gone crazy. He's hired a nurse to take care of her."

I was staring in disbelief. I'd thought that she was over there, living in the lap of luxury while I was facing death every day, but now I had been rescued and she was dying. Tears were running down my face in spite of all my efforts to hide my feelings. I loved Syble still, even though she had broken my mother's heart and sent her to an early grave and brought great shame upon us both. Finally, I began to sob as I put my face upon my knees.

The cowboy came over and put his hand on my back and I didn't even pull away from him. My grief was too great.

"The most amazing thing," the cowboy continued, "is that since I've experienced my redemption, my heart has softened toward Syble and I would like her to be redeemed and find peace before she dies. God used you to bring redemption to me, so maybe He could help her through you, also."

I suddenly sat up and stopped sobbing. "I must go see her immediately," I said.

"Tomorrow," the cowboy responded. "I have to wait for the trapper to come back.

"Now, I hate to put you through another emotional experience, but I wonder if you could show me where your husband died and where he's buried. I've got to get to the bottom of this whole thing. Did he say anything to you before he died, or was he completely gone when you found him?"

"I can show you," I sighed as I got up. "I buried him in a shallow grave. Evening was coming on and my daughter was in the wagon. She was only seven years old. I didn't dare leave her home alone and I was afraid—very afraid. I went to look for him when he didn't come home for supper. I found him just before he died. I think he had been hanging on, waiting for me to come. He was shot in the neck, but somehow managed to stay alive till I got there."

"Did he say anything?"

The question jarred me out of the silent remembering I had fallen into.

"'Don't give up the land,' he whispered. I had to put my ear right near his mouth to hear him. 'It's gold,' he added after a long pause.

"That's why I've fought so hard to keep this place," I added.

"Is that all he said?"

"Later, he said a couple of strange words. 'Pocket,' I think he said. 'Pocket,' but I might have misunderstood. Then, after a pause, he said, 'Silver' several times, then 'Jesus, Jesus, Jesus' as he left his body."

“Would you be willing to leave Jennie Lu here with Jimmy while we go find the grave?”

“No, she’s got to come with me. It’s not that I don’t trust Jimmy. I just can’t leave her behind, even for a short time.”

“Okay, I’ll saddle the horses.”

CHAPTER 7
His View

When we got to the grave site, I noticed that something or some-one had been digging around here and there. I said nothing to the women. They were already nervous. Actually, I was nervous myself. The Lady showed me where she had hidden the grave. She didn't know why she had felt compelled to hide it. It was covered with brush, and some cactus were growing on it. No one would have ever known it was there.

On the way back, I proposed a plan to the Lady. While she and Jennie Lu were visiting her cousin at my ranch, I would come back and build a coffin for her husband's body and move him to the ranch and bury him there.

"Would you be willing to do that?" she asked, incredulously.

"Yes," I answered. I was very curious about that "pocket" issue. I wanted to check all his pockets, but I didn't mention it to her. It looked to me like someone else was trying to find his body and I wanted to find out who it was and why.

Back at the ranch, the ladies were preparing for their trip, (I had told them to plan to stay a few days) while us men were having a conference in the barn. The trapper was back from his trip into town.

"They are planning for a showdown," he said. "I don't think I dare go back for any more ammunition. The guy that runs the store is getting suspicious. He was really grilling me about why I was back for more ammo. He sells jewelry and guns and ammunition. I never saw a man wearing so much silver as that guy. He had a silver belt buckle and silver buttons on his shirt and a couple of silver rings on his fingers and a silver hatband. No wonder everyone called him, 'Silver.'"

"What?!" I exclaimed.

He just gave me a blank stare.

"What did you say they called him?"

"Silver."

I sat down hard on a bale of hay. Things were starting to make sense real fast.

"Don't worry about going into town anymore," I said. "We'll get everything we need from our ranch."

"Your ranch?" he sounded puzzled. "Where's your ranch?"

"Just over that ridge."

"I thought you were a drifter."

"I was tryin' to be, but didn't get too far. Tomorrow, I'm taking the ladies there and bringing half my hands back here by the back way. I'm hopin' the fight will happen while the women are gone."

"It sounded to me like they were plannin' on next week. They think you are the only man here, so they're mighty sure of themselves."

"Good. Let's keep it that way. I don't want to scare them off and delay this thing. That will give me enough time to do some investigating on my own."

The next morning, we started out early for my ranch. The Lady and I were both amazed at how quickly we passed from her land to mine. There wasn't much territory in between.

"I can't believe we live this close to each other," she said.

"When your husband was dying and he kept saying, 'Silver,' did it seem like he was trying to say more?" I suddenly asked her.

"Yes. It was like he would build his strength to try to tell me something, but only got the one word out, then he would sink back into unconsciousness. Then he would summon all his strength to try again. I bent near him to hear more, but it was too faint. At the very last, I thought he might have said, 'did it,' but I couldn't be sure."

"Did you know there is a man they call 'Silver' in town?" I asked.

"No!" she almost shouted. "Oh, Jed, Jed, you were so trusting of everyone in that town," she cried.

"What do you mean?" I queried.

"My husband was raised in Tateville and he thought everyone there was his friend. He trusted them all and kept no secrets. He was like a child in that respect. I tried to caution him, but he wouldn't listen. He thought I was just suspicious because of being hurt so badly by Syble.

"He was keeping a secret from me at the last, though. He kept telling me he had a surprise for me, but I never found out what it was. His death was the only surprise I got. Sometimes I actually get angry at him, then sometimes I just cry."

"Who is this Silver guy, anyway?"

"He has a store in town that sells guns, ammunition and jewelry," I answered.

"Jed did mention that someone had started a jewelry store. I couldn't imagine how anyone around here could afford jewelry. He said I might be surprised."

I just kept listening and encouraging her to talk about her late husband. It seemed to do her good and I was gleaning information that might help me solve this mystery.

"What did you think he should keep secret?" I asked.

"I didn't think he should tell everyone in town how many cattle we had and how he was always prospecting for gold. He used to get a little, panning in the stream, and he would go sell it in town and tell everyone. He saved it all up and bought more land because we needed it and because he believed there was gold on that land. I don't think he ever found any, but he talked about it in town. I didn't think he should. I said he should sell it over in Titustown or somewhere else where he wasn't known."

I listened intently. I was starting to get a picture that made more sense.

When we got to my ranch, I took the women to the house immediately. It was apparent that the nurse knew the Lady. She called her Caroline and they exchanged hugs. Jennie Lu was introduced and shown a room where she would be staying.

CHAPTER 8
Her View

The McLane ranch looked just as nice as I remembered it. It brought tears to my eyes as I remembered happier times. Jimmy's parents were such nice Christian people. They had shown such appreciation for all my help to Jimmy. I remembered Mrs. McLane telling me about her older son and wishing he would come home and marry me so I could be her daughter.

When I entered that lovely ranch house, I was surprised to see Amy Tuttle. We had gone to school together. She was taking care of Syble. We agreed to send Jennie Lu to her room immediately since we didn't know how Syble would act.

Syble's room was in stark contrast to the rest of the house. Everything had been ripped from the walls. The bottom section of one window had been broken and boarded up. All the furniture but the bed had been removed.

Syble was lying across the bed on her stomach. She was as thin as a reed. Her hair was a matted mess. She was banging her head on the bed. She turned toward me with wild eyes.

"Hello, Syble," I said.

She stared at me for a long minute before she spoke.

"Caroline, is it you?" she whispered.

"It's me," I answered.

"Caroline, I didn't think I would see you again. How can you stand to look at me?"

"You're my sister. I love you."

"I made the wrong decision, Caroline, and now I'm dying. I'm going to hell. Sometimes I can feel the flames. Pray for me, Caroline, if you still love me."

I sat on the bed and held her in my arms and began to pray.

"Dear God, I forgive her and I ask You to forgive her. Jesus died for sinners."

"Please, God, for Jesus's sake, please save me. Please don't let me go to hell. I'm sorry, I'm sorry, I'm sorry....If only I could go back..." her voice trailed off.

I could feel her relaxing in my arms. The wild look went out of her eyes.

"Tell John the man he shot deserved to die. He killed two men for no reason," she said. "Tell him I'm sorry." Her voice trailed off as she seemed to go to sleep in my arms. I laid her on the bed and looked at Amy with a question in my eyes.

Amy came forward and felt her pulse.

"She's just sleeping. She hasn't slept for many nights. She says demons are tormenting her."

As we went out of the room, Amy told me that she had tried to tell Syble that God would forgive her if she'd ask, but she didn't believe her.

"I guess seeing that you forgave her made her believe that God could forgive her, too. I'm glad you came."

Just then, I looked up and saw John standing just inside the door. I walked over to him and took his hand.

"Thank you so much for what you've done for Syble. I'm so glad she's not dying alone somewhere. Did you hear what she said about the man you shot?"

John nodded his head and held my hand as he blinked back tears.

"Redeemed again," he whispered.

"I have some food here on the back of the stove," Amy spoke up.

"I can't take time to eat," John answered as he was giving money to Amy. "I have to hurry back to this Lady's place. I'm taking half the men with me and leaving half of them here to take care of you ladies. If Syble dies before I get back, they'll take care of everything. Don't tell anyone where I am. Don't go into town for any reason till I come back. If you need something in town, send one of the men." He started talking to Amy, but when he finished, he was talking to me.

"God be with you and keep everyone safe," I said as I nodded.

"Yes, and you also," he said as he went out the door.

On impulse, I ran out after him and called out.

"Please be careful. I don't want anyone to die because of me."

He stopped and turned slowly around. He walked back and stood before me and looked into my eyes before he spoke.

"Lady." His voice was low and intense. It hit something in the pit of my stomach that made me feel weak all over. "I would gladly die for you. I know no worthier cause to die for."

I stared at him with my mouth open. I couldn't think of a response. I was totally stunned and speechless. He took my hand in his and lifted it to his lips. Finally, he released it and said with a smile, "I have been redeemed!"

He turned and strode away.

I went back in the house quickly and found a chair to sit in. My mind was racing.

Whatever had come over "His Grouchiness"?

"Mother, come see our room."

Jennie Lu was peeking around the corner to see if she dared come in.

"Come eat something first," I suggested. "Amy has food warming on the stove. Let's eat before it dries out."

We sat down to eat and tried to answer all Amy's questions without saying too much about the mess back at my place.

After we ate, we got a tour of the house. There were plenty of rooms, but Jennie Lu and I chose to stay together in one room. We would both feel more secure together. Amy said she slept downstairs on a couch to be near Syble.

Jennie Lu and I went out to take a walk in the cool of the evening.

"Isn't this place wonderful?" Jennie Lu exclaimed. "It feels like we've gone to heaven. I don't feel afraid here."

When we got back in the house, Syble was awake and calling my name. I hurried into her room.

"I'm here," I assured her.

"Is it really you? I wasn't dreaming?"

"It's me."

"Is it true you have forgiven me and God has forgiven me, too?"

"Yes, it's true. John has forgiven you, too. He brought me here to help you. He wants you to be at peace."

Syble fell back on the bed and sighed. Then she sat straight up.

"My mother!" she said, pointing at the ceiling. "—And your mother, Caroline—see them? They're holding hands and beckoning me to come. They still love me. They want me—I'm going."

She fell back on the bed into unconsciousness.

Amy ran to her and felt her pulse. "Her heart is still beating, but very faintly. I don't think she'll last long," she said to me as she covered her with a sheet.

Syble lay in a coma for the rest of the week.

I had many long talks with Jennie Lu that week. I had to explain all the facts of life to her so she would understand what was happening to Syble.

"So, Mother, is that what they wanted to force you to do?" she asked. "To be like Syble?"

"Yes, I think so."

"Did they know about Syble? Is that why?" she asked.

"I don't think so," I answered. "I still don't understand it all."

Jennie Lu came and put her arms around me.

"I'm so glad you stood your ground, Mother."

"God helped me. It was for you and for Him, but it's not over yet."

"I think Mr. McLane will finish it. I think he's just as determined as you are."

I said nothing. I was still in awe of the dramatic change that had come over him.

CHAPTER 9
His View

I arrived back at the Stone ranch in the middle of the night with six of my men. We went straight to the barn. There was a full moon, so they had already recognized us and let us in immediately.

"Boy, am I glad to see you guys," Jimmy spoke quietly as he helped unload the wagon. "I've been getting nervous."

"Let's all get bedded down and try to get a few hours' sleep before daybreak. We'll talk tomorrow," I said, carrying my bedroll toward my stall where I'd been sleeping for months.

When I awoke, I could smell coffee. Our cook had already headed for the house and was preparing breakfast there. We all headed over.

As we ate, I explained things.

"In the future, we won't be seen in a group like this. There's people in town plannin' to burn this lady out and I don't want to scare them off by seeing a lot of men here. I want them to think it's still just one drifter hangin' around. I want this whole thing to come to a head out in the open. I want to find out what they are after. They are trying to force this woman to move into town, give up her ranch, and start a bar in town. But I think there's something else behind it.

"So you can keep cooking over here in the house just as if the Lady were still here. One man will come over and get the food and carry it to the barn. That will look normal. Only one man outside at a time during daylight. No one in here at night.

"Right now, I've got to go dig up the body of Jed Stone and bring it back here for a proper burial. I've already made a casket of some old boards in the barn. I'll need two volunteers to go with me. One as a lookout and one to help dig and carry. You boys start moving out of here one at a time through the back door."

Over in the barn, we put the coffin in the wagon. One man lay in the coffin and the other beside it. I got up to drive the horses.

"You okay with being in that box?" I asked.

"Just as long as you don't put the lid on it," he answered.

I had to chuckle.

I dropped one man off just over the ridge to watch while we drove the wagon on down to the stream. We cleared the brush and began to dig. The body wasn't more than three feet down. She'd done good to bury it that deep. It was in surprisingly good condition. Pretty much just dried and shriveled up. He had a gunshot wound in the back of the head and another in the shoulder.

I immediately began to check his pockets. From his right front pocket, I pulled a beautiful necklace made of gold and diamonds. I knew for whom that had been intended. But how could he afford it? In another pocket, I found a faded paper. It was some kind of receipt signed by a strange name. I couldn't make it out. It said something about gold. With it was a lot of money I didn't take the time to count.

We quickly lifted him into the coffin, put on the lid, and began to fill in the hole. We had barely got it onto the wagon when there was a whistle from the ridge. We ran up and threw ourselves down beside the lookout. We could see a man approaching on horseback, but he was starting to veer off toward the cliffs. We watched him for a few minutes, then I told the boys to take the wagon back to the ranch. I wanted to track this guy on foot.

I followed his trail until I found the horse tied outside a cave. This was the source of the stream by which Jed Stone had been buried. I ducked inside and waited for my eyes to adjust. I soon began to detect a distant glimmer and the sound of a pickaxe. I followed it very slowly. I soon saw the answer to this whole puzzle.

A man was digging and chuckling to himself about getting the gold while everyone was occupied with that stubborn woman.

"The longer she holds out, the more I'll get for myself before old Tate ever gets in here. What a stupid man he is!"

I watched him and listened to his muttering for a while, then quietly left. Now I understood the whole thing. It was all about gold and greed. That had to be the man they called 'Silver.' I was sure he was the man who killed Jed Stone. But I needed more evidence or an excuse to shoot him. And how did old man Tate figure into this?

When I got back to the ranch, it was suppertime. I went into the house so I could carry supper over to the barn. I glanced into the bedroom and saw that wedding dress hanging. I decided to come back after dark and carry some things out of the house and store them in the barn. After supper, I went into the house so I could choose what to pack while there was still some light. I decided to carry all the sewing supplies over to the barn, including the sewing machine. I also found some quilts that they had probably made. There wasn't much else in the house but a few pictures. I recognized the man whose body I had just dug up in a wedding picture with The Lady. He was a handsome young man.

I waited until dark, then I carried it all over to the barn while I had some men digging a grave. It was a strange feeling, having that dead body around. I was anxious to get it buried. It seemed I could feel that man's presence. We made a marker for the grave and got it finished and the marker in place as quickly as possible. We all had that uneasy feeling. We were relieved to get out of sight and into the barn. We all bedded down for the night. I lay there, feeling so relieved that I'd got that Lady and her daughter out of that house. I'd made up my mind to let them burn the house down so there could be no question about who was involved or what their intentions were. Besides, I wanted The Lady to stay at my place for a while. She needed a rest and this would force her into it.

I finally fell asleep as I thought on all these things. I was surprised when I awoke and saw the light of dawn. I didn't think I'd be able to sleep. I could see smoke from the chimney in the house. The cook was already on the job. I had some good men working for me. I had my parents to thank for that.

When I started moving around, the other men started getting up, too. I had a pot for them, so we wouldn't make so many trips to the outhouse. So when everyone had used it, I took it to the outhouse and then I carried a bucket of water into the barn so everyone could wash up. Then I carried more water for the animals. Some of the men were feeding them when I got back with the water. By the time we finished all that, I thought I'd better go over and check on breakfast. Sure enough, it was ready and I carried it over to the barn. It was a big pot of oatmeal and coffee and some bread of some kind. We would have fresh milk from the cows. He had also boiled some eggs, so we had plenty to eat. When I took the pots and dishes back to the house, Andy, our cook, was already making plans for lunch and supper.

"I need to have a talk with you," I said as I sat at the kitchen table. He came and sat down across from me.

"Don't like the food?" he asked with a grin.

"The food is great. I just want to talk over with you what I'm expecting and make some plans together."

Andy got serious real quick.

"Okay," he said.

"I'm expecting people to come from town and burn this house down any time now."

"We could stop them," Andy said, looking at me with a puzzled expression.

"I know we could, but I want to let them do it. I want to catch them all red-handed so there won't be any questions about who's guilty," I explained. "I want to find out just how far they will go."

We sat in silence for a few minutes while Andy thought that over.

"The problem is," I finally continued, "you will lose your kitchen. So I think we'd better move it into the barn after dark tonight. I hope we can get it done before they show up. This will also save the kitchen for the Lady."

"I'll have everything packed up and ready to go by suppertime. I'll cook the food this morning for both meals. We can eat it cold or warm it over there after we move the stove. We will move the stove over there, won't we?"

"Definitely! I'll get all the men to help and we'll have it done in no time!"

I studied the stove for a few seconds. It was a beautiful big old cast iron stove with a warming cupboard and even a hot water tank. The Lady certainly wouldn't want to lose it. I'd have to ask her the story behind it later. It looked too big and elegant for her little house. There had to be a story behind it. I wondered if it were a wedding present. That thought took me suddenly back to the night I watched her through the window, modeling her wedding dress. A thought began to tickle my mind, but I quickly pushed it down and snapped back to the present. Andy was watching me.

"Sure a nice big one," I said. "It'll be heavy, but we've got the manpower to move it."

"Good," Andy said. "I would sure miss it if I had to do without it."

That evening, right after supper, as soon as it was dark, we all went over to the house to move the kitchen. I felt a little guilty that I was letting those people burn the Lady's house down, so it made me feel better to save as much as I could for her. We moved everything in the kitchen but the curtains. We couldn't change the look on the outside. We even moved her cupboards if they weren't attached to the walls.

"Tomorrow we can help Andy set up his kitchen in the barn," I suggested.

"How long will I be cooking here?" he asked.

"Well, after they burn this house, I've got to see that it's rebuilt bigger and better. So it may be quite a while."

"I'll do a good job then of making a kitchen," he announced.

"Make it as good as you can," I agreed.

Andy began looking at the sink cabinet.

I think I can even move this," he murmured as he began disconnecting it from the wall.

"You might as well take all you can," I said as I began to help him. We soon had the kitchen stripped completely bare. We even moved the old couch and chair, though they were in pretty poor shape. We decided they were better than nothing.

"What about the food in the cellar?" Andy asked.

"Man, I am so glad you thought of that!" I exclaimed. "I would have forgotten until it was too late."

By the time we finished, we were all exhausted and ready for sleep. But we had barely gotten settled in and dozed off, when I was awakened by the sound of fire and the smell of smoke. All the other men were on their feet at the same time as I was. We were all strapping on our guns and heading for the back door of the barn at the same time. We had this well rehearsed. I didn't have to give any instructions. The men began to disappear into the darkness one at a time. I went out last and quietly closed the door. By the time I came around the barn, there was a pretty good fire going. I could see ten men. I counted them very carefully. I didn't want anyone to get away. They moved around to watch both doors and the back window. They were trying to stay in the shadows because they were afraid of the Lady's shotgun. The one that went around back to watch the back window had already been pistol whipped and tied up and gagged by my men. Pretty soon, I saw another man melt into the darkness by himself and I knew he was a goner, too.

"Down to eight," I muttered to myself.

Just then, old man Tate started to shout, "Caroline Stone! Your house is on fire! Come out right now." He waited, but when there was no response, he raised his voice louder. After about four attempts with no response, he began to panic. He ran to the side away from the fire and pounded on the door and then the windows.

"Caroline!, Caroline!" he screamed. "Don't kill yourself. I'll take care of you and your daughter. You'll be safe in town." He tried to open the door, but it was locked. He ran to the other door, but it was engulfed in flames. He began throwing stones at the windows and broke them. Then he started to climb in, but the guy they called Silver told the others to pull him down and hold him.

"You're an idiot!" he said. "I ought to let you go in there and die with her. If she wants to die, it's her business. It'll just be less trouble for you and for me."

When Tate saw he couldn't pull himself free, he began to sob like a child.

"My God! My God! What have I done? How did I get so blinded?"

"The love of money is the root of all evil!" He kept saying over and over between sobs.

"Please, let me go in there and die with them!" he begged. "I deserve it."

The men holding him looked at Silver for instructions. He shrugged.

The house was nearly fully engulfed in flames by this time.

When they let go of Tate, I called out.

"Don't anyone move or we'll shoot. You're surrounded."

Everyone froze but "Silver". He was looking frantically in all directions. He started to run away from me into the darkness. Three shots rang out and he dropped.

"Take your guns off slowly," I instructed.

There was a quick movement by one man and another shot rang out and he dropped to the ground. The other men slowly removed their guns and dropped them to the ground. I then came out of the darkness and picked them all up, including the one in the hand of the man I had shot. I didn't want to take any chances.

Tate was still lying on the ground, quietly sobbing. I walked over to him and said, "The Lady and her daughter are not in that house."

He got quiet and sat up and stared at me. It took a few seconds for my words to sink in. Just then, Jimmy came into the firelight. Tate looked back and forth from one to the other. After a while, he got up very slowly, never taking his eyes off of us.

"Are you the McLane brothers?" he finally asked.

"Yes," I replied.

"I'm glad she went to you for help," he said.

"She didn't. God brought me to her."

He looked puzzled.

"It's a long story." I dismissed his questions before they came. "You'll hear it someday."

Just then, the sheriff came out of the darkness.

"Well, McLane, you were right and I was wrong," he said. "Silver had us all deceived. I didn't believe he would go this far. I didn't believe he was actually a murderer.

"Where are Mrs. Stone and her daughter?" he asked.

"They are at my ranch, being well cared for. And they will stay there while you men rebuild their house. I had to let you burn it down to wake you up."

"You sure woke me up," Tate said. "Silver had me convinced that I had a right to that gold because I sold the land to them and now that her husband was dead, I was going to be responsible, as a church leader, for the care of a widow and orphan."

"Silver killed her husband," I interjected.

Tate put his head in his hands and moaned. "How could I be such a blind fool? I'll gladly rebuild her house and supply the material."

"How about the rest of you?" the sheriff asked. "You want to rebuild the house, or go to jail and stand trial for your crimes?"

They all agreed to work on the house.

"We'll build it bigger and better than it was," I said as I pulled out my plans from my pocket. The men all gathered around to listen to my plans. They were like men who had woken up from a bad dream and were relieved that it was over. They were all excited about this new project and were making suggestions. It was like some kind of spell had been broken by Silver's death. It was an amazing thing to see.

"These were all basically good men," I thought. "I'm glad I didn't have to shoot them. It was like they were under some kind of spell or something."

When I had them all busy cleaning up the mess they'd made and had given instructions about making the foundation and cellar twice as big as it was before, my thoughts began to wander back to my own place. I kept wondering what was going on back there.

"What's on your mind?" Jimmy's voice interrupted my thoughts.

"Oh, I've just been wondering what's going on back home," I explained.

"Why don't you go check on it? We've got this under control now. The sheriff just headed for town with those two dead bodies, and Tate has gone home to get more food supplies and building supplies for us and I've got a list here of stuff that Andy wants from our ranch. One of us needs to go back. It might as well be you."

"Okay," I said as I headed for the barn. "Help me load up The Lady's sewing supplies. I need to keep them clean somehow."

We found old things in the barn in which to wrap the sewing supplies and especially that wedding dress. Then I called all the men together and explained the situation as best I could.

"I've got to tell her what happened to her house," I explained, "and help her bury her cousin."

I didn't mention that her cousin was my wife. I couldn't address that subject.

"Be sure to tell her how sorry we are for what we did," one of the men spoke up.

"Yes," they all joined in. "And tell her we're going to rebuild it. And we're sorry about her cousin."

I nodded as I headed for the wagon. "Jimmy's in charge until I get back," I threw over my shoulder as I walked away. I heard a few murmurs. I stopped and turned around.

"Has someone got a problem with that?" I asked.

"Not from this bunch," Andy spoke up quickly.

I turned to the others.

"If you've got a problem with the McLanes, you're welcome to head for town and report to the sheriff."

"No problem," they all chorused.

Jimmy walked with me to the wagon.

"There's a trouble maker in there somewhere, so be careful and watch your back," I said to him. "If you have a problem, don't hesitate to come get me. It's been a week since we left home and I feel like I need to go over there."

"Don't worry. I'll be okay."

With that, I slapped the reins and left the Stone place. I was surprised at how anxious I was to go home. How could I feel like this when I was so anxious to leave that place just a short time ago? As I traveled, I had to remind myself not to push the horses.

The sun was sinking when I rode into the yard. I noticed all the men were standing outside, looking toward the house.

"What's going on?"

"She's dying."

I jumped from the wagon and ran toward the house. During my trip over, I'd done a lot of thinking. I had finally realized that Syble wasn't the only one who had committed sins. She had hoped to leave her old life behind her by marrying me, but I had completely deserted her. I had even left her to die alone.

Caroline was holding Syble in her arms as I stood in the door of the bedroom. Syble was barely breathing. I pushed through that invisible barrier that I had never crossed since that fateful night. I fell on my knees beside her bed.

"Syble," I whispered. "I'm sorry I deserted you in your time of need."

She opened her eyes and smiled.

"I forgive," she whispered as she raised one arm toward me.

I gathered her into my arms and took Caroline's place. I began to sob against her hair. She smiled faintly and put her hand on my face. I held her like that until her hand slid from my face. Her breaths came farther and farther apart. Until finally, they ceased altogether. I held her a while longer, then I finally laid her down and straightened her body and folded her hands across her chest. I went out into the kitchen where Amy and Caroline had respectfully retreated.

"She's gone," I stated in a gruff voice. "I'll get the men to start digging her grave and send someone for the Parson tomorrow."

"We'll prepare her body," Amy volunteered.

"Thanks," was all I could manage.

I went to the barn and started barking orders. I knew I sounded bad, but it was the only way I could maintain my composure. While they were building the coffin, I walked around the place, seeking where I should bury her. Not by my parents. Not near the house. Then I saw it. The chair she used to sit in was still there under the cherry tree. She used to sit there and watch everything I did until I thought I would go crazy.

I sat down in the chair and broke down again.

"She was trying to win me back in the only way she knew," I muttered between sobs. I remembered how she would be dressed to kill in the clothes she wore in the tavern. "This is where I'll bury her."

I went back to the barn to get a shovel and some men came back with me to help me dig. It did me good to work at digging that grave. I seemed to be getting control of myself.

It was dark when we finished. I noticed the lamps were lit in the house and the bunk house. There was a full moon, so we had no problem working.

I finally headed for the house. I had to do a better job of showing appreciation and I had some unfinished business with the Lady and her daughter.

When I came in, they were sitting around the kitchen table, talking in subdued tones. I noticed they had closed the door to Syble's bedroom. I was glad of that. They offered me food and I didn't refuse this time. When I started to eat, I realized I was famished. I cleaned up all their leftovers for them.

"How are things back at our place?" Jennie Lu finally got the nerve to ask.

"Well," I said, "that's what I came to talk to you about, but I got distracted." My voice cracked, but I got my control back quickly. "I have both bad and good news."

They all looked at me expectantly, waiting. I took another drink of coffee.

"They burned your house down," I blurted out.

There were gasps from all the ladies and tears in Jennie Lu's eyes.

I reached over to pat her arm.

"We're already rebuilding it," I added quickly.

"But my wedding dress!" she almost moaned.

"I saved it for you."

The Lady was looking at me with those piercing eyes of hers. She was figuring some things out already.

I smiled and answered her unspoken question.

"Yes, I knew they were coming, but I didn't stop them because I wanted to catch them in the act to prove to the sheriff how wicked Silver really was and that he was the one who murdered your husband.

"We were able to arrest them all and I only had to shoot two men—Silver and one of his hired killers. Once Silver was dead, they all seemed to wake up from some kind of spell. They said to tell you how sorry they are and they're working now to rebuild your house.

"Since the trapper had told us they were coming, we were able to strip your house of everything but the curtains. We worked after dark so their spies wouldn't see what we were doing."

"You saved my kitchen stove?"

"Yes, they're cooking on it in the barn."

Caroline gave a sigh of relief. "I got that from my mother."

Just then, we heard the wagon being pulled up to the door.

"You wanted to unload this at the house?" a voice called out.

"Yes," I called back. "Bring it all in."

The ladies stared in amazement as the men brought in armloads of sewing supplies and then, last of all, the sewing machine itself.

When they had left to take care of the horses, Caroline asked, "Why did you bring all that over here?"

"Two reasons. First, I didn't want it to get messed up in the barn."

Caroline nodded and waited for the second reason.

I took her by the hand and led her back to the table.

"Sit back down for a few minutes," I said.

She obeyed, but slowly.

"Lady, it's going to take us a while to build your house, so I want you and your daughter to stay here at my house. I'll be very busy going back and forth and I need someone to look after this place."

"What about Jimmy?"

"He's going to be busy over there, too. He's excited about building your house. He says you did a lot for him when he was in school. When I come over here, I'll be staying in the bunkhouse."

"Who is going to cook for all those men over there?" she asked.

"Andy, our cook, is over there."

"Please, Mother," Jennie Lu begged. "I love it here. I feel so safe here."

The Lady looked back at me and shrugged. "I guess I'll have to do it," While her daughter was clapping her hands and rejoicing, I asked the Lady quietly, "Do you feel safe here?"

She nodded.

"I'm so glad to hear that. I want you to relax and get your life back to normal.

"Would you walk with me out to see the grave?" I asked.

She got up obediently, but glanced at the pile of sewing supplies.

"You can make any room into your sewing room," I said. "I want you to make yourself completely at home."

As we were walking, I pulled the jewelry out of my pocket and explained it all to her.

"Your husband is now properly buried near your house. And you have much more gold than you thought. That jewelry was the secret he was keeping from you and the fact that he had found gold. The sheriff found quite a bit that Silver had been stealing from you."

"So I'll be able to pay the men who are rebuilding my house?" she asked.

"No," I answered firmly. "They are doing that in place of standing trial and going to jail or worse."

She was silent for a while as she examined the beautiful jewelry her late husband had bought for her.

Finally she spoke, more to herself than to me.

"What will a poor woman like me do with this?"

"Lady, I don't think you understood me. You are not a poor woman."

She looked up at me with the most pathetic look I had ever seen.

"I don't know what to do with that gold, either. I think I'm afraid of it. It has already turned my friends into enemies, caused my daughter and I much suffering, cost my husband his life, and almost cost Jennie Lu and I our lives. Must I live with this fear the rest of my life, never trusting anyone ever again? I'm tempted to walk away from it, but then how many deaths would I be responsible for?"

I suddenly had a completely different view of the whole issue. I saw this potential for wealth as a huge responsibility rather than something that would make you carefree and happy. Yes, even as something dangerous.

We walked on in silence for some time. The Lady put the jewelry in her pocket with a huge sigh. "I will give it to Jennie Lu as a wedding gift from her father," she said with finality. "He meant well, but he didn't take it seriously enough," she said, almost under her breath.

By this time, we were at the grave. We just stood there in silence. We both had a lot of grieving to do and didn't know how to do it. I think we both had tears running down, but we made no sound until the Lady began to speak quietly.

"This grave looks like a door to me. A door I wish I could walk through, like Syble, before my time. But I dare not. Too much depends on me now. Not just my daughter now. I fought to live for her sake. But now, I feel a heavy yoke has been placed upon me and I must bear up under it for the work that God has chosen for me and I don't even fully understand what it is. But I am His servant and I will follow on as best I can. But I will never fear death again. I have gone with two people I loved right up to that door and saw them pass over. I am ready whenever my time comes to pass through that door."

I had to lean near her to hear what she was saying. I was very moved by it and it seemed to totally illuminate my mind to the fact that I also had been chosen of God for some purpose and I could never be the same again. I could not walk away from my responsibilities ever again and part of that responsibility was to help this Lady bear her burden and to protect her and her daughter.

Finally, I spoke.

"I want you to know that I am your neighbor and friend and I will always be here to help you. You will never be all alone again. I believe you and my brother are the reasons I was brought back here and I don't intend to ever leave again. I am so grateful that I came in time to make peace with Syble before she died."

The Lady looked up and smiled.

"I appreciate your friendship. It makes me feel a little better about this whole thing and I also am glad for your time with Syble. She told me that all she ever wanted was someone to love her. After she'd walked away from the only people who ever loved her, my mother and I, she started looking for love in all the wrong places and then she met you and thought she could start a new life, but her old life wouldn't let her go. Right at the last, she finally got what she wanted and it gave her peace. I'm so glad."

I offered her my arm as we headed back toward the house and she placed her hand on it.

"Is the war over between us?" she asked.

"Absolutely!"

Just then, we heard a horse and rider approaching. It was the man I had sent to town.

"The parson says he'll try to be here by ten o'clock in the morning," he said.

I said "Good Night" to the Lady and headed for the bunkhouse. I was suddenly very tired.

CHAPTER 10
Her View

After the funeral, Amy went back to town with the Parson. That left Jennie Lu and me all alone in the McLane's big ranch house. We got immediately busy setting up our sewing room. We talked about how wonderful it felt to have all the trouble over. I found myself singing as I worked. I hadn't felt this good since the early days of my marriage. I found that Mrs. McLane had a sewing room, so we just moved all of our stuff into it. It had a door into the bedroom that Syble had destroyed which we could just keep closed because there was another door into the living room with its big windows with a view of the barns and the barnyard. From the window in the sewing room, you could see the road and the beautiful countryside. I realized that from this sewing room, Mrs. McLane could keep an eye on everything that was going on.

Jennie Lu decided she would have her own bedroom now. This was a sign of the confidence we were both developing. She even went outside and wandered around by herself. She came running back to tell me she had found a swing out behind a building she thought was a woodshed. I followed her out to see it. We worked together to clear the area of weeds and trash. I realized this play area was in view of the kitchen window. That relieved any worries I had about her being out alone. I was still thinking about her safety. Would I ever get over what we'd been through? Probably not.

When we had the place cleaned up, I tested the swing to see if the ropes would hold. Jennie Lu gave me a few pushes. It felt good. I hadn't been in a swing for years. Then I pushed her, but she was soon swinging on her own. Her laughter was music to my ears. I wanted her to have some pleasant childhood memories.

As I was walking back to the house, I noticed some flowerbeds that needed to be weeded. They seemed to call me and I couldn't resist. I found a shovel and hoe in the building that Jennie Lu had thought was a woodshed. I got one bed all cleaned up and looking nice before I went in to fix lunch. It had been a wonderful morning. I felt so good, I had to hug myself. When Jennie Lu came in to eat, I hugged her.

"Isn't it wonderful?" she exclaimed. "Do you think heaven would be better than this?"

"It does feel a lot like Heaven," I agreed. "I wonder how long we'll have to stay here."

"A long time, I hope," Jennie Lu exclaimed.

"Don't you even miss our own place?" I asked.

Jennie Lu was quiet for a while. "I'm beginning to remember when we were happy there and I had a father who loved me. I miss that," Jennie Lu admitted. "But I don't want to go back there because all the bad stuff will probably start again," she added.

"I know the feeling," I sighed. "But I believe it's over. The man who caused it all is dead."

"He is?"

"Yes, he is."

"Hallelujah," Jennie Lu exclaimed as she sat down to eat. "Where'd you get this food?" she asked between bites.

"I'm just using what's here in the pantry. There's not much. We just barely got a cellar full of food at our house and then we had to leave."

"I know! Oh well, you're good at making do. This is a good lunch."

I squeezed Jennie Lu's shoulders before I sat down to join her.

"You're a good daughter," I said. "I don't know what I would do without you."

"Hopefully you'll never have to find out."

I smiled, but felt a pang inside, knowing how soon Jennie Lu would leave me to make a life for herself. I remembered how I had found my mother weeping on my wedding day. We had started down the road when I remembered a treasure I had forgotten and ran back to get it. She had wiped her tears away and said she was just being foolish. But I had never forgotten it. I knew my day was coming. How many times I had longed to be back with my mother. But you can never turn the clock backward. I would do my best to make some happy memories for my daughter while I still had her.

"What are you thinking about, Mother?" Jennie Lu's voice interrupted my reverie.

"I was just remembering my mother. I wish you could have known her. But I'd better get to eating before my food is cold."

"If I help with the dishes, could you come out again and work in the flowers while I swing? That seemed so wonderful to me. We've been hiding in the house for so long."

"There is nothing I'd rather do. Put some water on to heat while I finish up here. I think there is still fire in the stove. I have beans on for supper, so I just have to keep that fire going. We can remind each other to run in and put a stick of wood in the stove every little while and check that the beans haven't gone dry."

When we got outside and I had given Jennie Lu a few pushes, I started on the second flowerbed. Mrs. McLane had beautiful flowers and shrubs, but no one had cared for them for a long time. Some of the weeds were bigger than the plants I was trying to preserve, so I had quite a job on my hands. I didn't get all the roots out but I got most of them. When I was done, that side of the house looked very nice. It gave me a good feeling to stand back and look at it. There were window boxes, but I didn't know what I could do for them. It would cost money to plant flowers there. In the garden shed, I found some paint that had been used for the fence and the window boxes. I decided to give them a fresh coat. Jennie Lu wanted to help, so I let her. We both went in and put old clothes on out of the rag bag. I wore some of the men's clothes I used to wear at our place. No one was around to see me. We had a lot of fun and got paint all over ourselves. When we were through, the house looked very nice, but we were a mess.

While we were standing there admiring our handiwork, we heard a male voice behind us.

"Well, you ladies sure did a good job on that house."

We both whirled around in shock. Who could it be? It was the cook for the ranch hands. He smiled at our confusion.

"I just came over to invite you both for supper," he said. "I thought I'd better give you time to clean up before the rest of the men get back here. They found a cow with a broken leg yesterday so I butchered it today. I'm smoking some of it, but we're having a big barbeque tonight and you ladies are invited. In fact, there's no reason why you shouldn't have supper with us every night. Or if you don't like our company, you could take some food over to the house. There can't be too much to cook in that house. No one has cooked in there for a long time."

"There isn't much but we've been getting by. I've got some beans on for supper. I guess some barbecued beef would go good with them since I couldn't find any meat to flavor them with."

"Well, I can take them over and add them to mine, if you don't mind. I used the last of my beans and I was afraid I didn't have quite enough."

"Of course. I'll go get them."

"No, let me get that pot. It's probably very heavy."

The cook named Jerry walked into the kitchen with us. He looked around and smiled.

"It sure is nice to see this house with a woman's touch again. You've done a great job already."

"Thank you. I love doing it," I answered as he carried our bean pot out the door and we began dipping water from the water tank so we could try to clean up.

"These clothes will never come clean," we both agreed with a chuckle, "but that was fun."

We put our dresses back on and combed each other's hair.

"I'll wash these old clothes and keep them in case we decide to paint again. There's not enough paint to do much more, though."

"I think Mr. McLane can buy more if he wants to," Jennie Lu commented.

I didn't answer, but I realized that she was probably right. It was hard to quit thinking in terms of poverty and hardship.

I walked over and looked out the window in time to see the men bringing the wagons in from the fields. They were all dirty and probably very tired. The wagons were all piled high, some with hay, some with corn. The cook had a big pot on the open fire. He began to shuck some of the corn and throw it into the boiling water. It made my mouth water, just to watch.

"I'm sure glad you didn't refuse to go over for supper," Jennie Lu spoke up beside me. "I was afraid you would."

"I almost did, but I couldn't refuse the chance for some meat. Besides, Mr. McLane told me we should eat over there until we could go to town for supplies. I just haven't had the nerve to go over there yet."

"That cook seemed like a nice man," Jennie Lu offered. She was reading between the lines. She saw that I was still wearing the gun that John McLane had given me.

"Yes, he did," I agreed.

Just then, he turned and looked our way and motioned for us to come. So we turned toward the door and walked out together.

"It feels like the beginning of a new life," I murmured as we went through the door.

"Amen!" Jennie Lu agreed.

That night, we had a very comfortable time with a group of men. At first, I was very self-conscious, but they were all very friendly without being pushy. I was able to relax around them. It really was like the beginning of a new life. Jennie Lu and I began to help Jerry by serving the food and later, we helped with the dishes. He was getting older, so I knew this was hard work for him. The younger cook, Andy, was over at my place cooking for those men. During the evening, I learned that Jerry's wife, who used to help in the kitchen, had passed away. There was a log cabin out behind the barn where he lived and they had lived there together for many years. Her grave was under a big tree near the cabin. After I heard his story, I made up my mind that I would help with the cooking as long as I was there.

"What time do you start fixing breakfast?" I asked him.

"About five o'clock."

CHAPTER 11
His View

I got up early and headed for the Stone place. I felt like I needed to hurry back. I had a suspicion that my troubles were not over there. I was so glad that the Lady and her daughter were not there to see and hear all that went on. I knew there was at least one troublemaker still among the men from town.

From the ridge, I looked back at my ranch. A lantern had been lit in my parents' home and smoke was rising from the chimney.

"She's an early riser," I muttered to myself. I was glad I had asked Jerry to make sure they had food. She would be too proud to go over there, even though I had told her to. And I knew there was very little in the house.

The closer I got to the Stone Place, the more I felt that heavy sense of foreboding. My thoughts began to run over all the evil that had happened there. I hoped that my memories were giving me this heavy feeling and not the present situation. But as soon as the place came in view, I knew something was wrong. The sun was high in the sky, but none of the men from my ranch were working on the house. I changed my direction and skirted the place so I could check it all out before I was seen. The men from town were working on the house, but they definitely were not following my instructions. So I continued around to the back of the property and approached the barn from the rear where I would be out of sight. I tied the horse a little distance from the barn and walked the rest of the way in. I let myself quietly in the back door.

All of my men were around the table, having a meeting. Jimmy was talking.

"If John doesn't come today, I will go after him," he said. "I agree that we can't have any part in what they are doing, but I don't want to get into a big fight with them either."

"I'm here," I spoke up. "What's going on?"

The men jumped and turned around and started to laugh with relief.

"Man, are we glad to see you," several of them exclaimed.

Jimmy started to explain what was happening.

"There is one man out there who keeps complaining and stirring up trouble and he finally convinced all the others to go along with him. He says they shouldn't have to dig that cellar bigger than it is or make the house any bigger. They should only have to replace what was there. But then he acts like he's being generous and says he's willing to extend the house out over the ground a little bit just to be nice, but they have to leave the cellar just like it is. Cleaning it was a big enough job."

I got up and looked out the window.

"Is it that guy with the red plaid shirt on?" I asked.

"That's him," they all answered.

"That was one of Silver's hired guns, I think. We shot the other ones, but he was smart enough not to run. I figured he was going to cause trouble. He's probably still got a gun on him somewhere, so I'll have to be careful."

"What are you going to do with him?" Jimmy sounded alarmed.

"Just take him in to the sheriff and let him handle it," I replied.

That seemed to help Jimmy relax a little.

"Well, you be careful."

"We'll go out there and keep him covered," one of the men offered.

They all showed their agreement by getting up and strapping on their guns. I could tell they were relieved to be doing something.

"You stay in here with Andy," I said to Jimmy. "I don't want you involved in this."

He didn't argue, but I saw he was puzzled.

We all went quietly out that back door and started fanning out around the group at the house site. No one seemed to notice until I called out.

"Okay, everyone stop working and put your hands on your heads." They all complied but old red shirt. I saw his hand moving toward his shirt front. I shot at the ground by his feet and his hands flew up. I walked over and ripped his shirt open and took his gun while my men were closing in.

"Put your hands behind your back," I ordered. I tied them with rope while someone brought his horse.

"I didn't do nothin' wrong," he protested. "I been workin' hard here. Ain't that right?" he asked the men who were still standing there with their hands raised. They all nodded solemnly.

"It's your men's been sitting in the barn doing nothing," he continued.

I helped him up on his horse but I held tight to the reins.

"You can put your hands down now," I said to the other men, "but I can't believe you all are so easily influenced after what you've just been through. I thought sure you had learned your lesson. Silver had you all believin' that evil was good and good was evil. Now you let this guy do the same thing. When are you going to learn to see through these deceivers?"

Old man Tate just groaned and put his head in his hands.

I walked over and looked at what they'd done while one of my men held the horses.

"This is not fit for anything but a porch," I said. "But we won't tear it down. You can extend the cellar in the other direction and this house will have a porch on the side as well as the front."

Tate looked relieved and started to smile again.

"You men keep it up and that Lady will end up with a mansion," I threw over my shoulder as I walked away.

They all started to laugh and joke about the mansion they were building and all the tension was gone. Well, not completely. Old Red Shirt was plenty tense. I could see the sweat beading up on his forehead. I mounted my horse and took the reins of his and headed for town. After a little while, he spoke.

"Where we goin'?" he asked.

"To town," I answered. He started breathing a little easier. I guess he thought I was going to take him off somewhere and shoot him.

After a few minutes, he spoke again.

"What you goin' to do with me?"

"Hand you over to the sheriff."

"I ain't done nothin' wrong."

"We'll let the sheriff decide that. But if you ever set foot on the Stone ranch or my ranch, I'll shoot you."

There was no more conversation until we got into town. I went directly to the sheriff's office. He came out when he saw us approaching.

"Glad to see you, John," he said. "You're saving me a trip." Then he noticed who was with me and that he was tied. "What have we here?"

"I don't want this man working for me, so I'm bringing him to you. You'll have to deal with him according to the law," I said as I pulled him from his horse.

"Okay," the sheriff said as he led him to a cell.

The man began to protest.

"You are charged with theft and attempted murder," the sheriff said. "Working for Mr. McLane was your chance to avoid a trial and prison. If he doesn't want to work with you, then you'll have to go to jail and stand trial. The judge will decide your fate," he said with finality as he locked him in the cell. Then he turned to me.

"Come with me to my office. I have something you can deliver for me."

He showed me two large bags of gold coins.

"These belong to Mrs. Stone," he said. "I've been going through all of Silver's records and possessions. He kept track of all the gold he was taking from the Stones' gold mine. He was so proud of how he was fooling everyone that he recorded it all. He even wrote the date that he killed her husband and all his plans to turn the town against her. His plan was to force her and her daughter into prostitution so he could make money off of them besides stealing their gold. He wrote it all down. He said if they refused, then he would kill them. His financial success had really made him think he could do anything he wanted. It's amazing. I was even fooled by him until you set me straight. The papers are all there if you want to read them."

"I don't want to read them," I answered. "I'll take your word for it. You might need them in your case against that guy in there."

"His name's in there. All the men he hired are listed."

"I'll take the gold coins out to Mrs. Stone," I said.

I headed straight for my ranch. I didn't even take the time to eat. I was anxious to deliver that gold to its rightful owner. I was glad I had some food in my saddlebags. I munched as I rode. I'd be lucky to get home in time for some leftovers from supper.

CHAPTER 12
Her View

THE MCLANE RANCH

I got up at four o'clock so I could have some time alone, just me and God, before breakfast. At five, I headed over to help Jerry fix breakfast. He was shocked when I walked into the kitchen.

"You don't need to help me this early in the morning!" he almost shouted. "You go home and take it easy."

"If I can't help, then we won't be eating here," I responded.

"It's not that I don't want your help," he said, "but John McLane is going to be upset with me. He wants you to be resting here."

"After breakfast I'll rest until supper."

"No, you won't. You'll be out there weedin' those flower beds!"

"That's rest to me."

Jerry just shrugged.

"You'll have to deal with John McLane," he said as he went back to work. He didn't have to give me too many instructions. It was obvious what needed to be done. When the men started coming in, we were ready for them. They were all surprised to see me. They came in loud and got real quiet when they saw me. They just ate their breakfast, said their polite thank you's and went back to work.

I insisted on helping with the dishes. I knew Jerry was being overworked because the regular cook was over at my place.

In fact, I was sure all the men were doing double duty and I was determined to help where I could. About halfway through the dishes, Jennie Lu came in.

"Mom, you left me alone over there," she accused. "Why didn't you wake me up?"

"It was too early. I wanted you to get your rest," I explained. "You weren't afraid, were you?" I asked in a low voice.

She shrugged and lowered her eyes.

"You know we're safe here," I assured her.

She raised her eyes to mine and smiled.

"I'm hungry."

"I saved you some food. It's on the back of the stove."

She went after her food while I finished the dishes. It wasn't long before we were both ready to head back. I rested for a while while Jennie Lu explored the McLane house.

Jerry was right. Those flowerbeds kept calling me. So I told Jennie Lu I was going out to work in them. She followed and was soon in the swing. As I worked, I realized I was happier than I'd been in years.

About the time I was beginning to feel hungry, I looked up and saw Jerry coming, carrying a pot.

"I made some soup for lunch," he explained, "and I thought you might like some."

"You're too good to us. Come in and eat with us."

I stirred up the fire and set the pot on the stove.

"I still have some bread from yesterday," I offered as I headed for the pantry.

"I'm surprised you could find enough supplies to make bread," Jerry said.

"Well, it's not yeast bread. But it should be all right with the soup."

"It's delicious!" Jerry exclaimed. "I need your recipe. The men would love this."

"I'll have to write it for you," I said as I began to look for a paper. "I learned it from my mother. I don't think she ever wrote it down. She just taught me how to do it. And I can't find a paper or pencil or any ink anywhere in this house."

After we'd finished eating, Jerry suggested that I come over to the bunkhouse kitchen and teach him how to make that bread.

"I have paper over there and you can start a list of things you need in this house," he added.

I stared at him for a minute. The idea of making a shopping list was something from long ago. I was about to protest that I had no money when I remembered John McLane's words: "Lady, you are not a poor woman!"

Well, I thought to myself, *I guess I could start a list in faith that some of that gold will show up sometime.*

CHAPTER 13
His View

When I reached the crest of the last hill before entering my ranch, I caught my breath and brought my horse to a standstill. The first building was my parents' house. It looked as though my mother was back. It brought tears to my eyes. I had to stop and get control of myself. Her flowerbeds were all weeded and the fence was freshly painted, and there was a child in the old swing. It was like going back in time. I could almost see her coming out on the porch to greet me with a big smile on her face, drying her hands on her apron. It took me several minutes to get over the pain that emotional shock had caused. I just sat there and wiped my eyes and watched the child swing. Finally, I moved on down into the scene. I stopped in front of the door and dismounted. The child came running.

"My mother's not there!" she exclaimed breathlessly. "She's over at the bunkhouse helping Jerry make bread for supper."

"Well, I've got to put something inside, then I'll go find her," I responded. I pulled the two bags of gold out of my saddlebags and headed inside. I couldn't wait to get them into a safe place. Like the Lady said, it's dangerous stuff. It only took me a few minutes and I was back outside, walking with the child toward the bunkhouse. She was chattering like a little squirrel, telling me the whole story of her mother's bread that Jerry liked so much that he wanted a lesson in making it. By the time we got to the bunkhouse, I was feeling a strange feeling, but I couldn't quite put a name to it.

I stood in the door and watched those two people laughing as they worked together. They were obviously enjoying each other's company. I had never seen the Lady so relaxed and I had never heard her laugh so freely. I was glad to see her so happy. But there was something else I was feeling. It was a little pang deep inside.

"Are you jealous?" I asked myself silently.

Just then, the child rushed past me.

"Mother, Mother, look who's here!" she exclaimed.

They both looked up and grew silent. The Lady smiled and greeted me.

I turned to Jerry.

"I didn't want her to come here to work," I said. "She's supposed to be resting."

The Lady answered before Jerry could say a word.

"There's no way that we are going to eat here if I can't help with the work," she answered flatly. "I know all your men, including Jerry, are doing double duty because of me, and the least I can do is help."

I started to answer her, but thought better of it when I saw that stubborn look. I knew I'd be getting into a fight I couldn't win, so I changed the subject.

"I need to discuss some things with you," I said. "Could you come back to the house with me?"

She turned to Jerry.

"Do you think you have the bread making under control now?" she asked.

"Oh yes," he answered quickly, obviously embarrassed. "I know how to do it now. Thanks for teaching me."

He didn't even dare to look at me.

"Well, I guess I'll go then."

I was seething inside, but I said nothing.

As we were walking toward the house in silence, I was trying to figure myself out. I realized that I admired this woman's stubborn, independent spirit when she was standing against the men of Tateville, but it was a little harder to admire when it was turned on me. But what I couldn't figure out was my feelings toward Jerry. Why did I resent the relationship that I saw developing between him and Caroline Stone? He needed a woman in his life and she needed a man in her life, so why was I upset about it? My thoughts were interrupted by the Lady's voice.

"Don't be upset with Jerry because I'm helping him. It wasn't his idea. In fact, he tried to talk me out of it because he knew you wouldn't like it, but I insisted. It's a big job for a man his age to cook for so many people. I'd never forgive myself if his health failed because of it. He reminds me of my father. My mother said he worked himself to death and I don't want Jerry to do the same thing."

A huge relief swept over me. And I began to assure her that I wouldn't say anything to Jerry and she could do whatever felt right to her. I was glad she was making herself at home.

"I assume that you're the one who did all this work at the house," I said as we entered the gate to the yard. "It sure looks good."

"I love doing this kind of work. It hardly seems like work to me. It actually helps me to relax and clear my head so I can think clearer," she explained.

"My mother was like that," I replied. "I sure miss her."

"I miss her, too. She was a good friend to me."

She turned to her daughter and said, "Jennie Lu, you stay outside and swing while I talk to Mr. McLane."

The child turned away without a word of protest.

"Your daughter is certainly well behaved," I commented as we entered the kitchen.

"Thank you," she responded.

I went directly to the little closet off the kitchen and opened the safe and brought out the two bags of gold. I set them on the table and began to explain where they came from.

"These belong to you," I concluded.

She reached out slowly to touch it as though she were afraid of it.

"Well, I can give it to you for letting us stay here," she finally spoke after a long silence.

"Oh, no," I exclaimed. "This is worth a lot of money. You could buy my whole ranch with this and still have lots left over."

The Lady turned pale and sat back in her seat. Finally, she spoke.

"I'll use some to buy supplies for this house," she offered.

"I can take you to town tomorrow to do that," I said. "You would only need to take a few coins in your bag."

"How many should I take?" she asked.

I gave her a handful and she put them away in her bag.

"Now, come with me and I'll show you where to keep the gold and how to get to it if you need it."

"This is your private place," she protested. "I shouldn't be using it."

"I trust you," I responded. "But do you trust me to have your gold in my safe?"

"I trust you," she answered after a long pause. "I'd probably be dead by now without you. But I never thought I'd ever trust any man ever again. I thought my father was the only trustworthy man I'd ever known."

"And Jerry reminds you of your father," I reminded her.

"Yes, he does. And I think I trust him also. But that has a lot to do with the fact that he's worked for you and your family for so many years."

"If he wasn't trustworthy, I would never have left you and your daughter here in his care," I agreed.

"Well, then why were you so irritated with him back there?" she asked.

She was looking right in my eyes and I couldn't look away. My mind was racing. She had me trapped. She was good at it.

"Well," I said, "to tell you the truth, I think I was just jealous."

"Jealous? Jealous of what?" She was incredulous.

"I could see that Jerry had a better relationship with you in a few days than I was able to have after all this time. You were totally relaxed with him and there always seems to be tension between you and me."

After my little speech, the Lady seemed to be speechless. She opened her mouth as though to speak a few times, but no sound came out. She was rescued by the sound of her daughter's voice.

"Mother, can I come in now?" she asked.

"Oh, yes, dear. I'm sorry. I forgot to call you," she exclaimed as she jumped up from the table, obviously relieved to change the subject. "Guess what! We're going to town tomorrow to buy supplies for this house, so you'd better help me make a list. We can even buy more sewing supplies and we can start your sewing lessons again."

"While you ladies are doing that, I'll go have a visit with Jerry," I said as I headed out the door.

I thought if the Lady sees him as a father figure, maybe I could get some fatherly advice from him. When I walked in the door, I saw apprehension in his face.

"John, I'm sorry about Mrs. Stone working over here," he started in.

"I'm not here about that, Jerry," I interrupted him. "I think you're doing a great job of making her feel at home here. I was just a little jealous of how well you're doing at it. She says you remind her of her father and that gave me the idea of coming to you for some fatherly advice."

Jerry wiped his hands on a towel and sat down at the nearest table. I sat down with him. I began to tell him the story of my encounter with Mrs. Stone. I told how I had learned to admire her courage, but somehow couldn't help finding fault with her when I was with her.

"And now that all the issues with Syble have been resolved, I thought all my problems would be over. But they're not. There is still some kind of tension whenever we're together. That surge of jealousy I felt seeing her with you is just one example. When I'm not around her, I think about her constantly and think of all the things I want to tell her. But when I'm with her, I feel tense and almost tongue-tied. What's wrong with me?"

Jerry looked at the table for a while before he spoke.

"It sounds to me like you're falling in love and you're fighting it," he finally blurted out. "Is there some reason why you're afraid to love this woman?"

I just stared at him for a while as the truth of his words sunk into me. Of course, I loved The Lady. She was the whole reason for everything I did now. Why hadn't I seen that before?

"Are you afraid she won't return your love?" Jerry asked.

"I think I'm even more afraid that she will."

"Why?" he asked.

"Well, that disease Syble had is catching. What if I have it? I can't pass that on to Caroline Stone. I can't marry again."

"I thought you never slept with her after you married her," Jerry said.

"I didn't," I replied, "but I'm ashamed to say that I did once before we were married. That's the real reason I married her. I was so ashamed of myself. I figured I was obligated to marry her. She led me to believe I was the first man who'd ever violated her and I was fool enough to believe her."

"Well," Jerry said, "you need to get to the Doc and ask him to test you to see if you have it or not. If you do, then continue to do what you're doing. Keep your distance and do all you can for her until you die. If you don't have it, then set yourself to stop fighting yourself and concentrate on winning the lady's heart and hand. I think part of her tension toward you may be that she's afraid to love you because she doesn't want to get hurt. You need to get after it if you want a child of your own. She's still young enough for that, but barely.

"And by the way, John, don't ever think I'm any competition to you. I'd never think of marrying a woman young enough to be my daughter. And I'm sure she doesn't think of me like that, either. That's why she's so relaxed around me. She doesn't have to worry about that."

"Jerry, I'm ashamed to admit to the Doc what I did," I confessed.

"You don't need to tell the Doc what you did. She was your wife and you need to find out if you got her disease. That's perfectly legitimate."

"Oh, yeah. Of course," I said. "He doesn't know all the details. Why didn't I think of that? I'll go see him when I go to town tomorrow. Thanks for all your help, Jerry. I see things a lot clearer now," I said as I got up to leave.

"The truth is, I love that Lady more than I've ever loved anyone in my whole life. And one way or the other, I'm going to live the rest of my life for her. So I might as well face that fact and deal with it. Right?"

"Right!" Jerry agreed.

"By the way, Jerry," I said as I paused in the door. "Don't ever think that you're going to lose your job here because I don't like something you did. You would have to do something horrendously bad to lose your job after all the years of faithful service to my parents. I expect that you will finish out your life right here, just as if you owned the place."

Jerry smiled and raised his hand in a salute.

"Thanks," was all he said, but I saw a lot more on his face.

It felt good to get on my horse and head out across my ranch to check on my cattle and my ranch hands. It felt so right. I couldn't believe that I ever wanted to run from it. I began to hum a tune as I rode. I thought about the Lady, and wondered if she'd like to ride with me sometime. I was amazed at how much better I felt after my talk with Jerry.

In the evening, I came in with the boys, tired and ready for some supper. The Lady and her daughter were both there, helping Jerry. I had to admit, the feminine touch was sure nice. The little girl was serving coffee to the tables and her mother was bringing out platters of food for seconds.

"Save room for dessert," Jerry called from the kitchen. "We have a special bread that Mrs. Stone taught me how to make. It's almost like cake. You're all sure to like it."

Sure enough, the bread was a big success. It was served with several kinds of jam and some applesauce. Most of the men ate several pieces. In fact, we put away all that they had made.

The next morning, I had the wagon at their gate as the sun was coming up, just as we had agreed the night before. The mother and daughter came out of the door as soon as I arrived. They were obviously excited. It dawned on me that it had probably been a very long time since they'd been shopping. When I brought up the subject, they were engaged in animated conversation the rest of the trip, trying to remember a pleasant shopping trip.

"Well, I know one thing for sure," Mrs. Stone said as the town came into view. "I haven't been to this town since my mother's funeral. I wonder if anyone will remember me."

"I remember Grandma's funeral. How old was I then?"

"You were five years old."

"Has it been that long?" I exclaimed. "Didn't you say she's twelve now?"

"Yes, she is. After my mother's death, I never went back. It's been a long, painful time, but I'm excited to be here today."

"I can tell, and I'm excited for you," I said as I reined in the horses in front of the bank.

"Bring in just three of your gold coins and exchange them for paper money to shop with today. If you need more, we can come and get more."

I wanted to make sure she was treated fairly, so I walked in right beside her. Her daughter was right by her on the other side. I could tell she was a little nervous.

"Well, hello, Caroline!" the banker exclaimed. "I've been wanting to find you, but didn't know how. Now here you are! What can I do for you?"

"I have some gold here that I would like to exchange for cash." She spoke very quietly.

"Come into my office."

When we were seated in his office and he began to count out the money, I watched carefully. I had already done some research and knew the monetary value of the gold. I was grateful to see that he was giving her exactly what it was worth. I noticed that Caroline sat back in her chair and turned pale as she watched the cash piling up in front of her. She was beginning to understand why people would kill for gold.

When the banker had put the gold away, he turned to the Lady.

"Caroline, did you know that your mother's shop is still right where she left it?"

Caroline shook her head.

"I haven't found anyone who wants to rent the space, so I left it just as it was. You are welcome to go look it over if you would like. Here's the key."

As he handed the key to her, he added, "I don't suppose you would be interested in reopening your mother's shop, would you?"

The Lady just stared at the banker for a while and my heart just about stopped.

"I'll have to pray about that," she finally answered and I was able to catch my breath. "But I would like to see it," she continued.

We all went over there, even the banker. I would have let her go alone, but when he asked to accompany her, I wasn't about to leave her alone with him. I couldn't quite figure him out. He was acting awfully interested in Caroline Stone. Had he figured out that she was now a rich woman?

CHAPTER 14
Her View

My mother's dress shop was just the way she left it. It wasn't even dusty. That puzzled me. Who had been cleaning it?

As I walked around and touched everything, memories flooded my soul. I could hardly hold the tears back. She and I had spent many wonderful hours there together.

"I didn't realize her shop was still here. I thought we sold everything when we sold her house to pay off her debts."

"I bought her shop," the banker explained. "You see, Caroline, your mother and I became very good friends after you left. In fact, I would have been your stepfather if she had lived. We had the wedding date set and I bought her this engagement ring."

He pulled it from his vest pocket and held it out for me to see.

"We had planned to go visit you and ask you to be in our wedding. Then she died suddenly and I was so devastated, I couldn't even go to her funeral. I blamed myself because there were little symptoms of heart trouble and I'd never insisted she go to the doctor. When I finally got the nerve to go talk to the doctor, he told me he couldn't have done anything to help her anyway."

"It makes me so happy to know that my mother was not alone after I left," I assured him, holding out my hand. "I used to feel so guilty for leaving her here all alone. I'm so glad that God sent her a friend."

"I loved your mother more than I've ever loved anyone and I hope you'll let me be your stepfather and a grandfather to your daughter."

There was a question in his voice as he held my hand. I nodded my head as I introduced him to Jennie Lu.

"This is Jennie Lucinda Stone," I said as I pulled her forward. She held out her hand but looked at the floor.

"My name is Zackery Jones. But I'll just be Grandpa to you and when you're a little older, I'll give you your grandmother's engagement ring."

Jennie Lu looked up for a second and smiled.

"But right now, I want to take you all over to the restaurant for a mid-morning treat. That lady over there makes the best pies I've ever eaten. And that includes you," he said, turning to John McLane. "I'm sure you've tasted her cooking before."

John smiled and nodded. "I was planning to head that direction," he said, "but first, I have to go see the Doc, so if you'll escort these two ladies for me, I'll meet you over there."

"It will be my pleasure," Mr. Jones announced, holding out his right arm to Jennie Lu, who put her hand very lightly on it. She'd never been escorted like that before.

"And now, my dear, if you'll take my other arm," he said, turning to Caroline, "we'll head for our treat."

Caroline obliged and they walked down the wooden walkway, three abreast, which forced the ladies to walk very close to the gentleman. Caroline was a little embarrassed, but Zackery Jones was grinning from ear to ear when they entered the restaurant.

"Well, hello, Mr. Jones," the waitress exclaimed. "This is the happiest I've seen you since Flora died. Who are these lovely ladies?"

"This is Flora's daughter, Caroline, and her granddaughter, Jennie Lucinda Stone."

"So you finally found them?"

"No, they found me, quite by accident. It's a long story. But we're here to celebrate with some of your mother's pies, Mary. What do you have to offer?"

"We have apple and cherry and custard, and my brother almost has the ice cream ready. He's been churning it ever since you sent word."

"Ice cream!" Jennie Lu forgot her shyness. "I've never had ice cream, but my mother told me about it."

"Well, now you are going to taste it."

Even the cook came out of the kitchen, beaming, when she heard Jennie Lu's exclamation.

"Just wait a few minutes," she said. "It's almost ready. Just give Mary your pie order so we can have that ready."

I went for cherry, Mr. Jones went for apple, and Jennie Lu followed my example. Just then, John came in and put in an order for custard.

I kept glancing at him, wondering if he were sick. I finally got up my courage to ask.

"Is there something wrong with you, John?"

"No, I'm just having a check up," he responded. "I got an appointment for later this afternoon while you ladies are shopping."

The pie was delicious and the ice cream was unbelievable. We gorged ourselves at Mr. Jones's expense. Jenny Lu had two pieces and mountains of ice cream. Mr. Jones was beaming. He didn't seem worried at all about the cost.

I kept wondering why John was going to the doctor. I thought he wasn't telling me the whole story. It made me nervous. If anything happened to him, I would be right back in trouble. Or would I? I could come run my mother's dress shop. I could pay someone to finish my house and keep the ranch. I had to remember I wasn't poor anymore. But I was still worried about John. I had come to really care about him. He had done so much for us.

But I put it all out of my mind so that Jennie Lu and I could enjoy our day shopping. I couldn't remember the last time I'd done any shopping. As I kept buying things, Jennie Lu's eyes got big with wonder. She began to ask if she could have some of the things she saw. When I would say yes, she would get so excited, she could hardly contain herself. I bought fabric to make new clothes. I bought her some shoes and socks and hair ornaments. I even bought her a dress that was already made. She wanted to change into it right away, so the lady in the store took her to a backroom where she could. She even helped her brush her hair and put her new barrettes in it. She came out looking beautiful.

I totally filled John McLane's wagon by the time I had bought everything on our list and a few other things as well. But I still hadn't used all my money. I was amazed. I even bought Jennie Lu and I some beautiful winter coats. I noticed that they had school supplies there, also. There was a little school at the end of the street.

On one of my trips out to load the wagon, John was there waiting. I expected a negative comment on all my purchases and I began to apologize for loading his wagon down.

"That's what I expected you to do," he said.

"It'll make fewer trips to town, at least," I said.

"I'm not worried about how many trips we make to town," he added. "In fact, I was just sitting here, thinking that you might want to send Jennie Lu to school this fall. Jimmy or I could bring her in every day and go get her in the afternoon."

"You mean it?" Jennie Lu exclaimed. "I've never been to school."

"If your mother will agree to it, we'll do it."

"I thought we'd be going home by then."

"Well," John began to explain, "I've been having compassion on some of those guys with families and letting them work half a day so they could take care of things at home. It all began with old man Tate. He said it was getting too much for his wife, running that store by herself. So I let him work his store in the morning and work on the house in the afternoon. One thing led to another and most of the men are working half days now. Some in the morning and some in the afternoon. So your house isn't getting done as fast as I would like. But I thought since you were doing so well at my place, you wouldn't mind spending the winter there. In fact, if it's all right with you, I thought we would just suspend construction once the snow flies and start again in the spring."

What could I say? Jennie Lu was jumping up and down with excitement and I sure didn't want to be the villain in this story.

"Well, we'd better go see what you need for school, then," I said.

We visited the school teacher and found out what Jennie Lu would need. Then we bought it all at the store. I promised the teacher

I would work with Jennie Lu and try to get her up to at least second grade by the time school started. She could already read a little from the Bible. She knew a little arithmetic from helping me in the kitchen. But we had our work cut out for us. I had to admit, Jennie Lu was not the only one who was excited. I was excited, myself. Most of all, I was excited about the books. I wanted my daughter to be able to read.

On the ride home, I almost fell asleep on John's shoulder. When I jerked myself awake, he just looked at me and smiled.

"It's been a long day," I explained, "and an exciting one."

When we arrived at the ranch, the men all came out of the bunkhouse to help unload the wagon. They informed us that Jerry was keeping food warm for us, so we'd better go on over there. With all that help, the wagon was unloaded in just a few minutes and we headed on over to see what Jerry had for us. It was good, but I was so tired, I could hardly stay awake to finish it. He had made some of that special bread for us, so I had to have some for dessert. He was standing in the kitchen door with his arms crossed, smiling from ear to ear, so I couldn't disappoint him.

John insisted on walking us back to the house. I told him it wasn't necessary, that we would be fine, but he insisted. When we got there, he went in and checked the house out. We had left the windows open when we left, so he started closing them all. I helped him. I kept glancing at him. He seemed to be glowing with an inner light of some kind. He came over to me before he left and took my hand and held it to his lips.

"Thank you," he whispered.

"Thank *you*," I corrected. "For giving us a wonderful day."

"I'm so grateful to you for agreeing to spend the winter here," he explained. "I was worried that you'd want to move into town when Mr. Jones offered your mother's shop."

I was speechless. I couldn't believe he actually wanted me here that much. Why did he want me here so much? Was it the gold? I suddenly felt confused and afraid. I guess he saw it in my eyes because he kissed my hand again and said, "Don't worry, my Lady, you'll understand me better as time goes by. You have nothing to fear from me."

"You're so…different!"

"You're changing me for the better. I'll never be 'His Grouchiness' again."

I gasped. How did he know about that?

He smiled as he closed the door behind him.

"Lock it!" he called through the door.

I obeyed. Then I headed for the bed. Jennie Lu was already there, sound asleep. Sometimes she slept in her own room and sometimes with me. I lay awake, trying to remember what we were discussing when "His Grouchiness" came up. I realized he had been outside the door, listening, and I was embarrassed when I remembered that we had been discussing marriage.

CHAPTER 15

In the weeks that followed that wonderful day, I concentrated on getting Jennie Lu ready for school. After I helped Jerry in the early morning, I worked on school all the rest of the morning. After a quick lunch, we either worked in the yard or in our sewing room, preparing her school clothes. Then I went over to help Jerry with supper.

John was coming and going all through August. Sometimes we took long walks after supper, so he could keep me updated. He said they had the cellar done and were working on the exterior walls. He hoped to have the roof on before the snow came. I got to design the interior just the way I wanted it. It was going to be a two story house with a big attic and a wraparound porch. I was getting excited about it. John was planning a way to burn wood in the cellar that would heat the whole house. He said his father did it in this house and it worked very well. They were never cold. He took me down in the cellar to show it to me. I had never been down there. It was amazing to see. There was a big workshop and a door that opened into another part where they stored vegetables from the garden.

"You should be using this workshop," I said. "You don't need to stay away from it because of me."

"I'll take you up on that if the need arises. We have another one over in the barn, but I may need to use this one sometimes."

By the end of August, I had the yard and its fence all repaired and looking nice. But then I discovered that behind the yard there was a large garden area. It had been fenced at one time, but the fence was broken down and the garden overgrown with weeds. In one corner, I found the rhubarb, so I weeded that corner first. I was able to glean enough rhubarb to make a couple of pies. Then I found where Mrs. McLane had an herb garden. So I began to try to restore that.

"Why are you working so hard on this place?" Jerry asked me one day when he came looking for me and found me in the garden.

"I don't know," I responded. "I know that no one will keep up with it when I'm gone. But I just can't stand not to do it."

"Well, I may keep this garden when Andy's back over here to help. I'll get the horse and plow it for you and then rake it out. You just show me the areas with perennials that you don't want plowed."

We worked together on that garden several afternoons. Jerry even brought manure over and plowed that in. By the time we were done, it looked really nice, except for the broken down fence. I was standing there admiring it, when I heard a horse approaching from town. When it was still quite a ways off, I could tell it was John. I was happy to see him, but I wondered what he would say about the garden. I watched him dismount and tie his horse in front of the house and walk back toward me. He stood and looked at the garden for several minutes before he spoke. When he turned toward me, I noticed moisture in his eyes.

"That looks so beautiful!" he said in a husky voice.

I didn't say a word. I wasn't sure how he really felt about it. He reached for my hand again and lifted it to his lips. I didn't resist, although I didn't really know what it meant. I'd never had my hand kissed by anyone before.

"I'm going to be here for a few days, so I'll help you restore that fence. Then it will really look nice. You've done a terrific job on this place."

"Jerry helped me with the garden. He said he'd try to keep it up after I'm gone and Andy is back here to help him."

"That's good. This garden used to produce a lot of food for us."

Just then, Jennie Lu came running around the house and threw her arms around John and gave him a big hug. "Come inside," she said, pulling on his sleeve. "I've got a surprise for you."

"And I have a surprise for *you*," he said.

When we got to the house, he went to his saddlebags and pulled out two little boxes.

"These are from Zackery Jones."

Jennie Lu took hers and read the tag herself.

"To Jennie Lu from Grandpa Jones"

She opened the box and found a beautiful jewelry box inside. In the jewelry box was a necklace.

"This one is for you," he said as he handed it to me. It was also a jewelry box from Mr. Jones, but inside was a picture of my mother. I gasped when I opened it and couldn't hold back a few tears. Both John and Jennie Lu came to look over my shoulders.

"That's your grandmother."

"You look a lot like her," John said.

We took our gifts inside and Jennie Lu got her reader and began to read for John. He was amazed at how well she did. Then she got her little chalkboard out and showed him how she could write.

He looked at me and said, "You've both done a wonderful job this month. I'm very proud of you."

"Do you think she'll be ready for second grade?" I asked.

"Easily! I think she'll be above that. Maybe third or fourth grade."

Jennie Lu was hugging her book and dancing around.

"Jimmy is coming over as soon as they finish the roof and he'll be staying here, so he can take Jennie Lu to school. I'll keep working over there until it snows. Then we'll bring all of your livestock over here for the winter.

"My kitten, too?" Jennie asked.

"Oh, my!" John exclaimed and headed out the door. We followed. He was opening his other saddlebag to reveal Jennie Lu's kitten, just waking up and stretching.

"I forgot all about her, but I guess she's all right."

Jennie Lu was delighted. She'd been missing her kitten.

"Now I need a box so I can keep her in the house."

"You come down to the cellar with me and if we don't find one, I'll make one."

I followed along and watched them searching for a box.

"Here's one," Jennie Lu exclaimed.

"That will work. That's the kindling box, but I'll make another one for kindling. Now, let's go outside and I'll show you where the sandy soil is. I used to play in it when I was a boy."

We walked out past the garden, through a stand of trees and on the other side, there was a sandbank on the edge of a little stream. It was a beautiful spot. There was a little wooden truck sitting in the sand. John picked it up and looked it over carefully.

"This must have belonged to Jimmy. Mine would have been rotted away by now.

"Now, remember, Jennie Lu, you can't empty the box here. It would ruin the sand and the stream. You can dump it in the trees."

Jennie Lu's eyes were glued to his face and she nodded solemnly.

"Now, let's go get the wheelbarrow and I'll bring some sand and put it in that barrel in the cellar. You can use that this winter when everything's froze up. Right now, you can come out here to empty your cat box and refill it, but not this winter."

We walked back together and into the cellar. He had opened the hatchway. I headed upstairs and left them alone. Jennie Lu never even looked my way. She was totally fascinated by John McLane. I could barely hold back the tears until I got upstairs. I hadn't realized before how much she needed a father. He was the reason she felt so secure and happy here. She knew he was watching out for us.

I sat on the couch and began to sob from deep inside. I remembered Jed. I could see his face smiling at me. He was such an innocent boy. I realized that I had never really grieved for him. I cried until I was totally exhausted. He missed out on so much and we missed a husband and father. And what about all the children that never got a chance to be born because he died so young? I started to cry again. It seemed my arms and my heart ached for the unborn children I would never hold. We had planned a large family, but he didn't even get one son to carry on his name. Every thought brought on another round of sobs.

I heard them in the cellar and I tried to get myself under control. I was relieved when I heard them leave for another load. The grief inside of me was so huge, I couldn't turn it off. When I thought I was through, I would think of something else and start all over again. I went from Jed to Jennie Lu and her missed childhood. Then to myself and my mother. Then my father who died young. Then to Syble and her mother. Then to Mrs. McLane, who died, longing for her son to come home. Now, he was here and she was gone.

Finally, when I lay quiet and exhausted, someone came in and sat in the chair across from me. His presence took all my strength and I was unable to move. I knew it must be Jesus. It seemed He was talking to me, but I heard Him inside, not with my ears. He assured me that all their losses down here were being more than repaid on the other side. He also assured me that He was guiding my life and that it was He who brought John McLane into my life.

"Don't be afraid to marry him, because I have ordained it and Jed is happy over here. I promised him when he was dying that I would take care of you and your daughter. Don't worry about the gold, either. It's for the future. I'll let you know when it's time to use it. For now, let John take care of you. I sent him."

He talked to me more and took away all my grief. Joy began to take its place. Just as He was leaving, I heard John and Jennie Lu coming up the stairs.

"Mother!" Jennie Lu screamed as she ran toward me. I sat up and put my arms around her.

"I'm okay," I assured her.

"Why are your eyes all red and swollen up?"

"I was grieving. But it's all over now."

"Why were you grieving?"

"I saw you with Mr. McLane and I realized how much you missed out on by not having a father. Then one thing led to another and I grieved over all the things I've never had a chance to grieve over before because we were living in constant danger and I could never give in to grief."

"But you're all right now?"

"Yes. Jesus came and comforted me. He turned my grief to joy."

"He came right here?"

"Yes. He was sitting right where Mr. McLane is sitting now. He left just as you were coming up the stairs. That's why I was laying there on the couch. When He was here, I couldn't move."

"'Lo, I am with you always,' the Bible says," Jennie Lu commented.

"Jennie Lu, how do you know that scripture?" I exclaimed.

"You taught me how to read, remember? And I've been reading the Bible every night."

"That's wonderful! And you're right. He didn't leave me. He just withdrew His presence enough that I could function."

"I was so afraid that you were dead." Jennie Lu started to cry. "I thought we were over that terrible fear, but it all came back on me."

Now Jennie Lu was sobbing.

"Just cry it out," I encouraged her, as I held her in my arms. "It's a sign we're getting over it. We never have to live like that again."

"I'm so afraid of being left all alone. They killed my daddy and they were trying to kill you. Then what would they do to me?"

"And God sent Mr. McLane along just in time. God was with us all the time. And it's all over now."

"And you'll never be left alone," John spoke up. "Even if your mother had died, you would still have me and Jimmy and Jerry and all the ranch hands. We're all committed to you. Besides us, there's your Grandpa Jones in town."

Jennie Lu sat up and wiped her eyes.

"I never thought of that. I have lots of friends now and Jesus is with me always!"

She jumped up and started for the door.

"I have to go find my kitten and put it in the cellar. Mr. McLane said to keep it down there for a few days. Then it would get used to using the box down there so you wouldn't have the mess up here."

I smiled my thanks to John, but I couldn't say a word. I was crying again. This time, it was tears of gratitude and relief. He came over and sat by me on the couch and wrapped his arms around me and held me close. It felt so wonderful that I cried even more.

"I want to be your daughter's father," he finally spoke.

"You're doing a great job."

"You don't understand. I want to adopt her."

I stopped crying and sat up.

"I can't just give her over to you! I can't give her away!" I was indignant.

"Caroline," he said firmly as he put his hands on both sides of my face. "I'm asking you to marry me. I want you and I want your daughter."

Tears ran out the corners of my eyes.

"I love you more than I've ever loved anyone in my life," he said. "I can't stand to see you crying like this. I want you to be happy."

"I am happy. It's because I'm happy that I'm crying. I'm crying all the past away. I'm erasing all those years that I never cried a tear. I don't have to be tough anymore. I have a strong shoulder to cry on. I can be a woman again. And yes, I will marry you."

"You will? I never thought you would agree so quickly."

"I wouldn't have a few hours ago. But Jesus said He sent you to me and that I shouldn't be afraid to marry you."

"Now I feel like I'm gonna cry. That means so much to me. He went before to prepare the way for me."

"But there's another thing I have to tell you," I said as I sat up out of his arms. "I'm not going to develop that gold mine. I'm going to close it down. I'll keep the gold in those bags as my pay for all that suffering, but I don't want any more."

I watched his reaction closely.

"I think that's a good idea," he said and he seemed to be sincere. "We've got enough to handle right now with these two ranches."

I breathed a sigh of relief. He wasn't marrying me for my gold. I sank back into his arms just as Jennie Lu came in with her kitten. She stopped and just stared at us.

"Are you…are you…" she stammered.

"Yes. Mr. McLane and I are getting married," I answered her unspoken question.

She let out a squeal and began to dance around the room.

"When? When?" she asked.

"We haven't decided that yet. So you go on with your kitten to the cellar and let us talk."

When she was gone, I moved to the chair so we could look at each other while we talked. We discussed the possibility of a summer wedding, so we could move right into my new house. Then we said maybe we should do it in the spring. Spring is so beautiful. Finally, John settled the issue.

"You know, Lady, I don't think I can wait that long. Now that I've held you in my arms and you've agreed to marry me, I want to get on with it. I'm already dreaming of sitting in front of that fireplace with you this winter. I think we should get married in September on my birthday. It'll be the best birthday present I could ever have. Then maybe for Christmas, we'll have a baby on the way, the Lord willing. Let's not waste any time. I'll be forty this year."

"Well, that doesn't give us much time to prepare," I protested.

"I happen to know that you already have your wedding dress made," he teased.

"Yes, and we've been working on a nice dress for Jennie Lu. It's almost ready. But what about you and Jimmy?"

"We'll either buy something in town or get by with what we have. We've got Sunday clothes."

"Well, okay then. You talk to the Parson about a date in September and I'll talk to Jerry about a dinner. Do you think lots of people will come?"

"Oh yes. I'll have to bring Andy back to help Jerry cook. Most of the town will come and probably some from over there, too."

Just then, Jennie Lu came back up the stairs. She was very quiet.

"When is the wedding?" she asked.

"Sometime in September."

"Does that mean my name will be McLane instead of Stone?"

"Your mother's name will be McLane when she marries me," John explained. "And when I adopt you, your name will be McLane also."

Jennie Lu just stared at the floor.

"What's bothering you?" I asked.

"I want to keep my father's name," she blurted out. "I'm his only child. He used to love me. There's no one else to carry his name."

"I understand how you feel," John spoke up. "And you can certainly keep his name. We'll keep his name over there on the Stone Place also."

"Oh, wonderful!" Jennie Lu exclaimed and clapped her hands. The smile was back on her face.

CHAPTER 16
His View

As soon as I left the house, I headed for the kitchen, hoping to find Jerry. As I suspected, he was still there, cleaning up and preparing for tomorrow. He was just finishing up as I came in.

"Do you have time to talk for a few minutes?" I asked. He had just blown out one of the lights. He carried the other one over to the table and sat down, pulling out another chair for me.

"Of course!" he said. "I've been wondering what was going on with you."

"Well, I've been going to see the doctor every week and he's been checking me out. Last week, he said he's pretty sure I'm clean. So I decided to take the chance and try to get the Lady to marry me."

Then I proceeded to tell him the whole story of what had just happened. When I got to the part about the Lady's supernatural visitor and how He had prepared the way for me, Jerry broke into a big smile. I could tell it was as much of a relief to him as it had been for me. That visitation had removed all lingering doubt about whether I should marry or not.

Jerry jumped up and held out his hand. I did the same.

"Congratulations," he exclaimed and began to pound me on the back. I gave him a big bear hug. I was so happy, I could scarcely contain myself. Something that I thought I had lost forever had suddenly been restored to me.

"I've been redeemed!" I shouted.

Jerry got suddenly serious.

"When's the wedding?" he asked.

"September 28—my birthday!"

"Man, I've got to get prepared. We'll have to feed the whole town."

"And part of Tateville," I added. "I'll send Andy back over here in a couple of weeks and all the men will help at the last."

Jerry looked relieved.

"Thanks," he said.

When I left Jerry, I headed straight for my bed in the bunkhouse. But I had a hard time getting to sleep. My mind kept rehearsing every detail of that day. When I remembered sitting in front of the fireplace and her words of admiration for my stonework, I got an inspiration for some stonework I would do over at the Stone Place.

"That'll be very appropriate," I thought. "Stone work at the Stone Place."

Then I began to dream about a honeymoon.

"I know I want her to myself for a while," I mused, "so we can get used to each other."

"What?" someone in the next bed muttered.

"Oh, sorry, I was thinking out loud. I didn't mean to wake you up."

"Ummm…" he muttered as he went back to sleep.

I gave all my concerns to God and finally got to sleep.

And I was up as soon as the sun was up. I headed for the kitchen and sure enough, she was there, helping Jerry. I convinced her to take a few minutes to talk to me.

"First, I want to say that you won't be seeing too much of me for the next month. I'm going to try to concentrate on getting your house closed in for the winter. And I need to stay away, so I won't get too forward with you, now that I know you're going to be mine. Do you understand?"

I held her hand as I spoke and she just nodded.

"Now I have one very big request," I said as I pressed her hand to my lips. "I'm wondering if there is anyone you would trust to care for your daughter, so I could have you all to myself for two weeks after our wedding?"

CHAPTER 17
Her View

My first reaction to his request was totally negative. There was no way I was going to leave my daughter with someone for two weeks. But as I looked into his pleading eyes, my heart began to soften. I remembered that she would be in school in town and how good Amy Tuttle had been with Syble. Then I remembered Mr. Jones, who wanted to be her grandfather and the school teacher who had been so helpful. Finally, I said, "I'll talk to Amy Tuttle about it," as I leaned over and kissed his cheek, then jumped up before he could grab me.

"Now, I've got to help Jerry," I said as I headed for the kitchen.

CHAPTER 18
His View

I sat and watched her prepare breakfast in the lamplight with the warm touch of her lips on my cheek. The morning sun broke through the shadows and illuminated her hair, making the red glow.

"I am so grateful to you, Lord God," I whispered. "You have redeemed my life that was totally destroyed!"

After breakfast, she headed for the stables. So I followed.

"Are you going to town right now?" I asked when I caught up with her.

"Yes, I thought I'd just take the buggy since I won't be buying supplies."

"I'll get it ready for you and ride along beside you on my way over to your place. I need to do some business in town anyway."

"That would be wonderful! While you're doing that, I'll go over to the house and make sure Jennie Lu is ready. She doesn't know I'm doing this today."

"I sure appreciate the way you get things done right away like this. This way, I'll know what to expect."

She gave me a big smile as she turned away and headed for the house.

"She really loves to hear compliments from me. I'll have to remember that in the future. More compliments and less criticism, if I want to make her happy, and I do want to make her happy!" I was muttering to myself as I got the horse and buggy ready. On the ride to town, I mainly listened as The Lady explained things to her daughter. Jennie Lu was very quiet the whole time. I could see that she was a little scared of being away from her mother. I could understand how she felt, but I was praying that her mother wouldn't change her mind. I wanted those two weeks alone with her!

Amy Tuttle was very enthusiastic about the whole idea. She was thrilled that we were getting married and she definitely wanted to keep Jennie Lu for two weeks.

"We'll have so much fun together! Your Grandpa Jones will probably buy us ice cream every day after school. You won't even want to go home after two weeks in town."

Jennie Lu laughed and I could see some of the tension going out of her. I breathed a sigh of relief. I gave her and her mother a hug before I headed out of town.

When I got to the Stone Place, I found everything progressing according to the plan, so I was able to concentrate on the stonework I wanted to do for My Lady. I spent the next month concentrating on that house. I went back to Titustown every Sunday for church and met My Lady there. We would spend several hours together, then I would head back to the Stone Place and she would go back to my ranch.

When September rolled around, I sent Jimmy back over there to help with getting Jennie Lu to school, but I stayed on at the Stone Place. I almost had the stonework done and it looked really nice. I put two chimneys in that house as well as the fences and the pillars on each side of the gate. The men were working on the roof. We were working hard to seal it up before winter.

While I was working, I did a lot of thinking and dreaming. I began to dream of taking My Lady on a train trip back East to visit her relatives and mine. I had heard about the train that had been brought out here not far from us. You could get back East much quicker on that train than in a wagon. So I began to ask questions in town. I finally rode over to see the train for myself and talk to the people who were managing it. It was an exciting development, but I wondered if Caroline would be afraid of it. I took a short ride to test it out. I was amazed at how much ground could be covered in such a short time. I had heard both good and bad stories about the trains. So I took the time to investigate myself, before I said anything to Caroline.

CHAPTER 19
Her View

When Jimmy came back to the McLane Ranch, life got a lot more exciting. He spent a lot of his time with us girls. He was so full of energy that he could keep up with Jennie Lu and took a lot of weight off of my shoulders. I trusted Jimmy completely. I even allowed him to take Jennie Lu for horseback rides when I felt too tired to accompany them. He was also stripping out the inside of the room adjoining the kitchen where Syble had died. He said his brother had told him to do it and do with it whatever I suggested. I recommended making it into a dining room. We all wanted to erase the bad memories from that room, but none of us were admitting it. Jimmy and I decided to replace the broken window with a double window and make the door into the living room into an archway the size of double doors. I was thinking of making it an open space that would not remind us of the closed up little room that had housed such misery. When John came for a visit, he approved my plan and added the suggestion of two archways, one into the living room and one into the kitchen.

Soon, it was time for school to start. John came back for the big day. We all rode into town with Jennie Lu. Not only was she starting school, but she was moving in with Amy Tuttle for a few weeks. We took her school clothes to town and left her wedding clothes at the ranch. Grandpa Jones was waiting for us at Amy's house. He planned to treat us all to ice cream. He kept assuring me that he would check on Jennie Lu every day while we were gone. Everyone we saw in town was congratulating us on our upcoming wedding and acting so happy that I was back in town. I didn't have the heart to tell them it was a temporary situation. Their friendliness was overwhelming to me. I kept blinking back tears. It was such a relief to see that everything was normal here. It made my other life seem like a bad dream, but I could not forget how quickly the love of money could change people. I knew I would never be the same trusting person I had once been.

When it was time to say goodbye to my daughter, I found it very difficult. I stood on the boardwalk and looked at her standing in the door of Amy's house. My heart was in my throat. How could I do this? John and Jimmy were in the carriage, waiting for me, but I couldn't pull myself away. I just stood there. Finally, Jennie Lu ran over and gave me a hug and walked with me to the carriage.

"I'm going to be fine, Mother," she whispered in my ear. "It's okay. You're doing the right thing."

John was standing by the carriage and put his arm across my shoulders and helped me in. I heard him whisper his thanks to Jennie Lu. She stood on the walk and waved until we were out of sight. Only then did I turn and give John a weak smile. I felt weak and empty inside. Jimmy drove the carriage and John just held me in a tight grip. No one said a word. I hadn't realized what a trauma this would be for me. I guess my daughter had become my whole life and my reason for living. There were no tears, just no feeling at all—like my insides had been ripped out. I didn't shed a tear or say a word all the way home, but I began to shiver like I was freezing. John just continued to hold me tight.

CHAPTER 20
His View

When I saw how hard it was for My Lady to say goodbye to her daughter, I began to wonder if I'd made a mistake in pressuring her to do it. I told Jimmy he'd have to spend the night at the house. I didn't want her to be alone in that big house tonight and I couldn't stay with her by myself, so he'd have to stay with us.

"I'll sleep on the couch and you can use Jennie Lu's bed or one of the other bedrooms."

He nodded.

"I'll take care of the horse and carriage, then I'll come back here."

I helped My Lady down and walked with her into the house, straight to the fireplace.

"You sit there while I build a fire."

I wrapped a shawl around her and started the fire. After a while, the shivering stopped and she finally spoke.

"I didn't realize until now that I had developed an unhealthy relationship with my daughter," she murmured. "I'm glad you made me see it."

I had to lean close to hear her. A big relief swept over me. I had been redeemed again.

"After all you two have been through together, it's only natural that you'd get very protective of her," I said.

"Maybe so, but I don't want to be so controlling that she can't grow up and live her own life. I think I was heading in that direction, but you stopped me. Thank you."

I just pulled her close and kissed her and thanked God for redeeming an old sinner like me. I was amazed that what I thought was a mistake had turned out to be a good thing. But I was still afraid to tell her about the train trip back East. So I waited.

Just then, Jimmy came in and suggested we make some coffee and pop some corn in the fireplace. He'd brought some over from the other kitchen. So we let him do it. That was something my mother would always do for us, so Jimmy knew right where everything was and how to do it. I just sat and held My Lady as tight as I could. This was as close as she'd ever let me get to her. In just a few days, we would be married. I wondered what it would be like. When she fell asleep in my arms, I just lay my head against hers and tried to sleep. Finally, I eased her down onto the couch and I lay on the floor beside her. I kept the fire going and went to my mother's linen closet and got some blankets and pillows. I covered her and she roused up a little, so I gave her a pillow.

"Just stay right there," I whispered. And she settled right back down.

About midnight, I woke up and saw that she was gone and the fire was dying. So I revived the fire and settled down on the couch to finish out the night. In the morning, I was awakened by the sound of pots and pans in the kitchen.

"Don't cook for us!" I exclaimed. "I want to take you over to see your house, so we can have breakfast with the men and head right out."

"I'm a little embarrassed to face the men," Caroline admitted.

"Why? We didn't do anything wrong."

"Well, it's going to look to them like we did."

"That's why I had Jimmy spend the night—to avoid the appearance of evil," I said with a grin.

Caroline laughed.

"I'm glad you know your scripture." Then she got serious and said, "I'm also glad you didn't leave me alone last night, no matter how it looked to others. I needed you last night."

Just then, Jimmy came bounding down the stairs and announced that he enjoyed sleeping in his old room again.

"Well, after your brother and I are married, there's no reason you can't move right back into this house."

"You mean it?" Jimmy exclaimed.

"If it's all right with Caroline, it's all right with me. This is as much your house as it is mine. We'll share it until Caroline and I move over to the Stone Place. Then you'll have it all to yourself.

"Today, I want to take her over to see her house, so I need you to stay here and help the men finish getting ready for winter around here and Jerry might need some help getting ready for the wedding."

CHAPTER 21
Her View

The Stone Place was so beautiful, it left me speechless. I just stared at it for a long time, trying to imagine myself living there. It was almost a mansion compared to the old house. The dog ran out to greet us and there was a cat sunning herself on the porch. There were animals in the barnyard. I just stood by the gate and took it all in. It was so wonderful that it made me ache inside.

The interior of the house wasn't finished yet but I got a good idea of what it would be like in the future.

"If you're going to close it down for the winter, what will you do with all the animals?" I asked John.

"We'll have to bring them all over to our place."

"Oh, good! I was hoping you'd say that. I miss having animals around, especially the chickens and the dog."

After I had admired everything and expressed my gratitude to everyone, especially John, we headed for Titustown to check on Jennie Lu. When John suggested that we go home that way, I got really anxious to get going. I knew it would be the long way around and could make us late, but I wanted to see my daughter and know she was happy.

We got into town just as the children were being released from school. Jennie Lu was excited to see us, but she was even more excited about her school experience.

"The teacher says I'm in fourth grade and she'll work with me to help me catch up to my age group. She thinks I can do it by the end of this year. And, Mother, you've got to come see the nice room I have at Amy Tuttle's house."

"Well, get in and we'll go see it," I laughed. "That's what we're here for—to see how you're doing."

"I'm doing great," she exclaimed as she jumped up in the carriage and gave me a hug. "I'm so glad you let me do this. It feels like I'm starting a new life."

I felt a pang inside, but said nothing. I just moved over to make room for her. I felt John's strong arm across my shoulders as I moved up next to him. He gave me a squeeze. I guess he could sense my feelings.

Jennie Lu had told us every detail of her first day at school by the time we got to Amy's house. Then she showed us her upstairs room. It was almost like an apartment. She had the whole upstairs to herself.

"Miss Tuttle said I can have a friend over anytime I want to. Why don't you stay with me tonight, Mother. You could help me with my school work and visit with Miss Tuttle in the evening. She's taking care of some sick people right now. We could fix supper for her. She'll probably be tired when she comes home."

"That's a good idea," John joined in. "I can get a room at the hotel for tonight. I'll go see about it right now while you girls visit."

When John was gone, Jennie Lu and I worked on her school books for about two hours. We had a good time together. Then we decided it was time to prepare supper for Amy. She had left a menu on the door of the ice box.

"I'm glad you're here," Jennie Lu said, "because I didn't know how to make this. I would have had to wait for Miss Tuttle."

"Well, we'd better make plenty, because John will probably be back for supper."

When Amy came in, supper was almost ready.

"Well, isn't this a pleasant surprise!" she exclaimed. "I hope you come often."

Just then, there was a knock on the door. It was John and he had Mr. Jones with him.

"Do you girls have enough for two hungry men," John asked, "or shall we go to the restaurant?"

"We have enough. I was expecting you to show up. Were you able to get a room at the hotel?"

"I never got that far. I met Mr. Jones on the way and he insisted that I stay with him."

"I wouldn't miss the chance to have company. I get mighty lonely."

"I totally sympathize," I responded to him.

"John has been telling me your story and I don't think I've ever known the loneliness you have known, Caroline. If I had only known, I would have put a stop to that a long time ago."

"Well, John came in the nick of time and put a stop to it and now we're starting a whole new life together and you're both invited to the wedding."

"I wouldn't miss it for the world," Mr. Jones said, "and I hope you, Miss Tuttle, will accompany Jennie Lu and me out to the McLane ranch for that wonderful celebration," he said, turning toward Amy, who blushed and nodded her agreement.

"Well, we appreciate your kindness, but since the wedding will be on Sunday afternoon, Jennie Lu will be at the ranch. But you could bring her back to town after the wedding if you'd like to. That would be a help," John interjected.

"That's what we'll do, then."

Before the men left for the evening, Jennie Lu was over in the corner with her books again. It made me realize how serious she was about catching up with her class. I noticed she would look at me every once in a while. So when the men left, I asked her if she needed help. She came over to the table and Amy and I were soon involved with her schoolwork. It was mainly a matter of telling her a certain word and the meaning of it. Finally, Amy brought out her dictionary and set it on an end table. She showed Jennie Lu how to use it.

"I'll leave that right there so we can both use it," she promised.

I could tell that Jennie Lu was excited about this new tool. She started practicing with it right away. Amy showed us her collection of books. She had quite a few.

"When your reading improves, you can read my books," she promised Jennie Lu.

Before I went to bed that night, I realized that Jennie Lu was in the right place for this time in her life. She was so excited, she could hardly contain herself. She was going to have a hard time coming back out to the ranch.

"Thank You, God, for what You're doing for my daughter," I prayed that night. "But I need Your help to cope with all these drastic changes in my life. Help me to know what's right and wrong."

In the morning before we left to take Jennie Lu to school, I gave Amy two gold coins.

"These should cover your expenses for taking care of Jennie Lu," I said. "I appreciate what you're doing for me. Mr. Jones can turn them into cash for you, but I would appreciate it if you would keep this between you and me and Mr. Jones."

"Caroline, you know you can come here anytime and you don't have to pay me. We're friends."

"I know, and that is a gift to a dear friend."

CHAPTER 22
His View

We took Jennie Lu to school and started for home. I noticed that My Lady was very quiet and deep in thought. I decided to try to draw her out.

"What's bothering you, Caroline?" I asked.

"I'm just amazed at the way Jennie Lu is fitting into being in town and how she's so excited about school. I'm thinking she's not going to want to come back to the ranch."

I began to feel alarmed. I remembered Mr. Jones's offer of her mother's dress shop.

"Let's not jump to conclusions," I advised. "We can take her back and forth to school."

"Don't worry, John. I'm not thinking of moving to town. I'm just realizing that my daughter and I are two different people. She will probably go a different direction than I have gone. She's going to be a very independent person. This trip to town and going to school has unlocked something inside of her and she'll never be the same little girl I once knew."

I saw a tear and heard a catch in her voice, so I reached for her and pulled her closer.

"I know it's a good thing, but it's happened so fast that it's hard for me to process," she continued. "I'm sure glad I'm going to have you in my life as she moves out of it."

I began to feel that redeemed feeling again. But I still didn't dare to mention our trip back East.

There was a long silence as I held her close. Then she started to assure me that she was all right now, if I wanted to go back to the Stone Place. I told her I would stay in the bunkhouse with the men, but I wasn't going back to the Stone Place until after the wedding. I had an uneasy feeling about leaving her alone.

"It'll be nice to have you near," she murmured as she snuggled up against me. "You comfort me."

We rode the rest of the way in silence until we were in sight of my ranch.

Then I spoke my thoughts. "I wish I hadn't said the harsh words to you that I said when we first met."

My Lady sat up and began to laugh.

"I'm glad you did," she said. "It'll give me something to tease you about for the rest of my life. I can call you 'His Grouchiness' whenever you get too high and mighty."

"Well, you were trying so hard to be ugly and I could see that you weren't ugly and it made me grouchy."

So we both rode into the yard, laughing at ourselves.

CHAPTER 23
Her View

We spent the rest of the week working on our wedding preparations. I felt totally at peace and happy. But a strange thing happened on Friday. When I was getting dressed in the morning, I thought I should put the gun back on my leg. It seemed that something or someone was telling me I would need it.

"Well, no one will know I did it if I don't need it," I reasoned with myself as I strapped it on.

After breakfast, John said he needed to go out to the pastures and check on the cattle. He didn't plan to be gone long. I watched him leave and headed for the house. I was sitting at the table, going over the list of things left for me to do when I heard a horse approaching. It seemed to be coming from the direction of the Stone Place rather than town. That made me curious, so I stopped to listen. It came right to my door. Soon, a man came bursting in without even knocking.

"Mrs. Stone!" he burst out. "I know you have a gold mine and I want to manage it for you. I'm very experienced at it."

"No, you're mistaken. I don't have a gold mine," I responded.

"Are you Caroline Stone?" he asked.

"Yes, I am, but I don't have a gold mine, and I don't need a manager."

"Don't lie to me, Lady," he growled. "I know all about that gold mine and I intend to have my share of it."

"Your share of it?" I was shocked by his boldness.

"Yes, my share of it! When Silver took over that gold mine, I bought half of it from him. In fact, I own half of you and your daughter's income as well. Now, I'm willing to give up my interest if you give me all of the gold you now have. I know the sheriff sent that gold over here to you, but it's mine. I'll have it or I'll have you and your daughter and make some money off of you."

He was so obsessed by gold that you could not reason with him. He actually believed he had a right to my gold. I was tempted to give it to him and tell him to leave, but I knew he would be back and we would never be at peace knowing that. A tremendous calm came over me and I realized I was going to have to shoot this man, but I didn't want to do it in the house.

"I'll have to go into town and see the banker," I answered.

He pulled his gun out and said, "Don't try to pull any tricks or I'll shoot you." He got right behind me and put his gun in my back as Jimmy came running over from the barn.

"Jimmy, could you get the carriage ready for me, please?" I asked very calmly. "I have to go into town and conduct some business with this man."

Jimmy gave me a puzzled look, but went back to the barn and was soon back with the carriage. As I lifted my skirts to get into the carriage, I quickly pulled my gun out of its holster and hid it in my skirts. I watched as the man started to climb in after me and when his gun was turned slightly away from me for a second, I pointed my gun at him and pulled the trigger. It knocked him backward onto the ground, but he was pointing that gun at me when another shot rang out from somewhere, which finished him off. John came riding in and asked if I was all right. When I said yes, he turned to Jimmy.

"Get into town as fast as you can and see if Jennie Lu is all right. If she is, bring her out here to her mother and ask the sheriff to come out also."

Jimmy jumped on a horse and took off at a gallop.

John turned to me and put his arms around me. "You were awesome," he said.

"I didn't know if I could ever really shoot someone."

"You did a great job. I didn't know you were still wearing that gun!"

"I wasn't—until today. This morning, I felt impressed to put it back on."

"I'm sure glad you obeyed that impression. I had a similar experience when I was trying to go out in the pasture. It felt like when I tried to leave you back at the Stone Place. I felt so miserable that I had to turn around and come back. I saw that man following you out the door and I recognized him immediately. I knew he probably had a gun on you and he was too close to chance a shot. I thought I'd have to follow you to town at a distance, but I kept my rifle on him and when your shot knocked him back, I was ready.

"Why were you heading for town?" he asked as an afterthought.

"I told him I'd have to go to town to get the gold. It was in the bank. I didn't want to shoot him in the house and mess up the house."

John started to laugh.

"Only a woman would worry about messing up her house at a time like that."

Just then, a group of riders came over the hill. They were all from Tateville. They came galloping up to us.

"There's been a jailbreak," they shouted. Then they saw the body on the ground and said no more.

Finally someone spoke.

"He killed our sheriff. His body looks like he was tortured before he died."

"That's probably how he got so much information," I said.

"He was acting like he was really wanting to change—even requested visits from the preacher. So the sheriff was fooled and got careless," Mr. Tate explained.

"Was he the only one who escaped?" John asked.

"Yes."

"Do you know if 'Silver' had any other accomplices who might still be on the loose?"

"Not that we know of," was everyone's reply.

"Well, I'm going to have to go over there and find those papers that your sheriff tried to get me to read. He said Silver kept record of every detail of his operation against this Lady. I want to make sure we don't have any more incidents like this one. But for now, you men can all come into the bunkhouse and have some coffee and rest before you head back. I'm waiting to hear from my brother. I sent him to town to check on The Lady's daughter."

John put his arm around me and steered me toward the house. I didn't resist. I was feeling pretty shaky.

"You go inside and I'll take care of this dead body. I guess I'll just cover it until the sheriff gets here."

John stayed with me until we heard horses coming. Then we went to the door. We were surprised to see several horses and a carriage. Grandpa Jones and Amy were in the carriage with Jennie Lu. There was a group of five men riding with Jimmy. One was the sheriff.

"I didn't expect you to bring a posse," John said to the sheriff.

"We wanted to be sure that nothing happened to Jennie Lu," Mr. Jones spoke up. "So we all came along."

Jennie Lu jumped down from the carriage and ran to me. We just held each other and cried.

"Are you sure you're all right?" she finally asked.

I just nodded as I looked around at all these wonderful neighbors who cared about my daughter. I could feel that something inside of me was being healed.

"Well, let's all go into the bunkhouse. There's a group from Tateville in there. They came to warn us but they were too late. We'll let the sheriff do his job while we have some coffee and whatever the cooks can drum up," John said.

"Jimmy, there's a pot of chili on the stove. Would you carry that over to the bunkhouse, please?" I asked.

A friend from town offered to help.

"Sure," I said. "It'll be easier with two hands."

Just then, the sheriff asked me to tell him my side of this whole incident, so I went into the kitchen and sat down. Jennie Lu stayed right by my side. I guess she wanted to hear it all, too. When I had finished, she said, "I missed it all," with a sigh.

I looked at her for a minute as I got a revelation of how good it was that she wasn't here.

"I'm so glad you weren't here," I finally said. "He might have been able to use you as a weapon against me to get what he wanted."

The sheriff nodded his head.

Jennie Lu frowned and looked puzzled.

"If he'd been holding you captive, I couldn't have shot him. And he might have taken you with him as a hostage." I shivered at the thought.

"Oh," Jennie Lu said.

"That's what we were all worried about," the sheriff agreed. "That's why we brought such a big bodyguard for you. We knew what that guy was after. I'm glad your mother was able to shoot him. I'm going to go with John tomorrow to investigate the records in Tateville and try to put a final end to this mess.

"For right now, we'd better go get some of that chili before it's all gone," he said with a smile.

When we walked into the dining room, we were treated like celebrities. The sheriff hushed everyone and lifted his coffee cup and proposed a toast.

"To the toughest lady this side of the Mississippi," he said. "May she continue to win all her battles."

Everyone cheered as they raised their cups.

I could feel my face getting hot, but I couldn't help but laugh.

"Speech! Speech!" they all began to chant.

I raised my hand for silence.

"All I can say is I'm very grateful to God for sending John McLane into my life and for protecting my daughter and me and bringing us through all our trials and for all the good friends we now have. And I want to invite you all to our wedding a week from this Sunday."

There was more cheering and assurances that they would all be here for the wedding.

Jerry had managed to put quite a meal together for everyone. I was amazed and said so.

"As soon as I saw those guys ride over the hill, I started frying potatoes," he explained. "I knew what was coming. When the second bunch arrived, I started peeling more potatoes. Your chili was a Godsend. I had some leftover that I added to it."

I gave him a hug. "You're a Godsend," I said.

I went to find John. "I think Jennie Lu and I will head for the house now," I said.

"Not without me," he responded. "The sheriff and I have agreed that someone needs to be with you as a precaution. So he and I will both sleep there tonight. Then we'll head for Tateville in the morning. The men from Tateville will sleep in the bunkhouse and the men from Titustown will head for home tonight."

"Okay," I said. "I'll wait for you, then."

"We can go right now. I'm ready when you are."

So I thanked all the people again, gave Amy a hug, and headed for home, holding Jennie Lu's hand on my left and John's on my right. I was glad to see that the bloodstain was removed from the earth.

John built a fire and we sat there for a while, listening to Jennie Lu read the Bible to us. She had improved tremendously in one week.

"Jennie Lu," I exclaimed, "you are doing wonderful. I'm so proud of you. I can tell you are really working hard at this."

"It's the most important thing in the world to me, Mother. Just a little while ago, it looked like I would have no future. Now I want to take advantage of this time to make something of myself. I want to erase all that wasted time. I want to prove that I cannot be defeated, just like you."

I hugged her with all my strength.

"Jennie Lu is the talk of the town," the sheriff said as he walked into the room. "The teacher has been telling us all how well she's doing and how much potential she has. We're happy to have her in our town and we're determined that no one is ever going to hinder her again. We all feel so bad about what happened to you both when you left us. We all are so sad that something so terrible was going on so close to us and we didn't know it. I've been talking to the men from Tateville tonight and they agree that we need to start meeting together and be accountable to each other since we are so close. They've asked me to come over and set up the sheriff's office and help them protect their people. If we'd been working together, I could have seen the danger and saved their sheriff's life.

"John, I've been talking to your brother about training for that job. I think he's interested. We need a person of integrity and because of what's gone on there, we all agree it would be good to have someone not from that town. Most of the local people have lost confidence in their own men."

"I don't think Jimmy's ready for such a huge responsibility," John said.

"That's where you come in. Would you be willing to help us out while I'm training your brother?"

"We'll talk more about it tomorrow," John said. "Let me sleep on it."

"Sure. I'll sleep on it, too. And we can discuss it more tomorrow on our way over there. I just hope we don't have to go on a manhunt."

"So do I," John agreed. "I've got a wedding coming up. But I'll do whatever I have to do. I want this cleared up. Even if I have to postpone the wedding." He glanced at me as he said it.

I just smiled and nodded my agreement.

CHAPTER 24
His View

I was awakened just as the sun was coming up by a gentle touch on my face. I opened my eyes and looked into the eyes of My Lady. She was sitting on the floor by the couch. There was a troubled look in her eyes.

"What is it, Caroline?"

"I feel there is still an evil presence on this ranch," she whispered. "Maybe I'm just being foolish and fearful."

"No, you're not. I know you better than that," I said as I sat up. "It must be one of those men from Tateville or else someone is hiding out here. Either way, I'm not leaving until we resolve it. I'm not leaving you here as long as you have that feeling."

We were sitting at the table, waiting for the coffee to perk when there was a knock at the door. We both jumped. I motioned for Caroline to get out of sight before I opened the door a crack. Mr. Tate was standing there. I opened the door a little more and looked around. He seemed to be alone, so I invited him in. He began immediately to tell us his story.

"Ever since you asked us if there was anyone else who was working for Silver, I've been going over every possibility in my mind. All of the men with me are local men who were deceived by him, but not employed by him. There was only one man that I was not sure of. He was new in town, so I wasn't sure where he came from. He always stayed to himself and was very quiet. He's been working with us on Caroline's house. I never saw him with Silver, but I wasn't sure of him. So I watched him. I put my bed right beside his so I'd wake up if he tried to get out in the night. Even put a burr in his saddle blankets. Sure enough, he got up in the middle of the night. When I woke up, he said something about needing the outhouse. So I laid back down until he went out, then I got up and put my guns on and followed him. He was saddling his horse. I asked him where he was going and he jumped on the horse and tried to leave, but the horse bucked him off and I had my gun on him and I told him not to move. By then, some of the other men were out there and they tied him up for me. So we've got him over there, tied up for you."

I could hear Caroline let out a sigh of relief as she poured us both coffee.

I told Mr. Tate about her premonition and said, "You've saved us from having to spend a lot of time and money on a manhunt."

"Have I been redeemed?" he asked Caroline.

"You certainly have," she said and shook his hand.

Mr. Tate and I walked over to the back of the bunkhouse so I could search the man's saddlebags. The sheriff soon joined us. We found some pages that had been torn from Silver's record books. They listed the investments of the man I had shot yesterday and another man who, after searching his personal possessions, I was able to identify as the man we now had in custody. There was blood on the papers.

"It looks like this man was involved in the murder of the sheriff of Tateville and deserves to hang," I said.

"It sure looks that way," the sheriff agreed. "We'll take him back there with us and look for more evidence."

After breakfast, Caroline assured me that she felt totally at peace now and told me to go on to Tateville and get everything cleared up. So I gave instructions to the hands that she and her daughter were never to be left alone on the ranch.

"There should always be two men here, besides Jerry, until I get back," I said. "Jimmy is going with us to Tateville."

Mr. Tate asked us to take the dead body back to Tateville, rather than sending it to Titustown as we had planned. He explained that the people of his town were very upset and needed to see that justice was being done. So we took a wagon and put the body in it and made our captive lay in the same wagon.

When we arrived in Tateville, it seemed the whole town came out to meet us. They were a lot of grim-faced people. We uncovered the body so they could all walk by and see it. We pulled our captive out of the wagon and made him stand nearby while all the people passed by. Several people witnessed that they had seen these two men running from the sheriff's office on the day of the murder.

The last witness was a young boy of about twelve years. He had to be helped by his mother and another person. He trembled and shook like he had the palsy. Mr. Tate explained to us that he was hiding in the closet during the murder of his father. He had seen everything and was unable to recover from the shock. He looked at the dead body and nodded his head.

"He killed my father," he whispered. Then he turned toward the captive and started to shake violently. He had to be held up. He pointed a trembling finger.

"He tortured my father. He used a poker from the fire and he pulled his fingernails out. He put the hot poker in his eyes at the last." At that point, the young boy began to vomit. He vomited right on the man, who could not get away from him.

"Do you have anything to say?" I asked the man. He shook his head.

I turned to all the people and introduced the sheriff from Titustown. "He will be working with you to re-establish law and order in your town this winter and spring. In the summer, I will be moving into the Stone Place with my wife, the former Caroline Stone. Then I will take over the sheriff position in this town if you people so desire."

The people began to applaud.

"So now I will ask the sheriff to pass judgment on this man who was arrested on my ranch."

The sheriff came forward.

"I sentence you to death by hanging," he said to the man, who showed no reaction of any kind.

The young boy began to stand on his own power and follow as the sheriff and some other men escorted the convicted man toward the gallows. He stood very near and stared at the man who was about to die. He stood near the base of the gallows and watched every move.

The convict was given another chance to speak.

He looked down at the boy and spoke for the first time anyone could remember.

"I'm sorry for what you saw. I hope it doesn't do to you what it did to me. I watched my whole family tortured to death by Indians. It entered into me and took control. I'm glad it's over now. I ask God to forgive me and heal you." With that, he nodded toward the executioner and closed his eyes.

The boy stayed where he was and watched the whole thing. When it was over, he straightened his shoulders and walked away on his own power. I walked beside him.

"Your father was a good man," I finally said.

"He told me how he failed in the Stone case," the boy offered.

"But he corrected his error. We all make mistakes," I continued.

"Through all his torture, he never made a sound, because he knew I was in the closet and he didn't want me to hear. But there was a crack in the door and I saw it all. Thank you for bringing those men back here so I could see their end."

"You're welcome. I hope it helped."

"It sure has helped. I feel like I can go on living now. My mother wants to go back East, but I have a feeling I'll be back out here someday. Maybe I'll see you again then."

"I'll look forward to that," I said as we shook hands and he headed for his house where his mother waited in the doorway.

When I got back to my ranch, Caroline was waiting for me.

"You can go on with the wedding plans," I announced. "Every one of Silver's men are buried beside him in the cemetery in Tateville."

"What did you decide about the sheriff's proposal for you?" she asked.

"I told him I wasn't willing to work in Tateville until we moved into the Stone Place, so he and Jimmy would have to cover Tateville for now. I could cover for him here in Titustown if he needed me, but

I wasn't willing to leave you here and work over there, especially since we are just getting started in our marriage."

"Good, I appreciate that. I also appreciate the fact that I don't have to worry about my daughter in this town. This incident proved to me that she's very safe and well cared for there. It seems the whole town is concerned about her. They wouldn't even let Jimmy take her away. They all came along to make sure it wasn't a trap of some kind."

Tears swam in her eyes as she said that last sentence.

I put my arms around her and thanked God again for my redemption.

"Caroline, I'm so glad to hear you say that, because I have planned a surprise for our honeymoon and I was worried that this incident was going to ruin everything."

"What surprise?" Caroline asked as she tried to pull away from me, but I held her tight and started to kiss the side of her face and neck. When I felt her begin to relax, I went on.

"I want to take you back East by train so you can meet my relatives and I can meet yours. And we can spend a lot of time together, just you and me."

As I spoke, I felt her tense up and then start to relax again as I continued to kiss and caress her with my lips.

"You said Jennie Lu is safe in this town," I reminded her.

"I thought we would spend our honeymoon right here in this house," she said.

"I planned to spend the first night here. You'll be too tired to travel."

"Well, I'm sure it will be exciting," she said as she pulled away from me. "Now, come inside and help me decide how to get this house ready for us to live in it together."

CHAPTER 25
The Wedding
Her View

When my wedding day finally arrived, I felt that I was ready. I had prayed for good weather and it looked like God had answered my prayer. We had decided to get married at home since the church in town would not be able to contain the crowd. John's mother had a vine-covered arbor in the side yard which covered a bench swing. John took the swing out temporarily so we could say our vows there. I would walk from the front door of the house around to that arbor, escorted by Grandpa Jones, where John would be waiting with the pastor. Jennie Lu would follow me, escorted by Jimmy.

Jerry and Andy said they had enough food to feed both towns. I had made many loaves of my bread that Jerry loved so much. Jerry had made some, too and Andy had made a beautiful wedding cake. Grandpa Jones was bringing ice cream from town. Jerry said he could keep it in the ice house. There was still some ice there.

The men had butchered a cow and were planning to roast the whole thing over the outdoor fires. They had also bought a sheep and a goat from some neighbors who raised those. Some of the people from town were bringing chickens and turkeys.

Everyone was coming out to our place right after the morning church service. So after John and I had walked around and checked on everything, we headed inside to get dressed for the wedding. He had already moved all of his clothes into the house so he came in to get them and then headed for the bunkhouse to dress. He stopped in the door and looked back at me.

"This is the last time," he said.

We just stood and looked at each other for a while. It was a strange feeling—that something was coming to an end and we could never go back to it. The man who was about to walk through that door would never walk back through it. The next time he walked through that door, he would be my husband and I would be his wife and we would never be the same people again. Because of our past experiences, we were both aware of what a drastic change was about to happen.

"Are you sure you want to do this?" I asked. "There's no going back. You'll never be totally free again. I could go into town until my house is finished and we could continue to be friends. But you would be free to do as you please and I would be also."

"I've already thought all that through," John responded. "I've been totally free to do as I pleased and it wasn't all that great. I want you more than I want that. I'm absolutely sure this is what I want to do."

"You could marry a younger woman and have more children."

John walked over and put his arms around me.

"I've thought of that, too. But you're the one I want. I'm hoping for a child, but if it doesn't happen, I'll still be happy that I married you."

"You sure?"

"I'm sure! How about you? Are you sure?"

"If you're sure, then I'm sure. I've heard from the Lord, remember?"

"Yes, I remember, and I'm so glad."

John walked back to the door and turned to look at me again.

"Tonight, you and I will become one flesh. Somehow the two of us will become one person. It's a mystery and I don't know how it works, but I'm anxious to experience it," he said.

"Okay, let's get on with it, then," I laughed as I pushed him out the door. I could already see a carriage coming from town which I was sure was Grandpa Jones, bringing Amy Tuttle to help us.

Jennie Lu was already in her wedding dress when I went up to her room. She just needed some help with buttons in the back. She looked beautiful in it. We had curled her hair, so I was busy taking those curlers out when I heard the knock on the door. I called down to Amy to come in and come on upstairs.

Jennie Lu was almost in tears because she didn't like the look of the curled hair.

"I can fix it," Amy assured her. "I'll pile some on your head and use a little moisture on the rest and it'll be beautiful."

I ran downstairs to get a glass of water. Sure enough, when Amy finished with it, Jennie Lu was smiling.

"Now it's my turn," I said as I uncovered my wedding dress. Amy caught her breath.

"Who made this?" she asked. "It's beautiful."

"We did," Jennie Lu beamed. "My mother and I worked on it together."

She looked at me and smiled and I knew she was remembering. Remembering things that it was best not to talk about at a time like this. We would always have that between us—that no one else would ever fully comprehend.

"Someday, I'll wear it for my wedding, the Lord willing," she said.

"If you put it in a trunk, you can probably preserve it," Amy advised.

When Amy was fixing my hair, Jennie Lu watched every move carefully.

"I'll learn how to do it, then I can fix your hair for you sometimes," she explained.

When Amy was through with me, she and Jennie Lu both said I looked like a queen.

"You're learning a lot from Amy, aren't you?" I said to Jennie Lu.

"Yes, and I plan to learn more. She said she will teach me to be a nurse like she is. I really want to learn that so I can help people."

"That's wonderful," I said, but I wondered how that was going to work with living at the Stone Place.

"How did you learn so much about fixing hair?" I asked Amy.

"When I was back East, going to nursing school, I worked part time for a lady who fixed people's hair."

"Oh," was all I could say about that. "How old are you, Amy?" I asked.

"I'm forty."

"How can you be that much older than me when we went to school together!" I exclaimed.

"I came into school late, like Jennie Lu. But I didn't let anyone know how old I was. My stepfather believed that women didn't need to go to school. He believed our place was in the home, raising children and keeping house. When he died, I went to school, and I kept going to school. I never married. It was probably because I resented him so much. I wanted to prove him wrong. But now I see he wasn't so far off as I thought. I see you and Jennie Lu and wish I had a daughter. But now, it's too late for me."

We were silent for a while. Then I said, "It may be too late for a child, but it's not too late to marry. And there are orphans out there that need a home."

Amy just nodded and said no more.

Soon, I heard music outside. I couldn't believe it. I rushed to the window and saw a group of musicians seated in chairs on the lawn. Just then, I heard a knock at the door.

Amy opened it and there was Grandpa Jones. He had brought our flowers in from the carriage.

"Are you ready?" he asked.

"I think I am," I responded. "Who is responsible for the music?"

"I am. It's my wedding present. Do you like it?"

"It's wonderful!"

Jimmy came in right behind Grandpa.

"Both of you look beautiful!" he exclaimed.

"Thank you, Jimmy. Without Amy, we wouldn't look this good, though."

Grandpa offered me his arm and we stepped through the door together to face a huge crowd who began to clap. Grandpa held up his hand for silence and the band began to play the wedding march as we walked slowly around the house and toward the arbor in the side yard. I soon saw John and the pastor waiting for me. And there were more people around in the side yard. I was amazed at the size of the crowd. John wasn't kidding when he said the whole town would come. But I soon focused my attention on John and began to remember when he first came to my gate and rescued me with the crack of a whip. I didn't know until later that he was in just as much of a mess as I was. We were two desperate people who rescued each other. Right in the middle of my wedding march, I received a revelation of a truth that I believe came from God. It brought tears to my eyes. I could see so clearly that God stepped in to rescue John and redeem all his mistakes when he made up his mind to rescue me. I realized that God would always do that. If we took care of others first, He would take care of us. John had a problem he couldn't solve. God let him try to run away from it and used his run-away to lead him to a problem he could solve. I had a problem I couldn't solve, but when I reached out to help my cousin in the midst of her need, God solved my problem for me. It was like the pieces of a huge unsolvable puzzle had suddenly all come together and fit together perfectly. This is what they call "Amazing Grace" that brings about redemption. We had all been redeemed. Including the people of Tateville who I was able to completely forgive in that moment of Divine Revelation. I felt a few tears of joy spillover and run down my cheeks.

CHAPTER 26

The Wedding

His View

As I stood in the yard of my childhood home and waited for my bride to appear, I watched wagon after wagon come over the hill, loaded with old friends and new acquaintances. Memories flooded my mind, some good, some bad, but all part of my story of redemption. I hoped my parents were watching from heaven. Every time I raised my hand to wave a welcome to another group, I felt inside that I was waving at them. I wanted so much for them to know that their wayward son had been redeemed. This old place that had seemed like a prison to me, now felt like the comforting arms of a mother's love. Between wagons, my eyes wandered over the grounds that Caroline had restored. The whole place was beautiful again. No wonder my mother had prayed that I would marry her. I was determined not to let it get rundown again, even after we moved to the Stone Place.

Mr. Jones arrived with a whole group of musicians. I hadn't even thought of that, but what a wonderful idea. I helped them pick out an appropriate spot and set up their chairs. Soon they were making beautiful music. I saw My Lady peek out the window to see where that music was coming from. I realized some people were going to want to dance after the wedding. So I went to the barn and got some ropes so I could block off an area. Otherwise, the wagons would fill the whole yard. I saw Jerry setting up some tables outside, so I coordinated my cleared area with his. I knew some people would want to eat in their wagons and would pull them right up to the door of the dining room if I didn't stop them.

Mr. Jones came over to help me and wanted to know when he should go after my bride.

"Not until the people from Tateville get here," I said. "I wouldn't want them to miss it after coming this far." Just then, I saw five wagons coming over the hill, full of people.

"I think that's them now. I'm glad I got these ropes up before they got here." I had just finished roping off the walkway for my bride to follow from the door to the altar. I hadn't seen the need of it until I saw what a crowd we were attracting. I didn't want them to block her way. Finally, I went to stand by the pastor and nodded to Mr. Jones. He got the flowers from the carriage and went to the door of the house.

When my bride stepped through that door and everyone started cheering and clapping, I thought I would burst inside. I was so full of joy. I thought I had completely lost this part of life, but I had been redeemed. She looked so beautiful, I could hardly stand it. I felt like my life was starting over again.

Then the Wedding March started and she came walking slowly toward me. If only I could freeze this moment in time and keep it to show it to our children in the future. Then I realized that I couldn't even imagine what my mother looked like on her wedding day. But my father had the memory permanently stored in his mind and always saw her that way. I remembered the times he would see her coming and say, "Here comes my beautiful bride!" That's what I would do. I would store this memory away and always see my wife as the beautiful woman I was looking at right now. I couldn't help but smile as I remembered all her attempts to hide that beauty.

When we had said our vows to each other and I had kissed my bride and the band started playing, I took her in my arms and started to waltz with her back down that path. It wasn't long before everyone started joining in. Mr. Jones was the first to join us. He danced with Jennie Lu until Jimmy cut in and Mr. Jones found Amy and asked her to dance. We danced right over to the dining hall where a delicious meal awaited us. We had to go first so Jerry could start serving the rest of the people. It was going to take a long time to serve all these people so we needed to get started.

HER VIEW

John and I and Jennie Lu and Jimmy sat at a table prepared for us on the side of the room and all the people filed by us to get their food. Many brought gifts as they greeted us. Most of them were beautiful handmade linens that money could not buy. I was very grateful for them because I had very few of my own. Almost everything I owned had either been stolen or destroyed. I noticed that the people from Tateville were feeling awkward. They didn't know what to say and they were the most generous in their giving. I tried hard to convey to them that all was forgiven. It was wonderful to renew old friendships. Mr. and Mrs. Tate, with the help of several young men, brought in a beautiful braided rug. They said the ladies' group at the church had made it for us. They had made it big enough for our living room at the Stone Place. I was amazed.

"Let's haul it over to the house and see if it fits there," I said. "I want to use it right away if I can. I love it!"

It was too big for the living room, but fit perfectly in the dining room. It looked so beautiful on the floor! I gave Mrs. Tate a hug of appreciation.

"Us girls didn't know all that was going on out at your place or we would have stepped in to stop it," she whispered in my ear.

"It makes me feel better to know that," I responded, "and it encourages me to stay involved in town business. Us ladies are needed, not just in the home."

Jennie Lu was standing beside me and had a very thoughtful look on her face. She was looking at that rug and nodding her head.

"We'll make sure that nothing like that ever happens again, won't we, Jennie Lu?" she asked, turning to my daughter.

"Yes," we both responded.

We headed back for the dining hall, greeting friends along the way. We enjoyed a delicious dinner and then came the time to cut that beautiful wedding cake. Everyone crowded around to watch me feed John and John feed me. Soon the music started again and a lot of people were dancing as John and I headed for our home. He grabbed me and waltzed me toward our house. A whole train of young people followed, carrying all our gifts. They piled them all on the dining room table.

As I thanked them all, John began to build a fire in the fireplace. We were home together at last. Jennie Lu came in and began to gather her things together.

"I'll be heading back to town with Grandpa Jones and Amy," she said. "I hope you have a wonderful time back East."

I gave her a hug and held on for a while.

"Don't worry about me, Mother," she finally said as she pulled away. "I'll be just fine. I love what I'm doing and all the danger is past for us. Just relax and enjoy your new life."

It made me laugh to hear my daughter sounding like a counselor or something. I gave her a smack on the bottom and said, "Just don't forget you are part of this new life, young lady. You aren't all grown up yet. You still need your parents."

"Amen!" John agreed.

Jennie Lu just laughed as she headed for Grandpa Jones's carriage. Suddenly, she turned back with a concerned look on her face.

"Who will take care of my cat?" she asked.

"I hadn't even thought of that," I confessed. "Go see if Jimmy will agree to do it for you."

I watched her run toward the dining hall and she looked like my little girl again. When she came back, I stood in the door. She jumped into the carriage and waved as she announced that Jimmy would take care of the cat. I watched and waved until they were out of sight. By then, many wagons were headed out and waved as they passed us by. John was standing behind me and was waving also.

"You make a handsome couple," one man shouted as they passed.

Finally, John pulled me back in and closed the door.

"Let's get you out of that wedding dress and into something more comfortable so you can relax for a few hours and enjoy our home before we take off in the morning."

But just then, there was a knock on the door. John went to answer. It was Jerry. He had his hands full of pots and pans.

"I brought you some leftovers so your bride won't need to cook tonight."

"Thank you, Jerry," I exclaimed. "That is so thoughtful. Will there be some for you and the other men?"

"There's plenty. We will have a great barbecue tonight to celebrate your wedding. We're all really happy about it. This means our boss will stay put and we'll continue to have a job!"

John began to laugh and slapped Jerry on the back.

"You got that right. After this honeymoon trip, I ain't goin' nowhere. I'm stayin' right here to run two ranches and keep my wife happy. Maybe with God's help, we'll end up raisin' some kids to carry on after we're gone."

"Amen," Jerry responded. "I'll be right here to help anyway I can."

"And we're glad about that, Jerry," I joined in.

Soon I was heading upstairs to change my clothes. John had closed the door after Jerry. I heard him running up the stairs.

"I came to help," he panted. "I wouldn't miss this for the world. I want to help you remove that wedding dress. Someone else put it on you and I'm going to take it off. It's symbolic of your passing from them to me."

"John," I laughed, "I didn't know you had this dramatic part to you. I'm already learning things about you that I didn't know."

Soon we were sitting in front of that fireplace, talking about our dreams and plans for the future. The hours passed quickly and we soon felt Jerry's food calling us. John got the fire going in the stove and I began to warm the food. Then he took the barbecued part and held it over the fire in the fireplace. It was just as delicious warmed up as it had been earlier.

"This is our first meal together as husband and wife," John said. "We will remember it and reproduce it on our anniversary."

I stared at him in amazement. He was already establishing traditions for us.

"Barbecued meat every anniversary," I commented.

He just nodded.

CHAPTER 27
His View

The trip back East went very well. Caroline and I enjoyed ourselves on the train and met lots of interesting people. Some of them will probably be our friends for life. Several have promised to visit us in the future. We encouraged our relatives to try a train trip and several seemed interested.

We had agreed beforehand not to discuss the details of Caroline's ordeal. We shared only that her first husband had been murdered and that the guilty people had been apprehended and executed. We never mentioned the gold or how we met. We shared only that our two ranches were near each other which led them all to believe that we had known each other for a long time. We agreed that some things were better left unsaid. I never mentioned my first wife until someone asked me if I'd been married before. Then I said I'd been married for a short time to Caroline's cousin who died soon after we were married. This seemed to satisfy everyone's curiosity as to why we married so late in life.

I was amazed to discover that my mother's sister was still alive. She was in good shape mentally and brought out all the family pictures for us. She also had all of my mother's letters. I was hesitant to read them because I knew she would mention me and my wayward ways. Sure enough, she asked for prayer for me when I headed for California. She even mentioned Caroline and her desire to have her as a daughter-in-law. When I told my aunt that my wife was the woman my mother had mentioned, she rejoiced and praised God for answered prayer. She sounded just like my mother and looked so much like her that it brought tears to my eyes. I met all her children and grandchildren before we left.

CHAPTER 28
Her View

It was easy for John to find his relatives because his mother had kept in contact with her family. Most of his father's family had moved even farther west than he had, so he didn't know what had become of them. But he found his father's older brother who was still alive and living alone.

When it came time to search for my relatives, I was a little hesitant because I had so little information to go on. My mother never discussed her family that much. She said some of them had married into the Cherokee nation and she didn't know if they had survived the Trail of Tears. So I really had nothing more than a name and a community to go on. But I finally did find a cousin who was a doctor. I didn't remember him, but he said he remembered pushing me in a swing when my family was visiting his, just before departing for the West. He was a very interesting person. His name was Joseph. We had some long talks. I told him of the needs in the West and he told me about his experiments with skin grafting.

When I told Joe what my mother had said about her family and the Cherokees, he got very quiet and just looked at me for a long time.

"Do you want to know the truth?" he asked.

I just nodded.

"Your mother and my mother were full-blooded Cherokee. That's why they never mentioned their maiden names. They wanted to keep it a secret. My mother finally told me before she died. They were both so light-skinned that no one ever suspected."

I was quiet for a long time—remembering things from my childhood that verified the truth of what Joe had said. I remembered how my mother used to like to squat down by an open fire and make bread. And sometimes I would hear her singing in a language I did not understand. But then another memory began to stir from deep inside that I thought I had forgotten. I remember hearing something like an argument going on between my parents far into the night until I finally fell asleep. But I remembered my mother talking about her people and crying. The next morning, my father had hitched the horses to the wagon. My mother put blankets in the wagon and some food, then they headed out. As we traveled, more people put blankets and food in our wagon. Finally, we came to a place where lots of people were walking and there were lots of wagons. I realized now that we had visited "The Trail of Tears".

The most amazing part of my memory was that my mother came back with two babies and she cried the whole way back home. My father said nothing. I remembered that we stopped at the first house we saw and got milk for those babies. We had those babies for what seemed like a long time. I remembered them sitting up and eating food that my mother had mashed up for them. But then we took a long trip to Oklahoma Indian Territory. I remembered a lot of crying and hugging when we gave those babies back to their mothers. And again, my mother held me and cried a lot on our way home.

When I related my memories to Joe, it made him very happy to know we had helped his mother's people in their time of suffering. I didn't tell him about the intense conversations I had overheard between my parents in the night when they assumed I was sound asleep.

"If we can't help my people then I must go join them," I heard my mother say. How I shivered in fear that my mother would leave me. I didn't know who 'her people' were. It made me into a clinging vine until I reached my teen years. I never wanted to let my mother out of my sight. My insecurity was only made worse by my father's sudden death when I was ten years old. Now at last, I was beginning to understand. I wish my parents had explained it to me when I was young. I remembered that after my father died, I didn't want to go to school, so my mother would get books from the teacher and we would study them while we worked together in her dress shop. We had some very good times together but there was always a sadness about my mother. I had always assumed it was her grief over my father. But now, I could understand that there was more to it than that. She probably carried a lot of guilt and grief about her people and she never felt free to share it with anyone. How alone she must have felt when I married and left her! She was suspended between two worlds and could never be totally at home in either one. If only she had told me!

CHAPTER 29
The Trip Back Home

Well, it was finally time to head home. I expected My Lady to be excited about heading back to check on her daughter. But I began to notice that she was very quiet. I kept trying to engage her in conversation, but she would answer my questions and go back to gazing out the window with that faraway look on her face. Finally, I could stand it no longer.

"Caroline!" I said, a little too forcefully. "Will you please wake up from your dream or at least share it with me? Aren't you happy to be going home?"

She turned slowly toward me and smiled slightly.

"I'm sorry," she almost whispered. "There is something I need to share with you—in private."

"Well, let's go back to that empty corner," I said, taking her hand and pulling her up.

When we sat down in the corner by ourselves, Caroline clasped her hands, resting them on her knees and looked straight ahead.

"Now, John," she started nervously, "if I had known about this before we were married, I certainly would have told you. And if you want to annul the marriage, I would certainly understand."

"What in the world are you talking about, Caroline?" I exclaimed.

"I'm half Indian! My mother was a full-blooded Cherokee Indian!"

I stared at her for a few seconds, then I exclaimed, "Is that all?"

She looked at me and nodded.

I grabbed her and began to laugh.

"Do you think I care about that?" I pushed her away and held her at arm's length for a few seconds.

"Now that you mention it, you do look a little bit like a Cherokee. I met lots of them on my way to California. Most of them were fine people. I was surprised that they would have anything to do with me after the way my people treated their people."

I held her in my arms while she told me her whole story, including her grief for her mother. I cried a few tears with her.

"Well," I finally said, "I'll be all the more determined to see that all the Indians in our area are treated fairly since I'm married to one. It's terrible what's going on in California. The gold fever is making monsters out of people. We'll have to be very careful how we handle that gold mine of yours."

Caroline put her finger to her lips.

"This train is making so much noise, no one could hear us," I assured her.

By the time we returned to our seats in the train, Caroline was her old self again. And as I expected, she was anxious to get home to her daughter. It made me feel good to see how important I had already become in her life.

The people on the train were excited about the wonderful invention of the telegraph that was going to make it so much easier to keep in touch with our relatives in the East. Everyone was very friendly and talkative the rest of our trip. It helped pass the time, but didn't contribute to us getting any rest. By the time we reached Titustown, we were very tired, but Jimmy and Jennie Lu were there to greet us and tell us that Amy had a meal ready for us. She had invited several people who wanted to hear all about our trip. So we didn't get home until late and we were happy, but exhausted.

CHAPTER 30
Her View

When we topped the hill and the house came into view, my heart leaped within me. It looked like home. All the lanterns were lit because Jimmy had gone before us to announce our coming. All the ranch hands were standing outside to welcome us home.

"Oh look," I exclaimed, "they brought Sadie and her puppies over. They've even built a chicken house near the garden."

As John was helping me down from the carriage, I heard a rooster crow.

"I guess we got that poor rooster confused with all these lanterns," Jimmy laughed.

"Everything looks so beautiful. I can hardly stand it," I confessed as a few tears overflowed my eyes. "It feels so good to be home."

All the men followed us into the house. There on the table was a huge bouquet of fall flowers and foliage. Leaning against it was a painting of the McLane ranch with these words on the bottom of the picture:

"Welcome Home Mr. & Mrs. John McLane"

"Where did you find all those flowers?" I exclaimed. "And who painted this beautiful picture?"

"Well," Jerry spoke up, "to answer your first question, we searched all over this ranch for those flowers. Some came from the flowerbeds that you restored, but most are the result of a search party we sent out.

"As for the painting, this young man right here did it," he said as he pulled a shy young man forward. "John hired him right before your wedding and put him in my care. I noticed that he drew pictures when he wasn't working, so I bought him some paint and told him to do something for you."

"This is beautiful," I said as I looked from the picture to the young man. I looked for a name in the corner of the picture or on the back, but there was none.

"What's your name?" I asked.

"John Ross," he whispered. I moved a little closer so I could hear him.

"Are you named after the great Cherokee Chief?" I asked. He raised his head and looked at me.

"Yes," he answered.

"I also am Cherokee," I said to him. "You are safe here. Where are your parents?"

"Dead."

"How old are you?"

"I think maybe sixteen. I don't know for sure."

"Why did you come here?"

"My mother told me before she died that she had a sister in this town. She said that this sister of hers would help me if I could find her. She saved two of my cousins from the Trail of Tears when they were just babies. So I came to look for her."

"That was my mother. She died several years ago. But I will take her place and see that you get an education and are able to develop the gift that God has given you, if you will work hard and obey the rules here."

He smiled and nodded and I took that as agreement.

"You speak very good English," I continued. "Have you been to school?"

"My mother taught me to speak English and read and write before she died."

"She did an excellent job! I'll get some school books in town so we can finish what she started."

When all the men had left, I thanked John for being so kind to my young Cherokee cousin.

"I didn't know he was your cousin, but I suspected that he was an Indian. He seemed too young to be on his own, so I gave him a job. I hope it works out good for everyone."

"So do I," I agreed. "Now let's get to bed before the sun comes up and that rooster gets going again."

I was awakened the next morning by the sound of a rooster crowing and the smell of coffee perking. Jennie Lu's kitten jumped up on the bed and started rubbing against me.

I grabbed my housecoat and headed downstairs. There was a fire burning in the fireplace. The feeling of warmth and comfort was overwhelming. I turned and looked out the window to hide my tears. There I watched the chickens pecking in their yard and Sadie trying to get away from her puppies for a few minutes. Smoke was rising from the chimney in the dining hall and my young cousin was hitching horses to the wagons. I leaned my head against the window and closed my eyes to shut out this peaceful scene so I could get control of myself. Just then, I felt John's strong arm across my shoulders.

"Is that boy upsetting you?" he asked.

"No, it's this whole beautiful and peaceful scene. It seems I have died and gone to heaven. I'm overwhelmed. I'm trying to adjust my thinking. Sometimes I pinch myself to see if I'll wake up from this dream."

"I'm glad it's a good dream," he said. "I told them to bring all the animals over while we were gone and make this place look as peaceful and as much like home as possible."

"They've done such a good job, I don't know if I'll want to move back into the Stone Place," I laughed.

"For right now, I need to see what we've got that I can cook for breakfast. Is Jimmy eating with us or over with the hands?"

"I think he ate over there. He's going out with them to work in the fields and check on the cattle. I told him I was going to finish out this week here with you, helping you get settled in."

"That will be fun," I said as I started to prepare breakfast. My mind was already on all those wedding presents I needed to put away.

By evening, we had it pretty well organized and a good supper on the stove. Jimmy came in and ate with us.

"This feels like home!" he exclaimed.

"This *is* your home," I responded. "I hope you'll always feel comfortable and welcome here. I don't want to take it away from you."

"You're not taking it away—you're giving it back to us," Jimmy said. "I'm sure glad John found you.

"That reminds me. We can't call that new boy 'John.' That's your name," he said, turning to John. "What shall we call him?"

"How about Johnnie?" John replied.

"Why don't you ask him what he would like to be called other than John," I suggested.

"That's a good idea. I'm going to run over and ask him right now."

I was doing the dishes when Jimmy returned.

"He told us some Indian name which none of us could pronounce, so I asked him what it meant in English and he said 'Little John,' so I guess that's what we'll call him. 'Little John.' If it's all right with you," he said, turning to John.

"Sounds good to me."

Jimmy ran up the stairs, whistling a tune, and John began to help me clean up.

"Are you happy?" he asked.

"The only thing that could make me happier would be having my daughter here."

"She'll be here this weekend. And she can come back now and we can take her into town every day for school like we had planned."

"I don't think she's going to want to now. She's learning so much from Amy Tuttle that she'll want to stay there."

"Well, you are the mother. You can decide."

"I know that, but I want to do what's best for my daughter. It's a hard decision. I'm praying about it."

"Let's pray together right now. Doesn't the Bible say something about two people agreeing?"

"It sure does. Let's pray!"

On Friday, we were at the school waiting for Jennie Lu, when she came out of the building. She was happy to see us and jumped right into the carriage, but I noticed she got real quiet on our way to Amy Tuttle's house.

"What's bothering you?" I asked.

"I don't know if I should go home with you," she responded. "Miss Tuttle really needs me now. She's got two babies to care for."

"She does?" I exclaimed. "How did that happen?"

"Right after you left, this man came into town looking for help for his wife. She was in labor and she had a two year old son and two older sons about six and eight, I think. She had the baby, but she died from loss of blood. Amy couldn't save her. But before she died, she asked Amy to take her children and raise them.

"The father agreed to give her the babies, but insisted on taking the older boys. He was headed for the gold rush in California. Grandpa Jones tried to talk him out of it. He said it wasn't a safe place for children. But the man wouldn't listen. We told the boys they could come back to us anytime if they needed to. They were crying when they left. It about broke my heart. I pray for them every day."

By the time Jennie Lu had finished her story, we were in front of Amy's house.

When we walked up to the door, I could hear a baby crying. Jennie Lu rushed in to help, but it was obvious that Amy had everything under control. The two year old was in a highchair and she was holding the newborn and teaching her to take a bottle. She finally took it and quieted down.

"I'm finally getting this under control," Amy said as we came in. "These babies have done a lot of crying in the last few days. I think they missed their mother. But they are starting to settle down now. Jennie Lu has been a tremendous help. She had to miss a couple days of school to help me. I don't know what I would have done without her."

I watched as Jennie Lu was feeding the two year old. He was obviously happy to see her. I could see why she was hesitant to leave, but I wanted my daughter back. I turned to Amy.

"Do you think you can manage alone until Monday?" I asked.

"I think I'll be fine. I've been doing fine the last two days, and Grandpa Jones said he would come help with the two year old if I needed him, or even take care of both of them if I had to go care for a sick person. Other women in town have offered to help also."

I was relieved.

"That's good to hear," I said. "This is a big job to take on so suddenly."

"It sure is!" Amy agreed, "but now I'm going to have a family, so I feel blessed."

"Is the baby a boy or a girl?" I asked.

"She's a girl. I named her Amy Lucinda, after me and Jennie Lucinda. We'll call her Amy Lu. The boy's name is Gerald Lee. His mother just called him Gerry. The last name was Slater. I wrote down the mother's maiden name. She asked me to try to let her mother know what happened."

"Do you think she'll try to take them away from you?" I asked.

"I hope not. Their mother wrote on a paper that she gave them to me to raise."

"Well, that should help."

Soon, Jennie Lu came back from putting the little boy down for a nap and we started for home. She was quiet for a while, but then she started to tell us about the death of the children's mother. It was her first time to witness a death since her father.

"I'm afraid for the little boys," she said. "Their father was half crazy with greed for gold. Grandpa Jones gave his horse to them and told them if anything happened to their father, that horse would know the way to bring them back here to us."

"Let's pray for them," I said.

As we prayed, Jennie Lu began to cry.

"Please, God! Please, God!" she begged over and over, "bring them back here safely.

"In Jesus's Name," she finally whispered and quieted down.

I just put my arms around her while she cried and agreed with her prayer by saying Amen.

It was great to have my daughter home again. I watched her swinging in the yard and playing with her cat and the puppies and just being a child again. That's when I decided I wasn't ready to let her live in town with Amy. She was growing up too fast there. We would go back to our original plan of commuting back and forth to school. I asked John about sending Little John to school also and he agreed to it. Jimmy would take them in and go get them in the afternoon. Little John could work after school and on Saturday to earn his keep. He readily agreed to our plan. Jimmy didn't hesitate one bit either. It sounded like fun to him.

Jennie Lu was the only one who was hesitant. She got very quiet for a while, but she finally came to me and gave me a hug.

"I'm glad you want me here, Mother," she said. "I'm just worried about Amy."

"I know," I responded, "but Amy needs this time alone to establish herself as the mother of those babies. You can visit them often, but remember there are lots of women in town that will be happy to help Amy with those babies. And I want you here with me because I'm your mother and you're growing up too fast. We already missed out on a lot of your childhood over at the Stone Place."

Jennie Lu was soon busy on the ranch and her crying spells over the Slater boys came less often. On Saturday, I let her go out with the men to help with bringing in the hay. John assured me he would keep a close eye on her.

When we went to church on Sunday, we visited Amy. She assured us she was doing fine. She wasn't ready to try to take those babies to church yet, but she was doing better at home.

October and November passed quickly. It was a wonderful time for us as we established ourselves as a family and got better acquainted with Little John. It soon seemed like he was part of the family. He and Jimmy competed with each other to see who was the best worker. They were practicing riding and roping and bull riding, because there was talk of a rodeo coming to town next year. I allowed Jennie to ride the horses, but said absolutely no bull riding for her.

When December came, we began to be excited about our first Christmas together as a family. I couldn't remember when I had last celebrated Christmas, so I began to decorate and kept going to town to start my shopping early. So I was there on that day when we saw that horse coming over the hill. It looked like some bags were on its back. It was walking very slowly with its head hanging low.

"That's Grandpa Jones's horse!" Jennie Lu whispered.

We all watched that horse walk slowly down the street and stop at Grandpa Jones's house. Then I realized the bags were moving and I started to run toward that horse. Jennie Lu was right beside me. When we got there, the oldest boy had managed to sit up, but he was wavering and his eyes were blurry.

"I think my brother is dead," he mumbled. "I tried to keep him warm."

"You did a great job," I assured him as I held him up. His knees kept giving way. Just then, two men came running from the store. They each grabbed one of the boys and started running with them toward Amy's house. She lived just across the street.

We pounded on her door as we were opening it. She looked up with a shocked look on her face, but immediately sprang into action.

We put the smaller boy on her couch and the older boy lay right down on the floor.

"Is my brother dead?" he asked.

Amy was feeling for a pulse and finally found one in his neck.

"His heart is still beating!" she assured his brother. She started stripping his clothes off and rubbing him down. Jennie Lu began to help her.

"Get them some water," she instructed me. I complied immediately. The older boy drank his down immediately and you could see his eyes clearing up. They began to drizzle a little into the corner of the other boy's mouth as they tried to warm him up. Amy was wrapping him in warm blankets and propped him up with pillows. She had been listening to his chest.

"I think he has pneumonia," she explained. "He can breathe better sitting up."

Just then, I noticed that he swallowed some of the water that Jennie Lu was drizzling into the corner of his mouth.

The older boy was soon fast asleep, so I covered him with one of the blankets.

Soon there was a knock at the door and I let one of the neighbor ladies in.

"I came to help you," she said to Amy. "I'll take care of the babies while you nurse these two boys."

Amy just nodded.

Before we left, I got Grandpa Jones to come help us bring a bed down into the living room for the older boy. We lifted him up and put him in the bed. He never woke up.

Amy wanted to move the small boy into her bed so she could be near him all night, and so her helper could have the couch. So we helped her move him.

"This way I can keep him warm," she said. "He's very near death. Everyone should pray for him."

"We'll get the word out," I promised.

We headed for the Pastor's home. When he heard our story, he headed for Amy's house.

"I'll pray for them right now," he said. "Then I'll spread the word around town."

Jennie insisted on following him, so I went along. When he started to pray, Jennie fell down on her knees and started to sob. Then she started to speak words which I couldn't understand and then began to groan from deep within. She couldn't seem to stop, even after the Pastor had finished his prayer. She continued for at least a half hour. When she raised up from the floor, that little boy opened his eyes for just a second and gave her a smile before going back to sleep. Amy grabbed the water glass and put it to his lips. He took a few swallows before sinking completely back into sleep.

Jennie Lu ran out into the living room and began to dance around in joy.

"He's going to live! Thank You, God!" she sang over and over again. Soon the older boy opened his eyes and smiled. Jennie fell to her knees beside his couch.

"Your little brother is going to live," she assured him, "and so are you."

"Good," he said before taking another drink from his glass. "I'm very hungry," he added.

Amy's helper was soon offering him some food.

He devoured every bit of it and fell back on the couch with a sigh.

"Thank you," he whispered as he went back to sleep.

Jennie Lu jumped up and hugged me with all her might.

"God heard my prayer!" she exulted.

The Pastor was just watching her with a look I could not decipher.

When we got over to the store where our carriage was, the boys were nowhere to be seen.

"They must still be over helping Grandpa Jones with his horse," I said. So we headed that direction. Sure enough, there they were, rubbing that horse down and trying to get it up on its feet.

"Why don't you just let it rest?" Jennie asked.

"I thought it would do better on its feet," Grandpa Jones responded, "but I guess we'll have to let it be for now. I'll try again in the morning.

"How are those boys doing?"

"They are going to live!" Jennie exclaimed. "I know they are both going to live!"

"Jennie Lu prayed through for them," I explained. "It was amazing to see.

"But now we've got to get going before John gets worried and comes looking for us."

We were almost home when we met John coming to look for us.

"What in the world took you so long?" he exclaimed.

"Don't be angry," I said. "The Slater boys came back almost dead on Grandpa Jones's horse."

"I'm not angry—just worried. What happened to their father?"

"We don't know that yet. Neither boy is able to talk. The younger boy was near death, but we saw signs of improvement before we left."

"Well, come to the dining hall for supper and tell us all about it. All the hands will want to hear the whole story."

After supper, when John and I were alone, I told him all about Jennie Lu's strange behavior.

"Is that mentioned in the Bible?" he asked.

"I remember hearing about groanings which cannot be uttered and then of course, they spoke in tongues on the day of Pentecost."

"Well, if it's in the Bible and she got results, then we shouldn't worry, but be glad. It sounds like God is using all she's been through to help others. She must feel very deeply for those poor boys because she's been there."

"That's how I feel about it, too. Thanks for the confirmation. We'll stand together on that if there is any negative feedback."

I went into town several times with Jimmy that next week to check on those boys. Every time I could detect improvement. By the end of the week, the older boy, whose name was Jack, was up and almost back to normal. The younger boy, Micah, was still very weak and sleeping propped up in Amy's bed. But he did wake up occasionally and smile at us. He was taking fluids which was a good sign. He was also coughing up phlegm.

As it grew colder, Grandpa Jones rigged up a small stove in Amy's bedroom with the pipe going out the window so she could make steam at night for that boy. She made a tent over the stove and the bed which improved his breathing. The people in the town brought them clothes.

One Sunday after church and a potluck dinner, we carried lots of leftovers to Amy's house. After they had eaten, Jack began to tell us what had happened to his father.

"We lived in a little shack in town and our father would leave us there while he went to look for gold. Sometimes there was nothing to eat. But there was a lady who worked in the tavern and sometimes she would bring us food, especially when our father was gone for days.

"Then one day, there was a gun battle and our father was shot in the street. The man who shot him took his gold and Grandpa Jones's horse. But while he was drinking in the tavern, I sneaked over and untied the horse. The lady saw me, but she talked loud to that man and kept him from looking our way. When I got the horse around to the back of the tavern where our shack was, she came out and handed me a bag of food.

"'Good luck!' she said.

"Then I got my brother and our one blanket and started out. My father's body was still lying in the street. There was nothing I could do about it.

"I let the horse go where she wanted because I remembered what Grandpa Jones said. When she found water to drink, we would drink, too. We did pretty good until the food was gone and our blanket got wet. Then we lost it, and it was getting colder. After a while, I was just trying to keep us both on the horse. That was all I could think about. I guess that horse kept us alive until we got here. Without that horse, I don't know what would have happened to us. We probably would have been sold as slaves like the Indians."

"Are the Indians being used as slaves over there?" I asked in shock.

"Yes."

I thought for a minute I might faint, but then I felt John's arm around me.

"We can't do anything about what's happening in California, but we can make sure it doesn't happen here," he assured me.

By Christmas time, little Micah was almost well. He had moved out of Amy's bed and was sharing a room with Jack. He was still thin and pale, but he was obviously going to make it. Amy planned to put him in school after Christmas. There was a strange quality about him. He wanted to go to church every time he got a chance and he talked about God a lot. He was especially fascinated by Christmas. He kept asking the reason for everything we did. It seemed that everyone in town was sending gifts to those boys. We thought that was the reason for his great interest, but we were wrong. It was the Christmas story that was captivating him.

One Sunday, we had the whole family out to the ranch for dinner and we got a surprise from Micah. We were sitting at the table after dinner and he spoke up.

"Jesus didn't tell me that He had been down here to this earth and lived here," he said. "I didn't know He had been a boy like me."

We all got quiet for a minute.

"Have you talked to Jesus?" Jennie asked.

"Yes, when I was sick I visited Him in Heaven. He took me for a ride on His white horse. I wanted to stay there because I wasn't sick there, but He said I had to come back because a friend was praying for me and His Father said I had to go back. I said my parents were dead and I didn't have any friends. But Jesus said I had some. Then my mother came and hugged me and said she'd be waiting for me when I finished my work down here. So now I've got to find out what my work is so I can do it and go back to heaven."

When he finished his story, we were all quiet for a long time. We didn't know what to say.

"Well, Micah," John said, "I think it will take you a lifetime to finish your work down here, just like the rest of us, so you'd better just start living your life. Your work will just happen."

Micah turned to Amy.

"Is that true?" he asked.

"Yes," she answered. "Just like raising you is my work down here. It just happened. I didn't have to go looking for it. But you know, Micah, you are very privileged to have had a private conversation with Jesus, face to face. That hasn't happened to very many people. Hold that memory as a special treasure."

"I will," Micah beamed. "I want to find out as much about Him as I can. He's the most wonderful man in the whole world and He loves me. My father didn't love me, but Jesus loves me."

When Micah ran outside to play, I noticed that Little John went out also. The rest of us were misty-eyed.

When Christmas week arrived, it began to snow and we all began to celebrate. Jennie Lu and I were celebrating our freedom and the salvation of the Slater children and the whole town was celebrating with us. John brought out the sleigh and took us for a ride over to check on the Stone Place. It looked so beautiful in the snow that it made me cry. On the outside, it looked finished and ready to move in, but John said there was lots left to do on the inside. We went on over to Tateville and were surprised that very few Christmas decorations were up. The town was very quiet. Jimmy was there, wearing a sheriff's badge. We stopped to talk to him.

"Why is this place so quiet?" I asked. "Aren't they celebrating Christmas?"

"We don't allow too much celebration around here after what went on here," Jimmy explained.

"I would think some celebration is what they need. Aren't all the bad guys gone? It's time to return to normal," I responded.

"I agree with her," John said. "Don't let that badge go to your head!"

We visited Tate's store and saw very few decorations.

"It's almost Christmas!" I exclaimed. "Where are your decorations?"

"We don't have a heart for it this year," Mr. Tate responded.

"The whole meaning of Christmas is a new beginning. God loves us and all the past is forgiven!" I exclaimed. "Where are those beautiful bells you used to hang around?"

"I'll get them from the attic," Mrs. Tate said as she started up the stairs. Soon she was bringing all the decorations down. I helped her decorate as we kept ringing the bells. Soon people were coming into the store to see what was going on.

"Let's make some Christmas cookies and give them away," Mrs. Tate suggested. Jennie and I helped her and we gave them out as fast as we could make them. John and Mr. Tate finished the decorations.

"Merry Christmas!" began to ring through the town.

Some of the people who came in asked me in a whisper, "Have you forgiven us?"

"Completely!" I responded.

Some men came and sat on the porch with their guitars and fiddles and began to play Christmas music.

Finally, Mary Black came in with her children. I'd been looking for her. I'd saved a bag of cookies just for her. I put it in her hand and said "Merry Christmas". Tears filled her eyes.

"Where is Zed?" I asked.

"He's outside. He's too ashamed to come in."

"Call him for me," I insisted.

When he came in, I took him aside and put a gold coin in his hand.

"This is so you can make a wonderful Christmas for the whole family," I said. "Get everyone a gift and buy food for a great meal. Use what's left for whatever your family needs—like food and clothes."

"Thank you," he whispered as he blinked back the tears. "I'll get my mother somethin' really special."

"She could use some new clothes and shoes and a warm coat," I suggested. "Ask Mrs. Tate to help you choose them."

Before we left, I gave Mr. Tate a few more gold coins designated for the neediest families in the community.

"Make sure they all have a wonderful Christmas," I instructed. "There's been enough suffering. Now is the time to rejoice."

"Will you ever come back to us?" Mrs. Tate asked.

"Yes, when my house is finished, I will move back over here."

We stood on the porch and sang a few carols before we left.

Finally, John said we had to go in order to get home before dark. He wanted to show me another way from Tateville to Titustown that was a lot closer, but there was no road there. We headed toward a low hill and from the top of it, I could see both towns. I was amazed.

"Someday, these two towns will be one town," I predicted, "and right on this hill, we will build a hospital. We need a road through here. It's so much closer this way."

"We'll start working on it right away," John promised.

"I could pay for it with my gold," I offered.

"I don't think that would be wise right now," John responded. "It would be better if the two towns worked on it together."

"Whatever you say."

"It will make it easier for the people from Tateville to get to the railroad so they should be willing to work on it."

When we got back to the ranch, Jennie Lu was sleeping on my shoulder. And I was feeling a little sick to my stomach. The lamps were lit because Jimmy had returned before us and he and Little John were waiting for us. They carried in the packages I had bought. I ate a piece of bread and butter and headed straight for bed. I couldn't be sick. Tomorrow was Christmas Eve. I had a lot of work to do to prepare our Christmas dinner. John was right behind me.

"Are you sick?" he asked.

"I'm feeling a little nauseated," I replied. "I'm probably just tired. I'm going to try to get rested up so I can cook tomorrow. I feel a little better since I ate that piece of bread."

As soon as I said I felt better after eating, something began to stir in my memory. Could it be? I tried to remember my last monthly time. There hadn't been one in December yet. What about November? When was it? I couldn't remember. I could remember October. Did that mean I didn't have one in November? Could it be that John's prayer was being answered? I didn't want to get his hopes up, so I didn't say anything.

John had just got into his pajamas when there was a timid knock on the door. When he opened the door, there stood Jennie Lu.

"Mother, are you all right?" she asked.

"I'll be fine," I assured her.

She came over and gave me a hug. I could see the old fear in her eyes. I moved over and pulled her down beside me.

"Did going over there stir up some bad memories?" I asked.

"I guess so," she answered.

After a few minutes, I started dozing off and Jennie got up and went to her own room.

The next morning, I jumped up, thinking all was fine, and that nausea hit me again. I ran down to the kitchen to look for something to eat but I started vomiting into the dish pan. Then I vomited up everything I tried to eat. Soon John was by my side and Jennie Lu was right behind him.

"Go lay on the couch," he suggested. "I'll bring the pan in case you need it."

I obeyed and after I settled down, I asked Jennie Lu to bring me a piece of bread. I lay very still and ate that piece of bread, and kept it down. I lay there for about a half hour, then I tried again to get up. This time, I made it. I drank some water and ate a little more.

Both John and Jennie Lu were looking at me with puzzled looks on their faces.

"Is it the flu?" John asked.

"No," I laughed. "I think it's morning sickness."

"It's what?"

"Morning sickness," I repeated.

"What is that? I've never heard of it!"

But Jennie Lu was starting to catch on. She started to laugh and dance around.

John still looked puzzled.

I went over and put my arms around his neck and whispered in his ear.

"I think I'm pregnant."

He pushed me away and stared at me.

"Are you sure?" he asked.

"No, I'm not absolutely sure, but it feels like it."

John started to grab me, but I said, "Don't get me going again. Go dance around with Jennie Lu."

So they did and I started breakfast. John already had the stove hot.

"We can have Christmas dinner with Jerry and whoever is left of the hands," John suggested. "Most of them are gone, but a few have nowhere to go or it's too far away. That way, you won't have to cook."

"Well, I will help Jerry cook. I don't want him to be alone on Christmas, but he doesn't have to do all the cooking for us, either."

After breakfast, we went over to talk with Jerry and got everything worked out. I started making pies while he went looking for a turkey. I did fine as long as I remembered to nibble on something often.

Christmas day was the most joy-filled day that I could ever remember. I'll never forget that day as long as I live. I spent the whole day thanking God for all His blessings. I gave gifts to everyone on our ranch. It was such a thrill to be able to do that. Such a short time ago, I was living in complete poverty, not knowing if we could live one more day.

The crowning moment came in the evening when we gathered around the fireplace to read the Christmas story. Little John was there with us and he spoke up before we prayed.

"Do you think God would forgive me for turning away from Him after my mother's death?"

"I know He will," I responded. "He forgave the people who were putting Him on the cross."

"I was so angry with God, that I said I would never pray to Him again, but since I came here, I see a whole new life opening up before me and it seems to me that God led me here, even though I was angry with Him. Could it be that Jesus still loves me?"

I led him in a prayer for forgiveness and re-dedication, and saw the joy come into his eyes. It was a beautiful ending to a wonderful day.

"I don't understand everything, but I know Jesus loves me just like that Slater boy," he said.

I hugged him and cried right along with him.

"Christmas will always be a special day for you."

He nodded his agreement.

CHAPTER 31
Her View

As winter bore down upon us, it became more apparent that *yes, indeed, I was pregnant!* John hovered over me like a mother hen.

"You take care of yourself," he would keep reminding me. "You're not as young as you used to be," or else it was, "Remember, you're eating for two people now."

By spring, the morning sickness was all gone and I was able to work in the garden. John wanted to get started on our house, but he was hesitant to leave me.

"Go ahead!" I insisted. "I'm fine and this baby isn't going to be born until August or September. I carried Jennie Lu for nine full months."

So work commenced on the Stone Place, but John was back home every night. We had long talks about that house. He wanted to build a stone base for a windmill over the well. I agreed to it. It sounded exciting. He said he could run the water right into the house and into the water tank that was attached to my stove as well and then over to the sink. He would also pipe water into the barn.

As I began to feel better, I went into town more often to check on Amy. She was doing great. She had both of the older boys in school, so they saw Jennie Lu every day. The babies were doing great also. Grandpa Jones would often take the older boys over to his place to visit his horse or some other excursion. He was making plans to take a train trip back East to try and find their grandmother.

On one of my trips to town, I got a letter from my cousin, the doctor. He informed me that his wife had passed away during the winter. He was having a hard time getting over it and was thinking of making a trip out West in the summer. I wrote back to him immediately, inviting him to come. I told him of Little John and his amazing artistic talent.

Soon I was too engrossed in my garden to make so many trips to town. Jimmy did most of it for me. He was constantly traveling to Tateville and the Stone Place so he just fit it all together and seemed to enjoy it. I enjoyed my garden. By May and June, it was beautiful. I spent most of my time there. Jennie Lu helped when school was out for the summer. Jerry helped me some also. He brought me a bench to sit on. We put it in the shade of a tree on the side. It was a big help. In July, the heat was amazing and I was getting pretty big so it really bothered me. Then I got a letter saying my cousin would arrive in August.

"Oh, no!" I exclaimed.

John came running. "What's the matter?" he asked.

"Dr. Joe is coming in August."

"I thought you wanted him to come."

"I do. But that will be getting close to my delivery time. I'm getting tired now. How will I be then?"

"Don't you worry," John assured me. "We have Jerry to help you or completely take over if need be. He was telling me today that you need to start resting more. He also thinks you should stay out of the heat of the day as much as possible. He thinks it is affecting you too much. Is he right?"

"Well, it *is* affecting me. Sometimes I feel like I'm going to faint."

"He suggested that you go sit down in the brook or at least in the shade and wash yourself down with cool water during the middle of the day."

"I might try that. I've got to think about the life inside of me, right?"

"Right. But I'm not concerned only about that life. I don't want anything to happen to you. You have changed my life for the better. I couldn't bear to lose you. I'm thinking maybe I need to stay around here."

"You don't need to do that until Dr. Joe comes. Then you can stay around to help me."

"Are you sure?"

"I'm sure!"

"Then promise me that you'll listen to Jerry while I'm gone."

"I promise! He's like a father to me."

CHAPTER 32
His View

Before I headed for the Stone Place, I went to see Jerry. I found him in his cabin. I told him about my conversation with My Lady and asked him to keep a close watch on her.

"Send someone for me immediately if you think I need to be here," I said.

"I will," he promised, "and when her cousin comes, I will do all the cooking. She's already having trouble standing on her feet for very long. It looks to me like the baby has already dropped down and is pressing on her bones."

"So do you think I should stay here?"

"No, I think you should start praying for her. This is going to be hard for a woman her age."

"I've been so excited about having a child that I haven't even considered what it could do to my wife. Now I'm getting worried. I don't want to lose her or see her become an invalid. I guess hearing about that Slater woman dying in childbirth woke me up. I certainly will pray."

"So will I and I'll try to get her to take it easy so she'll have strength for the labor."

"I've noticed that Jennie Lu is staying right around her mother and helping her more than usual. I guess she's a little worried, too," I said.

"I imagine she's more than a little worried," Jerry responded. "She was there for the Slater woman's death, wasn't she?"

"Yes, she was."

All the way back to the Stone Place, I talked to God. I confessed my sins and prayed for my wife. I reminded Him of how He was the One who brought us together and asked Him not to take her away from me.

"You know how much I need this woman. She has straightened me out and given my life purpose. And please God, let this be the last baby for her. I don't want to risk her life again."

When I got busy working, I was able to calm down a little but I still talked to God a lot. More than I ever had in my life before. At one point, I felt like He might have answered me. I felt something inside that said, "Is this what it took to get you to talk to Me?"

"I'm sorry," I responded, "for the way I've been. I'll be different from now on. I'll talk to You about everything. I'll seek Your advice about everything."

"Even if she dies?"

I began to sob. It took me a while to get through that. Finally I responded, "Even if she dies, I'll continue to talk to You and seek Your advice about everything."

After I made that commitment, I began to feel peace inside. I even began to hum as I worked. I could feel that God was real and everything would be all right.

But every night when I went home, it seemed that My Lady's belly had grown bigger. She didn't walk around much and her daughter stayed right by her side. I was relieved to see that.

"How is she doing?" I asked Jennie Lu when we were alone.

"I'm worried about her," she confessed. "She seems so tired all the time. She doesn't even work in the garden anymore. She just sits out there and stares at it."

"I'm glad she isn't working in the garden. You keep it weeded so she won't feel pressured to work in it. She needs to save all her strength for labor."

Jennie nodded. "I'm trying!" she said.

"You're doing great!"

When I was in bed with My Lady at night, I could feel that baby kicking.

"Does it hurt when that baby kicks like that?" I asked.

"Yes. Sometimes I think I'm all bruised up on the inside. At other times, I think I've got two babies in there and they're fighting like Jacob and Esau," she laughed.

"Well, it should be over soon. We're into August. I've got to go meet your cousin at the railroad station tomorrow."

CHAPTER 33

Her View

I watched John leave for town, then I headed for my bed. I felt very tired and I'd been having contractions for a couple of days. I hadn't told anyone because they didn't seem to be going anywhere. They didn't get worse, but when I had one, I couldn't walk for a few seconds.

"Will you please clean up the kitchen?" I asked Jennie Lu. "I have to lay down."

I went right off to sleep, but the contractions would wake me up. I'd catch myself groaning as I woke up, then I'd hush myself. I didn't want to worry Jennie Lu. But one time, she was standing in the door as I woke up. I just smiled and tried to reassure her. The next time, Jerry was there with her.

"How long you been having those pains?" he asked.

"I think a couple of days," I responded.

He turned around and headed downstairs without saying another word.

Jerry went right out and found Little John. He sent him to town with instructions to tell John to hurry and bring Amy Tuttle with him because his wife was having contractions. Then he filled the biggest kettle he could find with water and stirred up the fire under it.

"Where can we find some old towels and rags?" he asked Jennie. "Maybe even some old blankets."

Jennie Lu went searching and found several of everything he asked for.

"More rags would be good," he said.

So by the time the party arrived from town, Jerry had made preparations as best he could.

When Caroline heard the carriage arrive, she got up and tried to make herself presentable to greet her guest. She started down the stairs but had to stop in the middle because of a strong contraction. When she got to the bottom, she just stood there for a while, not knowing if she dared to walk. But she finally headed for the dining room. Dr. Joe saw her first and stopped in mid-sentence and scrutinized her as she walked slowly toward him.

"It looks like I got here just in time," he said as he took her hand. She bent over and groaned before she could give him a weak smile.

"I need to sit down," she whispered.

John grabbed a chair for her and let her lean on him after she sat.

"Let's use that table," Dr. Joe said. "That's a good height for a delivery table and she'll never make it back upstairs. Put some of those blankets on it for padding. Get her some pillows. Now all you men—out of here, but her husband.

"Get her a loose fitting nightgown," he said, turning to Jennie Lu, who ran up the stairs and was back in a minute.

"Now, I'm going to hold this sheet up for privacy and John, you help her take all her clothes off and put this nightgown on.

"Okay, now John and I are going to lift her onto this table. You girls lift her legs."

But before they could, Caroline stood up. "Maybe I can do it," she said. Just then, her water broke and went all over the floor. She started to tremble, but she held out her hands to the men. With their help, she stepped up on the chair and then onto the table on her knees. They steadied her as she turned around and sat on the table, then fell back on the pillows and dozed for a few seconds before another pain awakened her. Dr. Joe was watching her belly during that pain. He wore a serious expression as he washed his hands.

Jennie Lu was down on the floor, wiping up the water with the rags.

"There's blood in this water," she said.

"Yes, she's bleeding," Dr. Joe said.

"Let's see if we can turn that baby," he said to Amy. "Can you see that it's in there sideways?"

"Yes," she responded.

When they tried to turn the baby, Caroline let out a scream, then she passed out.

Dr. Joe turned to John.

"The only way I'm going to save your wife and baby is to do a Cesarean section."

"Do what you have to do. Jennie Lu and I will get on our knees over here and pray."

"I want to do it while she's unconscious, but if she starts coming around, make her breathe this," he said to Amy. Then he took his knife out of the hot water and made a quick incision and reached in and pulled out a big baby boy.

"Jennie Lu, come take your brother and clean him up. In order to stop the bleeding, I'm going to have to remove the uterus. It's very damaged. Oh my, there's another baby in that uterus. It's a little girl. No wonder we couldn't turn that baby. There was no room.

"Poor little girl! Your brother's been beating up on you. Here, Amy, you clean this one while I sew the mother back up. I think I've got the bleeding stopped. Let me make sure I've got all the pieces of that uterus out of there. That little boy is a wild Indian. He tore his mother up."

Everyone started to laugh a little and relax a little.

Dr. Joe was busy sewing while he talked.

Caroline started to moan.

"I'm almost done. Maybe we won't have to gas her," he said to Amy.

Caroline opened her eyes just as he was doing the last stitch. She caught her breath but didn't scream.

"You've got two beautiful babies," Dr. Joe said to her, "but you're going to be very sore for a while. I had to do a Cesarean to get them out."

John came over and sat beside Caroline.

"It was just like you said—two babies in there fighting," he said.

She smiled as she looked at the two babies Jennie Lu and Amy were holding.

"How will I feed them?"

"It'll take some practice, but we'll manage it together," John promised.

"I would suggest that you bring your bed down here until she has recovered," Dr. Joe said to John.

"Good idea!" John said as he headed up the stairs.

Dr. Joe bounded up right behind him.

"I'll help you," he said.

They soon had the bed set up near the fireplace and brought the baby bed down also.

While the men were working on that, Amy and Jennie Lu were busy cleaning Caroline up. Amy taught Jennie how to make a solution to clean the wound.

"You'll need to do this every day for a while," she explained to Jennie.

Caroline was holding her two babies while they were cleaning the mess. They soon had her presentable.

"Hold these babies so I can get down from this table," she said.

"Oh, no," both men said together.

"We will move you," Dr. Joe explained. "You just wait there until we have your bed ready for you."

"Help me, Jennie Lu! Let's see if this big guy here is ready to eat. He's wide awake and looking all around."

"He sure is!" Jennie exclaimed. "Look at him going for that milk! If he had his way, he'd probably clean out both sides and leave nothing for his sister." The men chuckled.

When he had nursed, Jennie carried him to the baby bed and tucked him in. She tried to help her mother get her baby sister to nurse, but she only wanted to sleep.

"Her brother has probably been keeping her awake with all his kicking," Caroline explained.

Again the men chuckled.

"I think you ladies have got it in for that boy," Dr. Joe exclaimed.

Jennie took the baby from her mother so the men could move her.

There was a lot of gasping for breath, but no screams.

"Now see if you can walk with us holding you up," Dr. Joe instructed.

Again she kept catching her breath and paused after every couple of steps but she made it over to the bed. She was obviously very relieved to get into it.

"Whew!" she exclaimed. "I'm glad I didn't have to go upstairs."

Jennie brought her the baby girl and this time she woke up and nursed. She even opened her eyes and looked at her mother.

"Baby girl, you're beautiful!" her mother cooed to her.

"Look! She smiled!" Jennie Lu exclaimed. "She loves the sound of your voice!"

CHAPTER 34
Her View

Later that night when everyone had gone to bed and John and I were alone with our new babies, John explained to me what had happened on that table.

"So you're saying that Dr. Joe saved my life and also our children's lives."

"Yes, and why do you think he came when he did?"

"God sent him."

"Yes, He heard my prayers. Jerry told me that something wasn't right with you. He was worried about the shape of your belly and he thought you were in a lot of pain. He told me I'd better pray. He woke me up. I'd been so happy about having a child that I hadn't considered the possibility of losing you. He scared me and I prayed like I'd never prayed before. I finally made a commitment that I would pray and obey even if you died. Then He whispered to my heart that He was sending someone to help you."

"And He did, just in the nick of time."

"You know what else Joe told me? He'd been studying about C-section deliveries but he had never performed one. Then last week, he assisted at one in an attempt to save a baby whose mother had died. He thought then if they had acted sooner they probably could have saved the mother too. So that's what he did with you."

"Well, what are we going to name these babies? We can't call them Big Guy and Baby Girl for the rest of their lives!"

"How would you like to name them after Dr. Joe?" John asked. "We could name them Joseph and Josephine and call them Joe and Josie."

"You don't want them named after you?" I asked.

"There's too many named John. It's getting confusing,"

"Well, whatever you say. But I think they'll be Big Guy and Baby Girl for quite a while."

"You're probably right. We might be calling them that when they're grown.

"I feel so blessed to have you and now these two children," John exclaimed as he was bringing them to me to nurse. They had both started to fuss at the same time.

"We are blessed!" I agreed. "We've been redeemed. You rescued me and I rescued you but it was really God who rescued both of us. He took all our mistakes and turned them into blessings!"

John helped me get the babies situated so they could both nurse. Soon I was gasping for breath.

"What's wrong?" John was alarmed.

"It's all right," I gasped. "Their nursing causes me to have contractions and I'm awfully sore inside."

John ran up the stairs to ask Dr. Joe, who confirmed what I had said. But he came down to check on me anyway.

"Are you bleeding?" he asked.

"Just a little," I said.

"That's normal, but we want to watch that you don't start bleeding profusely," he said.

Then John told him what we had decided to name the children and he was overwhelmed.

"I have no children of my own," he explained, "so this means a lot to me.

"If it's all right with you, I'll hang around here for a while to keep an eye on this situation and take notes on it for a medical report when I go back East."

"We'd love to have you," we both exclaimed.

So I had Dr. Joe around for almost a month, keeping a close eye on me, but he spent a lot of time in town also. Amy took him around to visit all of her patients and they became very good friends. He was very impressed with her nursing skill.

When he finally headed back East, he took Little John with him to finish his education and study art.

Before he left, Little John asked me to keep a picture for him of his mother that he had been carrying around. It looked so much like my mother that it took my breath away. He also presented John with a picture of me on our wedding day. It was so well done that it looked like a photograph. John was very grateful.

Grandpa Jones traveled back with them also. He intended to find the grandmother of the Slater children. We prayed together before they left that God would help him.

We didn't hear anything from Grandpa Jones for a long time. I was so busy with my babies that I hardly noticed. But Jennie Lu mentioned it once in a while. School had started again so she was going to town every day. One day she came back all excited. Grandpa Jones was back after being gone for three months. He had brought the Slater children's grandmother with him.

"He married her!" Jennie Lu exclaimed, "and she moved back here with him. She sold all her stuff and now she's living with him.

"She's real nice!" Jennie added as an afterthought.

"Is she trying to take the children?" I asked.

"No, she's real glad that Amy has them and she just wants to be their grandmother. She said she knows she couldn't do a good job with them."

Well, there goes my idea that Amy would marry Grandpa Jones, I thought to myself.

CHAPTER 35
His View

We didn't get into the Stone Place as soon as we had planned because of the babies. So I had more time to perfect things. I got the water system going and I was anxious to see how it would work through the winter. I buried all the water lines and I figured I could put heat in the pump house if I needed to.

I started hauling a lot of stuff over one wagon load at a time. I brought most of the wedding gifts including that new rug. Then I realized I needed to make some furniture. So I went back to my parents' ranch and used my father's tools. That way, I could be near My Lady if she needed me. So it was late into November before we were ready to move. I had made new high chairs and baby beds for the Stone Place so we didn't have to move those. We just took our clothes and some food.

Mrs. Tate had come out to see me several times to find out when we were coming. So when we arrived, they had a house warming for us. Most of the town was there with gifts and food. It was a wonderful time. I saw My Lady in tears several times. I brought the baby beds into the living room so everyone could get a good look at them and our babies. They were three months old now and very cute. Big Guy was still much bigger than the Baby Girl.

The next day when all the people were gone, Caroline went out and walked all around the place. I just watched from a respectful distance. She walked through the barn, touching everything as she went. She stopped to visit her old horse that was still there in the same stall. She whinnied a greeting to Caroline who stopped and fed her some grain. She said something to her but I couldn't catch what it was. Then she led her out into the yard. I had restored the fence so that barnyard could be used again. Caroline left the door open so the horses could go in and out at will.

"Is it all right if I let your horses out of their stalls?" she asked.

I walked up and put my arm across her shoulders.

"They aren't my horses. They're our horses. Everything of mine belongs to you. And yes, it's all right to let the horses out into the barnyard. I can get them easily from there if I decide to make another trip today."

My Lady continued to make her rounds of the place. She visited every out building and stopped and looked up the hill toward the stream that came from the cave where her first burial plot was, but made no move to go there—probably because of the sleeping babies in the house. When she got to the windmill, she went inside and laughed to see her same old pump.

"Do we have to pump the water up into that tank?" she asked.

"I could do that if I needed to, but as long as there's a breeze, the windmill will do it for me."

I showed her that I had disconnected the mechanism because the tank was full. Then I showed her how it worked.

"But you can still come and pump water from that well for old time's sake, anytime you want to. Just like when you scared me nearly to death right here."

"I'm glad I didn't succeed in scaring you away," she said. "You've restored this place beyond my wildest dreams."

I was just starting to kiss and caress her when she jumped and said, "I think the babies are crying!"

I followed her inside and sure enough, they were both crying. I don't know how she knew it. I couldn't hear them.

I picked up the Big Guy and got him amused while she settled in with our Baby Girl in her rocking chair. I had saved that chair from the fire and I was glad because they aren't that easy to make. When she got the babies all settled down, I began to show her the house. She loved the water system I had invented. She was also impressed with my heating system, but glad we still had a fireplace.

"I'll love to sit with you in front of that beautiful fireplace," she said.

There were four bedrooms upstairs plus ours downstairs right by the bathroom.

So we had a big house with lots of room for raising our children. But for right now, Caroline was going to keep those babies right in the room with us.

It took me about two weeks to finish moving everything and get us settled into our new home. I had to bring the animals back over and get them settled in also. We left two of Sadie's pups over there for Jerry to care for and brought Sadie and one pup over our way. We had given one puppy to the Slater children.

Jennie Lu was staying with Amy again until school was closed for Christmas. Then we planned to send her to the Tateville school. She wasn't too excited about changing schools but she wasn't arguing. She had caught up with the other students and would soon finish school anyway. She would soon be fourteen.

When Jennie was home for the weekend, we took a trip into town. We needed an extra person to hold one of the babies, so I could drive the team. I showed the girls that work had begun on the new road between our two towns. Then we went by the school and found the teacher there, so we stopped to introduce ourselves. We were surprised to see a male school teacher. He was friendly until we told him Jennie Lu would be coming to school in January.

"She doesn't need to come to school," he said. "She needs to be at home, learning to cook and sew and clean and raise children."

We were a little shocked by his bluntness so we excused ourselves and got away from there as quickly as possible. No one said anything for quite a while. I noticed a few tear drops from Jennie's eyes. So I reached over and laid my hand on her shoulder.

"Don't worry! We won't send you to school there. We'll work something else out. That man just lost his best student!"

"Amen!" her mother murmured, while patting her leg.

"There's a lot of other girls in this town," Jennie said with a catch in her voice.

"You're right!" I said. "Maybe we'll be able to make some changes in the future."

"I wish I could take them all over to Titustown to go to school. Miss Wright treats all the boys and girls the same."

I didn't respond to that comment but I was thinking about that road we were making and My Lady's prophecy that these two towns would be one someday.

CHAPTER 36
Her View

I saw a lot less of my daughter for the rest of the school year. She was staying in Titustown during the week and spending weekends with us at the Stone Place. I really missed her. Her absence made my big new house seem lonely. Sometimes I wondered if we'd moved there too soon. John had taken over the job of sheriff besides running our ranches, so he was very busy. It was fortunate for us that John had very reliable men working for him.

Besides missing my daughter, I also missed Jerry and the other men who worked on the McLane ranch. They worked on my ranch also, but I very seldom saw them. They went home at night over there. Even though I had a brand new house, the old memories would keep coming back. Sometimes when I went out the door of my house, I would get a feeling of fear even though there was no reason for it. I would look all around for a cause but could find none. My babies kept me busy, but not busy enough, I guess.

John helped them get town government set up in Tateville. Then he was elected Mayor. He set someone else in as sheriff and was just as busy as ever. But I was thankful that he was home every night. I remembered those long, scary nights from before he came.

The weekends were wonderful! So was Christmas. Jimmy was with us a lot. He said the big empty house over there was lonely also. I managed to get into town on the weekends because I had Jennie to help me with the babies. So I got some Christmas shopping done. Again, I was able to help the needy and tell the Tates to keep it to themselves. It gave me such joy to alleviate other people's suffering.

I guess John began to notice my loneliness because he talked to me one evening about bringing some of the hands over here to live. After we had discussed it for some time, I brought up the gold mine and the danger involved. We ended up leaving everything as it was. Loneliness was a price I had to pay. But we decided that as our babies grew older, I would go into town with him on some days. That worked out really well and I soon had a once a week meeting with the women in town. We read the Bible and prayed and we gave each other lessons in sewing and cooking and childcare. The day finally came when they asked me why my daughter was going to school in Titustown. So I told them. That led to quite a discussion. Some thought we should get a different teacher. Others said he was really good with the younger children. I discovered that he didn't want to teach the girls past the age of twelve.

John came in one day and discussed the possibility of taking the older girls to Titustown for school after the new road was finished. He promised that we would discuss the issue with the teacher in Titustown. We hoped to have it all settled in time for school next year. John promised to do his best to make it happen. He asked the ladies to use their influence with their husbands to get the road finished.

Tateville ended up doing more than half of the road. Titustown got embarrassed and put more effort into their part. Jimmy organized some crews to rotate their time so they could catch up. John led a procession of wagons across that new road into Titustown from Tateville. Everyone was cheering and then we all went to the restaurant to celebrate. It ended up being a meeting between the two towns. Miss Wright was introduced and she presented her plan for next year, especially for the older boys and girls. She had made arrangements to train some to work in the bank with Grandpa Jones's help, some would train for the restaurant and some would begin training to help Amy with nursing. John had agreed to start a training program in ranching for some of the older boys. I agreed, with Grandpa Jones's approval, to let Jennie Lu open my mother's dress shop to teach that business. I agreed to act as an adviser. The dress shop would be a school project. If we made any money, it would go toward paying for all these new projects.

Everyone was excited about next year. And I was delighted that I would have my daughter for at least one more year.

CHAPTER 37
Her View

That summer at the Stone Place was a wonderful time. I had Jennie Lu there to help me. We restored the garden and the chicken house. John brought a milk cow over and some goats. He also made a swing for Jennie Lu.

We started going one day a week to Titustown to get a head start on the dress shop. Sometimes we spent the night with Amy and the Slater children and headed home early the next morning. About once a month, we did it on Saturday and stayed over for church on Sunday, so we could see all the people and stay connected. Besides we missed the church in Titustown. The young pastor there would always call us to the altar at the end of the service to pray. We would all be invited to speak out our concerns for prayer. Then we would all pray together. Jennie would often fall to her knees and be moved into those deep groans and unintelligible words. Little Micah would join her. One Sunday, the pastor told us that Jennie had spoken Hebrew words on that day that she prayed for Micah at Amy's house.

"I don't claim to speak or understand Hebrew," he said, "but I learned enough of it while I was in seminary to recognize some of the words. She was addressing God in Hebrew. I don't understand what is happening to her, but I know it came from God. That's why I'm not trying to discourage her. I don't want to fight against God."

I thanked him for telling us.

Micah would always kneel right beside Jennie Lu and was soon joining her in the same kind of prayer. Micah's grandmother and I started praying right along with them. My broken heart over the plight of our native people soon began to pour out. There were no words to describe it. But praying for them gave me some relief.

But there were no such opportunities for prayer at the church in Tateville. Everything was very formal and the pastor there reminded me of the school teacher. He said women were to keep silent in the church. I knew he was somehow not understanding that verse of scripture but I wasn't qualified to argue with him. So we did our praying at our ladies' meeting. Soon every woman in Tateville was coming to our meetings.

When John started town meetings, us ladies were there. We insisted on having a voice in every decision. John agreed with us but some of the men did not. But John rebuked them sharply and reminded them of the mess they had just come through. He said that God created men and women to work together. So the women of Tateville had the right to vote. I was proud of John.

The summer went flying by and I was no longer lonely. My daughter and I had a great time together. My babies were growing like the weeds in my garden. And John and I were developing a stronger partnership every week. We were working together to make Tateville the wonderful town it used to be.

Soon it was time for school to start again. John hired Zed Black to drive the wagon to carry the students from Tateville to Titustown. That job would help his family and since he was going to be there anyway, he went back to school to finish his education. He wanted to learn more about ranching from John so that became part of his education. I was so happy that things were going to be a little better for Mary Black. Zed went to school in the morning and then worked on the ranch in the afternoon. John said he would pay him just like he did Little John. And the girls said if he didn't get back in time to drive the wagon, they could manage it.

One day when I went over to Titustown with the girls, I was surprised to see Dr. Joe back again. He told us that Little John was going to Europe to study art. He had received a scholarship and Dr. Joe had financed the trip. He also told us that the paper he had written about my C-section was very well received and he had received an award. He was back to check on me and the babies. So I invited him to come over to the Stone Place when school was over. While he was waiting for school to be over, he visited with Amy and helped her with all her patients. I could tell she was very happy to see him. He had brought her some medicine and some gifts for herself and all the children. Could a romance be developing?

That evening he had supper with us and afterward he asked us all kinds of questions and wrote down our answers. He examined our babies and pronounced them in perfect health. He said it seemed to him that I was also doing fine.

"We really appreciate you coming all this way to check on us," I said. "These communities could certainly use a doctor like you. So if you ever want to relocate, please consider us."

"Thank you for that invitation," he responded, turning slightly toward John.

"We would love to have you here," John agreed.

"I have already considered the possibility of setting up a clinic here," Joe assured us. "Amy Tuttle is an excellent nurse and your daughter shows great promise also. In fact, I wanted to discuss with you the possibility of sending her out to me after she finishes school here so she could have a year of nurse's training."

Jennie Lu was standing in the door, listening to all of this and I could tell she was getting excited.

"I don't want you to think this would be improper," Joe continued. "I have an older woman who cared for my wife until her death, who lives in my house and is my housekeeper. She would be in charge of your daughter."

"We will talk about it and pray about it," I responded. "I certainly appreciate the offer. I know Jennie Lu is very interested in nursing. But I'd like to know what the expense would be if we sent her."

"When I get back there, I'll check all that out—with the school, that is—there won't be any charge to stay at my house. I'll send you a letter."

"We'll want to cover her expenses," John asserted. "We aren't destitute out here."

"I know you're not," Joe laughed. "But she is my cousin and I'd like to invest in her future, too. I believe she will accomplish great things."

Jennie Lu was blushing by this time. But I could tell she really wanted to do this.

"Speaking of investing in someone's future," I said as I put a gold coin in Dr. Joe's hand, "this is my investment in Little John's future. Use it in anyway it's needed."

Dr. Joe just stared at the gold coin for a while, then he put it in his pocket and nodded.

"I'll see that it gets used for him as needed," he said. "It might pay for his return."

CHAPTER 38
His View

I didn't say too much about Jennie Lu going back east with Dr. Joe. I decided to leave that decision totally up to My Lady. I could tell she was a little uneasy about sending her so far away at such a young age. But I had so many decisions to make in the present, I couldn't even think about next year. No matter how hard I tried to get out of town government, I kept getting deeper and deeper into it. I just wanted to go ride the range with my men and check on our cattle and develop our two ranches into one. But I never seemed to have the time. I got rid of the sheriff's job in Tateville only to be given the mayor's job. Now I'm involved in developing the school system which I'm not even qualified to do but I feel like I'm forced to do it for the sake of the young people that I love.

Some of the people of Titustown have asked me to be mayor over there, too. But I said it would be too much. So they asked if they chose a mayor to run their town, would I advise him. So I agreed to that and I suggested that Grandpa Jones would be a good choice. So they voted him in and now I've got to help him get started. Not that I'm an expert on any of this, but they all seem to think I am.

So I asked Dr. Joe if he knew of any books on town government and if so, could he send me some. He said he would look in the library when he got home and see what he could find. So if he finds some, I'll have to find time to read them. I won't do it at home, though. I want some time with my family. They are the most important part of my life. They are God's special gift to me. When I thought I had lost that completely, God restored my life.

I think what I'll do is arrange a once a week meeting with both sheriffs and both mayors and Jimmy who is in training with the sheriff of Titustown. Then we can discuss all our problems and give each other suggestions. That way I won't have to follow them all around.

I was thinking of all these things as I was riding out to the McLane ranch to check on things out there. Everything looked fine as I rode in. Jerry was working in the garden and came over to the house to greet me.

"We sure miss you around here," he said. "How's your family doing?"

"Everyone is fine!" I said and began to explain to him how busy we were between the two towns.

"Well, it's better to be busy than to be lonely and bored," he said.

"You're right," I agreed. "I think Caroline was lonely and bored when we first moved over there. But now she's busy in both towns and happy as a lark. So I guess I'd better stop complaining and be grateful. You always straighten me out, Jerry," I said as I patted him on the back.

"Speaking of being grateful," Jerry said, "come over to the dining hall and see all the beautiful vegetables I have harvested from your wife's garden. She straightened me out and got me back to gardening. All the men are grateful for better meals. I'm preserving some for this winter."

I spent the rest of that day on the two ranches. When I headed for home, I went the long way around—out across the range—being grateful the whole way. I shed a few tears as the memories rolled over me. On the way, I came across a cow giving birth. I helped her and wondered how this happened. It wasn't the right time of year. So I decided to carry the newborn calf back to the Stone Place. I lay it across my saddle and started toward home. The cow followed me, bawling the whole way.

"You don't have enough sense to know when you're blessed," I said to the cow. "I'm taking you to a better place."

"She sounds a lot like you," seemed to float up into my mind from inside me.

I started to laugh and couldn't wait to share the story of my day with Caroline.

When the house came into view, I could see that the old trapper was visiting us again. He came by once in a while and set up camp in our barn for a few days. I had told him he was welcome anytime and to just make himself at home. So he did. I think our barn was like home to him. So it wasn't unusual to see the trapper. What really had me puzzled was to see that Jerry was there. I took the cow and calf into the barn and headed for the house to see what was going on.

When I walked through the door, I could sense that something was wrong. Jennie Lu was there and looked like she'd been crying. Caroline was sitting at the table with her head in her hands.

"What's wrong?" I asked immediately.

"It's all my fault! I've ruined everything!" Jennie Lu began to cry again.

"What's your fault?" I asked.

Jerry spoke up and began to explain things.

"I happened to notice that Jimmy had Jennie Lu in the carriage with him when he came back from town. He took her into the house. I thought that was strange since you had just left and her mother was not with them. I waited about a half hour, thinking they would be coming out and heading over here. But when it didn't happen, I went over there and walked in without knocking. Jimmy was embracing and kissing this girl very passionately. I told him I wasn't going to let this go on under my nose without her parents' consent. He got really angry, but I stood my ground and insisted on bringing her to her mother. Jimmy refused to come.

"And it wasn't all your fault," he said, turning to Jennie Lu. "I heard you telling him, 'We shouldn't be doing this' when I came in.

"So now that I've done my duty, I'm going back home and let you folks work this out," he said as he turned toward the door.

"Thank you so much, Jerry," My Lady managed to say before he went out the door.

After he was gone, we began to question Jennie Lu to find out what was going on.

"Jimmy doesn't want me to go back East with Dr. Joe," Jennie Lu explained. "He wants me to marry him as soon as I finish school here. I told him I'm too young to marry, but he said he can take care of me. He says I can get as much nurses' training as I need right here, helping Amy Tuttle."

"What do you want, Jennie Lu?" her mother asked.

"I want to be a nurse. But I love Jimmy and I can't resist him. And I don't want to lose him either."

"Do you realize that as soon as you marry, you will start having babies?" her mother asked.

"Yes, and I've read about the danger to mothers that are too young. I don't want to have babies yet. I want to help with your babies. But I do love Jimmy."

As they talked, I began to realize what I had to do. It was like a dark cloud over my head but I had to do it. I went to the barn and talked to the trapper while I saddled a fresh horse. Then I headed for my parents' ranch after telling My Lady where I was going. I told her I'd probably be gone all night. She just nodded.

When I got there, Jimmy was belligerent. But he calmed down real fast when I told him my decision.

"Since this girl is too young to marry and you have overstepped the acceptable boundaries, you are going to have to take your turn at leaving home for a while. I want you to leave for two years. You can come back on her sixteenth birthday. If you both still love each other, then you are welcome to marry."

Jimmy tried to argue but I was unmoved. I knew this was the only solution.

"Do you want to kill this girl?" I asked him.

"No," he responded.

"She's too young to bare children safely. Childbirth is a risk for every woman, but for a young girl, it's very risky."

Jimmy started to tremble. "I don't know how to live like that—out there on my own."

Fear was taking the place of his pride and arrogance.

"I've asked the trapper to teach you. He's at the Stone Place right now. We'll head over there tomorrow and you can take off with him."

"So soon?"

"Yes, there is no time to lose. There is no stopping once you start down that road you've started on. The end result is a pregnant female.

"Now, I can tell you a few things that will protect you and maybe save your life. Remember, I've been there."

I talked to Jimmy late into the night. I shared things I'd never talked about before. Before it was over, he and I were friends again.

In the morning, I helped him choose what to put in his saddlebags and what to pack away. It didn't take long. When Jerry came out, I told him what was happening and he just nodded.

"I'll get the best horse we have for him," he said, "and I've got some jerky I just made. Take as much as you can fit in those bags."

I could see that Jimmy was blinking back a few tears.

Soon all the men were coming out to wish him well and slapping him on the back.

"We'll all be praying for you, Jimmy," Jerry spoke for us all. There was a chorus of amens.

Jimmy would just nod, but he never said a word. I knew he didn't trust his voice. We headed for the Stone Place in silence.

When we got there, we headed for the barn. I introduced him to the trapper and asked his advice about anything else that Jimmy might need. He looked through all his bags and made a few suggestions. When they were ready to leave, Jimmy asked me to send Jennie Lu out to say goodbye.

I went into the house and explained everything to the ladies. They were both in tears.

"Two years?" they both exclaimed.

"Yes, two years," I replied firmly.

"You can go say goodbye," I said to Jennie Lu. She ran to the barn, sobbing.

I waited about a half hour outside with the trapper before finally going into the barn. Jimmy and Jennie Lu were just standing there in each other's arms.

"Okay," I said, "it's time to get going."

Jennie Lu turned and ran for the house. Her mother came out and put two gold coins in Jimmy's hand and gave him a hug.

"Put these away for an emergency," she whispered. "I love you and I'll look forward to your return."

"Thank you," he choked out.

I stood and watched as they moved out. I heard the trapper telling Jimmy he had two great years ahead of him.

At the crest of the last hill, they both turned and looked back. Jimmy waved at me and then toward the house. Evidently the girls were in the windows.

I went to the barn and got my horse saddled and took a ride by myself. I went up into the hills and from there, I could see them in the distance. I did a lot of praying. I followed at a distance most of that day. I kept asking God if I was doing the right thing or should I call him back? Finally, I had to turn back as evening was coming on. I could see that they were making camp for the night. It was dark when I got back to the ranch house. Supper was waiting for me on the stove. I ate without saying a word and My Lady asked me no questions. After supper, I rocked my babies in the rocking chair while she cleaned up my dishes.

"They're camped on the ridge where I camped that last night, or tried to camp, before I came back to you. I could easily go tell him to come back. But how could I keep them apart for two years while Jennie Lu finishes growing up?"

"I don't know," My Lady answered. "I've been trying to think of another way myself. I could send Jennie Lu back East a little early."

"No, she's too young. She needs to be here with you for at least the rest of this year.

"He brought this on himself by trying to propose marriage to a fourteen year old girl without consulting her mother. But it doesn't make it any easier. I feel like I'm tearing myself up inside. I should never have let the Sheriff put that badge on him. He was too young. It went right to his head and made him arrogant.

"If I brought him back, Jennie Lu would be pregnant by the end of the school year and that would be the end of her dreams.

"If he listens to me, he will be all right and he will gain a lot of valuable knowledge. But what if he doesn't listen? That is what worries me."

CHAPTER 39
Her View

I listened to John talk and didn't say too much. I knew he was rehearsing what he had already thought through many times. He was trying to fit together his role of big brother and stepfather. I didn't want to interfere in his decision making. I knew it was a very difficult time for him. I remembered the awful weight of making decisions that would mean life or death for my daughter. Now I watched him rocking our babies and was so thankful to have him in my life, especially at this particular time. I was so glad that I was not alone and I was determined to support his decisions.

On Monday, we all went back to our work and no one said too much about Jimmy. But he was never far from our minds. Sometimes at night, I could hear Jennie Lu praying and I knew she prayed for him. We all did.

But school and work and meetings kept us busy. Life went on and helped us get over our grief and worry. Soon, Christmas approached again. My babies were getting big and Jennie Lu was such a tremendous help with them. I don't know how I could manage without her. We did everything together, from the dress shop to the Christmas shopping. She was usually carrying one baby and I was carrying the other.

"Josie is going to think you're her mother," I would tease her.

Then, just before Christmas, who should show up but Dr. Joe. He brought his housekeeper along this time. I knew what that was for. It made me uncomfortable. I didn't want to think about being without Jennie Lu. But I was friendly, of course, and invited them to stay with us. Dr. Joe wanted to stay at the McLane ranch, so he would be closer to Titustown. But he wanted his housekeeper to stay with us, so we could get to know her. She was very nice and a big help with the babies. But she was puzzled when she heard Jennie Lu pray at night in her room. I tried to explain it the best I could, but she was still uneasy, I could tell.

"This is going to be a problem if Jennie Lu goes back there for school," I shared with John that night after we'd gone to bed.

"Well, you'll just have to talk it over with Dr. Joe and see what he says about it. Jennie Lu doesn't have to go back there. She's learning a lot right here, working with Amy."

So I did just that and Dr. Joe said there was no problem. She could pray anyway she wanted to in his house. But I knew there was going to be a problem with his housekeeper.

During the Holiday season, Dr. Joe and Amy announced their engagement. I wasn't surprised and I was happy for them both, but I was worried that we might lose Amy.

"Don't worry," Amy said when I questioned her, "that was the condition upon which I agreed to marry him. He would come here. I would not go there."

Dr. Joe talked to John about building an addition on Amy's house so he could have an office and a clinic. We were excited about that and agreed to help finance it. Joe would have the beds and other supplies sent out by train while he was still back East. He planned to stay back there at least another year to fulfill obligations he had.

Amy showed us books that Dr. Joe had brought out to help with Jennie Lu's education. They were the beginning courses in nurses training. He had persuaded the school to let her study under Amy and give her credit if she could pass the tests when she came back East. That would mean that she would only need to be gone one year.

"I hope, with the help of Amy and Jennie Lu, to start a school of nursing out here when I move. When we start that clinic, it will be too much for one person, especially a woman who now has a family to care for," he smiled at Amy as he spoke. "In fact, what she's doing right now is too much for her. I hope to get out here and help her as soon as I can."

After Christmas, Jennie Lu studied constantly. She spent a lot of time with Amy and I ran the dress shop with the help of the other students. I gave them sewing lessons and they helped me with the babies. I enjoyed my time with them, but I still missed Jennie Lu.

"Amy is learning right along with me," Jennie Lu explained. "She says a lot of the material is new since she studied nursing."

Many evenings, Jennie Lu spent the night with Amy so they could study right up until bedtime. Amy's children loved Jennie Lu and were thrilled to have her, but I missed her. Especially since John was gone more and more. He was getting more involved in government all the time. He was now involved at the State level.

One night when we knelt beside our bed to say our evening prayers, he began to sob. I was amazed because I'd never seen him like that before. He was holding both of our babies on the bed in front of him.

"Oh God! Oh God!" was all he was saying.

I waited for him to finish praying before I asked for an explanation.

"There's going to be a war!" he explained. "And it's going to be terrible. We could lose everything. I just don't want to lose our children."

"Over the slavery issue?" I asked.

"Yes, over the slavery issue. I told you we could make sure that nothing like that happened here but I didn't know what I was talking about."

"Surely it could be resolved peacefully!"

John just shook his head.

"Remember when that man came looking for you over the gold and you just knew you'd have to shoot him because he had gold fever and you couldn't reason with him?"

"Yes, I remember," I said as a shiver ran down my spine. "He actually thought he had a right to take my gold and my daughter and myself because he had financially invested in Silver's scheme. Money was all that mattered."

"Well, that's how the southerners are about slavery. They see it as the key to their wealth and so they justify themselves. They are trying hard to make us a slave state and those of us who are against it see it as a moral issue and so we can't compromise. So there is no hope for resolution. It will be finally resolved by war. I just realized this and it scares me. Some of them tried to talk me over to their side. They told me I could live like a king if I had slaves. I told them I already live like a king. Trying to talk to them is like trying to reason with a drunk man."

"Are they drunk on the blood of the saints?" I asked.

"I never thought of that before, but lots of those Negroes are saints and we've all got their blood on our hands."

Here John and I both fell to our knees and began to sob and pray to God for mercy. Soon, Jennie Lu came in and joined us. We prayed for a long time and when we finished, we had peace that God would see us through whatever happened. We also agreed that we would help any runaway slaves who came our way, no matter what the consequences might be.

CHAPTER 40
His View

After we made our commitment, I had a meeting with all our workers. I explained what was happening and asked them how they felt about the slavery issue. After we'd discussed it for a while, it was apparent that they were all in agreement with us with the exception of one man. He became so belligerent that I gave him his pay and asked him to leave. Which he did that very night.

After he was gone, I explained our position to our men and the commitment we had made. They all agreed to help.

"We could hide them in the root cellar," Jerry said. "Our barn is pretty full."

"The basement of the house would be better," I responded. "The root cellar is very damp."

As we continued to talk, I shared my feelings about the coming war and asked all the men to wear their guns at all times.

"Things are going to get really bad before it's over. A lot of people are going to die. I just hope it won't be any of you," I said.

"Or any of your family," Jerry added.

"In the time we have left, we'll do our best to stand against slavery and help our fellowmen and pray that when the judgment comes, God will remember mercy," I concluded.

There was a chorus of Amens.

It wasn't long after that meeting that my first opportunity came. We were sitting in our living room after our evening meal when there was a knock on the kitchen door. I told My Lady to stay put and I went to answer it after strapping my gun on again. I had just removed it. There was no one at the door so I took a step out into the darkness and looked around. Then I heard a feminine voice speaking to me from the darkness.

"Are you John McLane?"

I realized immediately that this was a Negro speaking to me.

"Yes," I responded.

"The John McLane who is against slavery?"

"Yes."

Then she stepped out of the darkness so I could see her.

"Are you willing to supply refuge for those of us who are escaping?" she asked.

"Yes," I answered again. "Come inside so we can talk."

She came in and told us her story. She had escaped from slavery and now she was helping other people escape. She needed places where they could hide and rest. Sometimes they rested in the daytime and traveled at night. Our ranch was an excellent location. I told her we had two ranches and they could use either or both.

"If things get really bad, there's a cave up on that hill."

I showed her the back door to the barn. Just then, dark forms started appearing out of the darkness and just about scared me to death.

"I can see why you would travel at night," I said after I'd recovered my breath. "You're almost invisible."

The lady just smiled. "Everything has its advantages," she said.

When they had all come inside the barn, I lit another lantern. There were five adults and a young boy.

"I'll start storing some food in here," I promised, "and set up that little stove again so you can cook. Right now, I'll go get you some food from the house and some blankets."

I kept glancing at the young boy who it seemed could hardly stand on his feet. The others were holding him up.

"He's the reason we stopped here," the lady explained. "He's too sick to go on and no one is strong enough to carry him. He wants to find his mother who escaped to the north last year."

"She just deserted him?" I exclaimed.

"He had been sold away from her. He ran away from his new owner and came back to find her gone. He's been on the run a long time. That's why he's so sick."

"Oh, I see," was all I could say. I headed back to the house and told the whole story to My Lady. She started digging out blankets and pillows and food with that hard look on her face that I remembered from the first day I saw her. I knew her fighting spirit had been aroused.

When we took the supplies to the barn, she informed the people that they were welcome to take the blankets with them when they left.

"I will replace them," she promised. "You can also take as much food as you feel able to carry."

They all grabbed a potato and started eating it raw. We could see that they were very hungry.

"If you can stay tomorrow, I will bring our nurse out here for the boy," Caroline said.

"We have to stay. We don't dare to travel in the daytime," the lady leader responded.

When I brought Amy to our place the next day, she confirmed our suspicions. The boy would not survive if he kept pressing on.

"It's just like little Micah," Amy said. "He has pneumonia from too much exposure. I don't think he'll survive in this barn either."

"Is it catching?" Caroline asked.

I knew what she had on her mind.

"I don't think so," Amy responded. "No one caught it from Micah. But of course there was a lot of praying."

"Well, we'll do a lot of praying for this boy, too."

She looked at me with a question in her eyes. I just gave her a slight nod.

"We'll move him into our house and nurse him back to health," she announced, "then when you come through here again, he can join you."

"I don't expect you to risk your family for us," the Negro lady responded.

"If I send him on with you, I'll be responsible for his death. We've all got blood on our hands already over this issue. Maybe if I do what I can now, there will be mercy for me when the judgment falls."

The Negro lady just looked at Caroline without saying a word for quite a while.

"I hope so. I will pray so," she finally whispered.

"Thank you," Caroline said.

So we moved the boy inside and began to pray for him and take care of him as best we could. It took several months but he finally got well. His name was Zacharias. He became like part of the family. At first, we kept him hidden, but as time went by, we got more careless. We even took him to town with us.

Then the inevitable happened.

Zed Black came riding over the hill, whipping his horse to the greatest speed possible.

"There's a whole bunch of men in town looking for Zacharias. They say he belongs to them. They threatened to burn our whole town if we didn't tell them where he was. They're headed this way."

I told Zed to put his horse in the barn so they wouldn't know he'd warned us. I told Zacharias to go into the house and stay out of sight.

"Tell my wife to pray," I said, "and get her shotgun ready."

I began to pray myself.

"Oh, Lord," I prayed, "please help me to avoid bloodshed. Give me Your wisdom."

Soon, I saw them coming over the hill. When they got close enough, I recognized several of them from the legislature, so I acted as friendly as I could.

"Mr. McLane," they said, "we hear that you are harboring a runaway slave here."

"Well now, I don't know about that," I said. "A few months ago, I found a nearly dead Negro boy in my barn. We nursed him back to health and he's been working for me. If that's what you're talking about."

"Well, I appreciate that," one of the men spoke up, "but you should have tried to find out who he belonged to. He's my property and I want him back so I can teach him a thing or two."

Just then, My Lady walked out the door, completely unarmed. She was all friendliness. I was shocked.

"You know, gentlemen," she purred, "I'm beginning to really appreciate having this Negro boy around to help me. I think I'd like to buy him from you. I know you've got plenty of slaves. Surely you could spare this one. How much do I owe you for him?"

"Well now, Mrs. McLane, it seems that you are a wiser woman than your husband is a man. You at least are beginning to make sense. But since I've come all this way to get him, it would cost you too much, I'm afraid."

"Well, just give me a try," she responded.

They named a ridiculous price, but she never blinked an eye.

"I'll pay it," she said. "Zacharias, come out here and tell me if this man is your former owner," she called.

He came out, holding Big Guy in his arms.

"Yes," was all he said.

Then my wife produced a paper for the man to sign after she'd given him his price. When everything was finished, Zacharias spoke up.

"I'll work hard for you, Mrs. McLane, for the rest of my life. I promise not to run away."

I was watching this whole thing in shock. I couldn't believe my wife was buying a slave. I was speechless.

Then her tone changed. I heard the woman I'd come to love speaking again.

"No, Zacharias, you are now a free man. You may go or stay as you choose," she said as she pulled out another paper. "This is your emancipation paper. You are no longer a slave."

Zacharias just stared in amazement and I began to smile. But that man who had sold that boy began to turn red in the face. He was obviously furious. He had his hand on his gun, but then Zed came out of the barn and startled him. Then some other men from town rode over the hill. And My Lady reached behind her and lifted her shotgun up under her arm.

"The transaction was more than fair," she said in that hard voice. "It's time for you to be moving on."

The man mounted his horse and rode away without a backward glance. All the other men followed him.

I let out a sigh of relief that ended in a whistle.

"You were awesome," I said as I ran toward My Lady and swung her around in the air. "You even had me fooled for a while."

"I knew there was no way we could fight them, so I had to join them. Thank God I had the money. All I went through to get that money seems worth it now."

I glanced at Zacharias and saw that he was still standing there, staring at us, holding Big Guy. It hadn't sunk in yet. He didn't understand what had just happened.

"You're free! You're not a slave anymore," I said to him.

"But don't I have to work and pay back that money?" he asked.

"No!" Caroline said. "I gave it as a gift to God. You're free!"

"Does that mean I have to leave?"

"No, Zach, you can stay here with us as long as you want to. You're like a part of the family. But you can leave to go look for your mother if you want to. You might be safer up north where there's no slavery."

I went over and thanked the men from town for coming out to back us up.

"I'm afraid there's going to be more confrontations like this," I said. "We'd better be armed at all times and continue to back each other up. You'd better follow those men right now and make sure they don't do any damage in town."

They all turned and started off at a gallop. They hadn't thought of that and neither had I until right at that moment. Zed Black went with them.

I learned later that they had barely got there in time to avert a disaster. Those men were trying to set the town on fire and had Mrs. Tate and Mrs. Black trapped in the store and wouldn't let them out, until they saw the men riding over the hill. They tried to fight for a few minutes, but gave up and ran, after one of their men was wounded.

After that, I had a meeting with my ranch hands and we all agreed that we needed to start having half of them stay at the Stone Place every night. We'd fix a place in the barn for them just like when we were building the house. Since it wouldn't be that comfortable there, they could take turns.

So life went on and we didn't see any more runaway slaves for several months.

CHAPTER 41
Her View

I started taking Zacharias to school with us. I asked Miss White to teach him to read and write and to add and subtract. She got some of the other students to help. I had a feeling he wouldn't be with us for long, so there was a sense of urgency. He worked hard and was a quick learner.

During our evenings at home, he began to tell us about his life. He said that the man who sold him to me was actually his father. That explained why Zach had such a light complexion. After a while, he told us his father had killed his little sister because she was too light. He didn't want people to think she was white and really his daughter when she was nothing but a Negro. That's why his mother had run away. She didn't want to have any more children by him.

"How old was your sister?" I asked.

"I think four or five," he responded. "He did bad stuff to her before he killed her. I saw it all."

"I'm sorry, Zach. I'm really sorry. I think I have a little understanding of how it feels to be what they call a halfbreed. Because that's what I am. I'm half Cherokee."

"Before I came here, I hated all white people. I thought they were all like my father. I hated being half white. I wished I could cut the white part out of me. I thought a lot about killing myself to do away with that white part. But now, I see that some are good and some are bad."

"It's all up to you and the decisions you make," I responded.

The school year soon ended and I was faced with the possibility of Jennie Lu going away. It was hard for me. I did a lot of praying with her and by myself. When I was praying, I would feel at peace about it. But my doubts and fears would soon return. The slavery issue only intensified my turmoil.

Dr. Joe came to visit at the beginning of summer. He spent two weeks helping Amy. He was encouraged by the progress on the addition being built on her house. He made suggestions and helped out where he could. Amy had us all over for a meal and he talked to us about sending Jennie Lu back East. I expressed my doubts and fears and he tried to assure me.

"I'll be back again at the end of summer and you can let me know what you've decided," he finally concluded.

I just nodded.

So we had another wonderful summer. Jennie Lu and Zacharias studied every evening, but we all had work to do in the daytime. Jennie Lu spent most days helping Amy, but she stayed with me when I went to town. She helped with the babies. John was very busy between the ranches and government. Zacharias helped wherever he was needed. Sometimes he was with me and sometimes with John.

He was able to read the Bible to us at night. He was thrilled and I was so proud of him. I tried not to get too attached because I knew he would be leaving. But I couldn't help but love him.

"I'm so proud of you," I finally told him and he just beamed.

"I'm glad," he responded. "I'll try to make you proud as long as I live. Even when I'm not here, I will think of what would make you proud."

I was almost in tears after that speech.

"The most important thing is that you live your life for God. That will make me proud," I said.

He nodded his understanding and agreement.

When I put my arms around him and gave him a hug, he began to cry. I held him for a few minutes. When I let him go, he tried to explain.

"You're the first white person who has touched me to be kind," he said. "Now I know it's all right to be part white. My father is a wicked man because he chose to be, not because he's white."

"You're right, and you don't have to be like him."

"I won't be. I'm going to be like you and follow God. I've got to find my mother and make sure she knows God the way I've learned here."

I gave him my Bible after signing it over to him, and prayed that God would guide him to his mother. He hugged that Bible to his chest as he headed for his room.

It was August when his opportunity finally came.

CHAPTER 42
His View

It was early in the morning after a hot August night that I thought I heard the barn door opening. So I went to investigate. Sure enough, the Negro lady was back with a group of runaways. They were surprised and terrified to find five white men in the barn. I explained it all to them and what had happened over Zacharias.

"Where is he now?" the lady asked.

"In our house, fast asleep."

"I didn't think he would make it," she responded.

"My wife and daughter did a lot of praying over him. They've also taught him to read and write and add and subtract. So his sickness turned into a blessing. I think God has a special job in mind for him. I believe he'll be a bridge between our peoples."

The lady just looked at me.

The men soon had a fire going and were cooking breakfast for everybody. I went back to the house and found My Lady doing the same for us. Soon the whole household was up and after I'd explained what was going on, Zach headed for the barn. When he came back, he was very quiet.

"What's the matter, Zach?" Jennie Lu asked.

"I just know I have to leave with them to find my mother. I've felt so safe here that now I'm scared."

"We'll be praying for you," Jennie Lu assured him.

"Once you get up North, you'll be safer than you are here," my wife assured him. "Someone down here could still try to force you back into slavery."

After breakfast, they were all settled in for a rest in the barn and my men had all headed out into the fields. I was tempted to go with them, but thought better of it. I decided to spend the day around the house, protecting my family. They had all decided to stay at home also. They knew it would be their last day with Zach. My Lady was making him a bag to carry on his back, while Jennie took care of the babies. Zach was helping me out where he could, but kept wandering back into the house. I could tell his emotions were all mixed up.

I had asked Zed Black to stay in town and work as my lookout. Their house was situated where they could see everything that went on in town and he could take off on horseback without anyone seeing him leave. So I wasn't surprised to see a galloping horse approaching. I had given him a good horse to replace the old worn out mare that he had before.

"A posse is coming," he said before he had dismounted.

"Hide your horse out behind the barn."

Zacharias was already in the barn waking everyone up.

"Head for the cave and don't come out for anyone but me," I instructed.

They were off at a run.

I rang the bell that I had installed on top of the windmill for such a time as this. I hoped the men would hear it.

"You stay here. Get in the house," I ordered Zach.

We had just barely cleared the runaways out of sight when the horses came over the hill. I hadn't even had time to explain things to Caroline but I was sure that Zach told her all about it. Of the men riding into our gate at least three were members of our legislature who had managed to get slavery legalized in our state. I was working hard to change that.

"Well, hello, gentlemen, what can I do for you?"

"Now, John, we have reason to believe that you are hiding runaway slaves on your property and we intend to search for them."

"Who gave you the authority to do that?" I asked.

"Your sheriff didn't feel up to making the trip, so we're acting in his stead," one of the men explained as he headed for my barn. He opened the door and called to the others. "Now look at this. Here is all the evidence we need. All of you come and look at this. They were obviously here last night. Look at these beds and there is still warmth in this stove from breakfast."

"John, we are placing you under arrest," one of the other men joined in, "but just tell us where they are and we'll let you go."

"Who gave you the authority to do this?" I asked again.

"Don't try to change the subject, John. Where are the slaves?"

"I've also heard that you have a slave here named Zacharias," one of the other men joined in. "He belongs to me and I want him back. If I have to, I'll search your house for him."

Just then, Caroline stepped out on the porch, carrying her shotgun. That man had been walking toward the door, but stopped in his tracks.

"Don't take another step or I'll blow your head off," she said. "You'll touch that boy over my dead body. I bought him at great price and I emancipated him and he's nobody's slave."

He tried to grab me and use me for cover, but I avoided him and moved away from the whole group.

"Now, Mrs. McLane, the man you bought him from was not his rightful owner. I had already bought that Negro from him, so he had no right to sell him again."

"Then your quarrel is with him. Go demand reimbursement and leave me alone."

He started to walk toward her and I saw her brace herself against the house wall and I caught my breath because I could tell she planned to shoot that gun. When the shot rang out, everything came to a halt. I was relieved to see that she hadn't actually shot the man. But it was close enough to give him a good scare.

"That was a warning," she said. "I'd hate to send you to hell for eternity no matter how much you deserve it but I will if you come any closer. I still have the other barrel loaded."

About that time, I saw my men come galloping over the hill with their guns ready. I was relieved to see that our visitors were putting theirs away. They knew they were in trouble.

"What's going on?" one of our men asked as he rode up.

"These gentlemen think that they can arrest me for having beds and a stove in my barn," I responded.

"What!"

"And they thought they could force my wife to send Zacharias back into slavery.

"Let me ask you men a few questions," I continued. "Just tell the truth.

"Who slept in those beds last night?"

"We did."

"And who cooked on that stove this morning?"

"I did," one of the men responded.

"You men live in that barn?" one of our guests asked incredulously.

"No, we just stay there when we're working over here. We live at the McLane ranch."

About that time, Mr. Tate and several men from town came into view. They rode into the yard and dismounted.

"Is everyone all right out here?" Mr. Tate asked.

"Well, these men wanted to arrest me and tried to force Zach back into slavery."

"What! I gave them no authority to arrest you. I told them I wouldn't arrest you unless they could prove you'd committed murder. They said they just wanted to ask you some questions. So I told them where you lived, but then I felt uneasy about it, so we decided to come check on you."

"Well, I think they were just leaving. Perhaps you'd like to escort them back to town."

"Be glad to, John, and I'm sorry I sent them out here. They fooled me, I guess."

When they were gone, I went to check on My Lady. She was in her rocking chair, looking a little pale. Zach was keeping the babies occupied. I could sense something was wrong.

"Are you all right?" I asked her.

"I think I may have cracked a rib with that gun," she said. "It hurts when I breathe."

"Shall I go for Amy?"

"I think I can help her," Jennie Lu spoke up. "I saw Amy and Dr. Joe fix someone with a cracked rib. Let me try."

I nodded. I could tell Zach was really worried, so I turned to him and suggested we take the babies for a walk. When we were out of the house, I headed for the cave, carrying Big Guy. Zach followed along, carrying Baby Girl. We soon had everyone back in the barn. The men had some food ready for them to eat. While they ate, Zach explained everything that had happened. After they had eaten, the men headed back to work and the escaped slaves bedded down to try to sleep. I stationed Zach in the yard as a lookout. I headed inside, holding both babies. Jennie Lu had her mother wrapped up from her waist to her armpits.

"Did you leave room for the babies to nurse?" I asked.

"We tried to," Jennie laughed. "I hope it works."

"I know I feel a lot better," Caroline assured us.

"Please don't ever shoot that gun again," I pleaded.

"I'll try my best to never do that again," she said. "But I can't promise. You never know what might happen."

I shivered as I acknowledged the truth of that statement. I cleaned the gun and reloaded it and hung it back over the door. And I prayed another prayer for God's mercy on us.

From that day on, I became a very active politician. I visited the district of each of the three representatives who had visited my ranch. I made sure that the voters knew what they had done. Every one of them lost their seat in the House of Representatives for our state. They had managed to make our state a slave state, but for a very short time. We soon had that turned around and many of the people who had moved up for that purpose returned to the South. When the slavery issue was settled for our state, I relaxed a little, but not completely because I knew a war would come eventually.

CHAPTER 43
Her View

When that group of escaped slaves left our ranch, Zacharias left with them. He realized what I meant about being safer in the North. He also realized that his presence was a danger to us. But he promised that someday he would return.

Toward the end of the summer, Dr. Joe came again and Jennie Lu went back with him. After she left, I cried my eyes out, but I soon got over it and went on with my life. The babies were big enough that they didn't have to be held constantly anymore, so I was able to put them in the wagon or the buggy and go to my meetings and go on with the work in both towns. Zed Black was back in school and working on the ranch. So he helped me a lot. He only had to stay home as a lookout if we had runaways at the ranch. That didn't happen very often. And it wasn't so tense now that we were a free state.

Dr. Joe came out to visit Amy every three months. He kept us informed about Jennie Lu and he directed the building of his clinic. He said that Jennie Lu was doing well in school and had become active in the woman's suffrage movement. She was such a good speaker that the other students were calling her Lucy, because she reminded them of Lucy Stone, a well-known women's suffrage speaker.

"Did she pass the tests on all the books she was studying before she left?" I asked.

"Yes," he replied. "She did very well. I think all her training with Amy helped her a lot.

"Here's a letter from her," he continued. "I almost forgot to give it to you. It's as thick as a book."

"And here's one for you to take to her—just as thick. We agreed to write something every day and send it to each other. Since you are here, I'll send it by you."

"I'm glad to be your mailman," he said with a smile.

At Christmastime, he was back again and this time, he brought Jennie Lu with him. It was so wonderful to have her home again. We talked for hours. One night, I heard her praying in the wee hours of the morning. It sounded like she was in agony. So I slipped into her room and knelt beside her to help her bear the burden. It soon passed onto me and we were both groaning deep inside. When the burden lifted, she told me that it was for Jimmy. She had seen him in a dream with fire all around him.

"It sure is good to be home where I can pray freely and even get some help," she said. "Dr. Joe's housekeeper gets really upset with me when I pray like that. She thinks I'm just being emotional. I've tried to explain it to her, but she doesn't want to hear it. She says God hears prayers that are spoken very quietly and calmly."

"I'm sure He does. But He's the One who puts this kind of burden on us, so we have to respond. We don't work this up out of our own emotions."

"I explained that to her but she doesn't believe me. She asked me what you thought of it and when I told her that you do it sometimes too, she was very disgusted. She thinks we're a bunch of fanatics. I'll be glad when this year is over."

"I hear you're involved in the Woman's Suffrage movement. That must cause a lot of tension, also."

"Not only that. I've been pretty outspoken against slavery. They have slaves there and I find that disgusting. So I'll be glad to leave and they'll be glad to see me go."

"John says there's going to be a war over slavery. He thinks there is no way it can be avoided."

"He's probably right."

When Christmas was over, life went back to normal, except that Jennie Lu was gone and we had to get the sleigh out for our trips to town. John stayed home more, for which I was very grateful because our babies were getting to be quite a handful. He said he had accomplished his goal in politics so he could let up some. He didn't want me traveling alone in the winter.

CHAPTER 44
Her View

The day finally came when Dr. Joe brought Jennie Lu home. The whole town was there to greet them. We had the wedding planned for that Sunday. The pastor had agreed to give that whole Sunday over to Amy's wedding to Dr. Joe. John and I were to be in it, along with Jennie Lu and all the Slater children. The church was doing the dinner. They planned to head back East for their honeymoon and Jennie Lu and I would take care of the children while they were gone. Dr. Joe had brought a lot of stuff out on that train, but he wanted to get more while they were on their honeymoon. He was bringing supplies for the clinic as well as his personal possessions. He said that Little John was coming back from Europe and they would bring him back after their honeymoon.

Both of our communities were so happy that we were going to have a doctor and two nurses among us. There was even going to be a clinic. Our other doctor and his nurse had moved back to the Northeast where they were from. They left a huge vacant spot for us. As I listened to all the excitement, something began to stir inside of me, but I wasn't ready to talk about it yet.

The wedding was beautiful. We couldn't fit all the people in the church, so we opened the doors and windows so those on the outside could see in. I was so happy for Amy and Joe that I could hardly contain myself.

"Your idea was better than mine," I whispered to God as I stood beside Amy.

The Slater children were also radiant. It was obvious that they loved their new father. They were also excited about spending time at our ranch. They loved all the animals. It was a wonderful three weeks for all of us. When it was nearly over, they were having mixed emotions. The older boy explained it.

"We're anxious to see our mother and father. We know they are a great big blessing from God to us. But we hate to leave this ranch. We wish we could live like this."

"Do you know that your new father and I are cousins?" I asked him.

"No," he answered in a puzzled tone.

"Well, he is and that means that you are my cousins now. That means that we are all family. You can come visit us as much as you want. If your parents agree, you could spend some of your school vacations out here with us."

"Really?" they both exclaimed.

"Really," I replied. They began to jump around and clap their hands. The baby didn't understand what it was all about, but she clapped her hands also. Then our two joined in.

"What's all the celebration about?" John asked when he came in from the barn.

When I had explained it to him, he agreed with me.

"That's right," he said. "We're all one big family now and when Little John gets back here, he's part of our family, too."

Micah fell right down on the floor and started to cry.

John picked him up and set him in his lap.

"What's wrong, son?" he said.

"I thought we were all alone—no father—no mother—no family—no one to care about us—I was dying all alone. I just wanted to go to heaven. But now, I have a big family, a better family than I had before. If I hadn't had all that trouble, I never would have had all this."

"You've found out a very important truth," John said. "It's called redemption. God takes everything that happens to us, even our mistakes and turns them around for our good. The Bible promises that He makes all things work together for good to them that seek Him and pray to Him."

"What's it called?" Micah asked.

"Redemption. It's like the old hoe I found today. It was all rusty and the handle was broken. But I didn't throw it away. I cleaned it up and put a new handle in it. I redeemed it. It was ruined and wasted, but I redeemed it. Once I was ruined and wasted, but God redeemed me."

Now the older brother started to cry. He fell to his knees.

"I've been mad at God all this time," he explained. "Do you think He'll forgive me?"

"Why don't you ask Him?" I suggested.

"I'm sorry, God. Can You forgive me?"

"Pray in the Name of Jesus," I suggested.

"In the name of Jesus," he added.

He was very still for a while. Then he prayed again.

"I'll trust You with the rest of my life and try not to question You," he promised. Then he raised himself from the floor with a sigh of relief and showed us a big smile.

"He forgave me. I feel good inside again."

I gave him a hug.

"I knew He would," I said.

"I couldn't even see how much good He had done for me until Micah started saying it. I was hard inside. I felt sorry for myself all the time."

"Micah is a good preacher," I said.

We kept the Slater children a few extra days so Joe and Amy could get settled in. We had agreed to come to Titustown to church that last weekend and bring the children home then. When we got there, Amy was the only one in church.

"We've already got an emergency situation that Joe is taking care of," Amy explained. "It's someone from a neighboring town that they brought over in the middle of the night last night. We haven't even got the clinic set up yet, but we just put up a bed over there and put him in it."

"I hope it's not catching," I said.

"I don't think so. It seems to be an infected wound. But that is a concern we have, especially since the children are so near."

I got that stirring deep inside again.

CHAPTER 45
His View

Well, I'd managed to get our state back to being a free state.

The road was finished between Tateville and Titustown.

Our educational system was upgraded and was meeting the needs of the children from both towns.

We had town government set up and running smoothly in both towns.

Both of our ranches were doing well and we had helped quite a few people escape from slavery.

So I was feeling pretty good about myself and felt that God was blessing me. Now, I was anxious to see my younger brother. Jennie Lu's sixteenth birthday was approaching, so I expected him to appear very soon. If I could close that chapter successfully, I would be very happy. My Lady was planning a huge celebration. She had invited all the young people from both towns and most of the adults.

"We're celebrating her return, her birthday and her graduation from nursing school," she explained.

We all kept looking for Jimmy, but no one said anything.

When the party was over, Jennie Lu went to her room. She never came out all the next day. In the evening, she came out to empty her chamber pot and stood and looked out over the ridge where Jimmy had disappeared. I knew she was assuming that he was dead. But after she'd gone in, I looked a little longer as the darkness was deepening. I thought I saw a tiny flicker of light, so I saddled my horse and headed that direction. When I topped the ridge, I could see a campfire off in a little hollow. As I drew nearer, I recognized

Jimmy sitting by that fire. A huge relief swelled up from within me, but irritation was rising up right behind it.

"Jimmy!" I almost shouted. "What are you doing out here? We've all been grieving, thinking you were dead."

Jimmy didn't even respond until I had dismounted and walked toward him. Then he turned very slowly and looked at me.

I gasped and stopped in my tracks. The other side of his face was so deformed that he was not even recognizable. He wore a patch over that eye. He looked like a monster on that side.

"What happened?" I whispered.

"I was beaten unconscious, thrown in a fire and left for dead. But for some reason, I rolled out of the fire alive. Indians found me, took me to their village and took care of me until I recovered."

I fell to my knees and covered my face with my hands.

"Oh God! Oh God! Oh God!" I moaned. "You've redeemed all my mistakes up to now, but I don't see how You can redeem this one." I put my forehead on the ground and sobbed. When I quieted down a little, Jimmy spoke again.

"When I first became conscious again, I did just what you are doing. I blamed you. But finally I had to face the fact that I brought this on myself because I ignored your warnings. You told me not to get into any position that exercised control in those gold mines, because it was too dangerous. But I was so sure of myself that I couldn't turn down that job offer, and two of the men conspired to kill me."

"What happened to them?" I asked.

"When I finally returned, they were terrified. I looked like I'd risen from the dead. Which I nearly did. I don't know how or why I survived. But anyway, I brought charges against them and they were finally hung. But I felt sorry for them at the last and I went and found a preacher to come and talk to them before they died. That gold fever is a terrible thing. It makes you go crazy.

"So now you see why I haven't showed my face," he continued. "I think it would be better for everyone if they continue to think I'm dead. When they finish grieving, they can go on with their lives. I wouldn't have come back at all but I made a promise and that kept bothering me. But when I saw that beautiful young lady and all those handsome young men flocking around her, I couldn't bring myself to go in. I knew she would feel obligated to marry me and I don't want that. I'm just sorry you found me and will have to keep this secret all your life. I thought I was far enough away that you wouldn't be able to see me. I plan to move on in the morning."

I sat and talked with Jimmy for at least a couple of hours. I finally convinced him to come spend the night in the barn and say goodbye to the girls in the morning.

"If you're truly not blaming me for this," I said, "then don't put this terrible burden of guilt on me to carry for the rest of my life."

I think that was the argument that finally convinced him. I promised to prepare the girls before they saw him and let Jennie Lu know that he had no intention of marrying her. He had just come to say goodbye.

When we got back to the Stone Place, I let him quietly into the barn. I showed him where the beds were and explained that whole situation to him while we fed the horses and rubbed them down.

"I'm glad you're doing that," was all he said. Then he stood there, waiting for me to leave.

"Promise me you won't leave until tomorrow after breakfast," I said.

"Do you read minds?" he asked.

"I read yours," I responded.

I stood with my hand on the door until he finally answered with a sigh.

"Oh, all right," he sighed. "I promise."

I gave him a hug and said, "I love you, Jimmy."

He hugged me back, but didn't say a word.

I went out as quietly as possible and entered the house just as quietly. While I was hanging up my hat and jacket, I was startled by her quiet voice.

"Did you find him?" she asked very quietly.

"Yes."

"Where is he?" she whispered.

"In the barn."

"Why?"

I took her by the hand and led her to the bedroom.

"Let's get in bed and I'll explain it all to you," I whispered.

When I had told her the whole story, we held each other and cried together, trying to be as quiet as possible.

"Heavenly Father," she prayed, "in the name of Jesus, I ask You for the wisdom to keep him here with us."

"Amen," was all I could choke out.

We wept and prayed until the wee hours of the morning. Then we were both awake at dawn.

My Lady started to prepare breakfast, but was soon interrupted by our babies. That brought Jennie Lu down from her room.

"I'll help you," she said. "I guess I've hid long enough."

While she was feeding those babies their cereal, I began to tell her the story. She never said a word through the whole thing, but the tears began to roll down her cheeks. I couldn't hold mine back either. I thought I had cried all the tears I had but they started again.

"I don't love him for his looks," she finally managed to say.

"You've never seen anything this bad," I replied. "He looks like a monster. I'm sure he will terrify these babies."

"Well, breakfast is almost ready, so go get him and Jennie Lu, put the babies in their beds in the bedroom with some toys."

When I brought Jimmy over, Jennie Lu was still in the bedroom with the babies. I knew she was praying.

Caroline hugged Jimmy and told him how glad she was to see him and tried to ignore his terrible scars. He had bags of skin hanging down in places. But when Jennie Lu came out, she went right to the scars and began to examine them. She acted just like the nurse that she was.

"You know, Jimmy," she said, "I think Dr. Joe can help with this. Before we left the East, he and another doctor were doing some experiments with something they call skin grafting. I saw one man that they helped a lot."

Jennie Lu bent down and looked into his eyes. I noticed that he had removed the patch.

"Can you see out of this eye?" she asked.

"Yes," he said, "but I can't close it, so I usually wear a patch to protect it. But I wanted to see everybody as good as I could for one last time this morning, so I took it off."

"I know we can fix that eyelid so it will work again. That's just scar tissue holding that eyelid up."

Jennie Lu sat down at the table facing Jimmy.

"As far as your leaving is concerned," she continued, "I think my mother and I should have something to say about that. We were the ones who prayed you out of that fire. Your life is now an answer to our prayers."

She pulled her journal from her apron pocket. She turned to the page and read to him the date and what she had written. It told about the vision she had seen of him surrounded by flames and how her mother had helped her pray until the burden lifted. There was complete silence for several minutes.

"So I've been redeemed and my life is no longer my own," Jimmy finally whispered. "Is that what you're saying?"

"Yes, and I want you to forget about running away to hide. If you have to hide, you do it right here and give us a chance to see if we can fix you up some. I believe we can, with God's help. That damaged side will never be as handsome as the other side, but it can be improved."

"Amen!" My Lady agreed. "And I have something stirring inside of me that I have been praying that God would send the right person for and I think you are that person."

I stared at her and held my breath. I had no idea what she was talking about.

"Do you remember that gold mine that caused me so much trouble?" she asked.

"Yes," he responded.

"Well, I believe it's time to open it again to finance the building of a hospital. To do that, I need someone who knows the danger and won't be subject to gold fever. But he also needs to know how to manage it. He also needs to know the people around here and who can be trusted. I believe you are the man God has prepared for this job."

There was complete silence for quite a while. Jimmy finally spoke.

"Why do you need a hospital?"

"Your brother says that a war between the north and the south over the slavery issue is coming. He says it cannot be avoided. We will be right in the middle between the two sides. There will be many wounded people. Even now, our clinic is too small and we just barely got it built. People were coming before we had officially opened it."

"Well, I guess I could do that from hiding," Jimmy mused.

I let out a huge sigh of relief. My Lady had done it again. I was redeemed!

Jennie Lu kissed Jimmy right on the mouth. I guess he kissed her back because she said, "I'm glad your mouth still works!"

We all laughed, even Jimmy.

She insisted on taking him to see Dr. Joe immediately.

"You can hide in the carriage," she insisted.

"Let him get cleaned up first and then take him in the evening," My Lady suggested, "so he'll have the cover of darkness when he has to get out."

Jennie Lu agreed to that and Jimmy was relieved. He couldn't take his eyes off of her. He just sat and watched every move she made.

"Can I see the babies while they're sleeping?" he finally asked. "So I won't scare them," he added.

I took him into the bedroom where they were.

"I hope nothing like this ever happens to them," he whispered.

I remembered Jimmy as a beautiful little boy and a sob caught in my throat. I had to go out to keep from waking them.

CHAPTER 46
Her View

Jennie Lu and Jimmy didn't come back that night. I didn't expect them to. Jennie Lu told me later that she had slept on Amy's couch and they had put Jimmy on a vacant bed in the clinic. Early the next morning, Dr. Joe had gone to the train station to send a telegram to his friend back East, explaining Jimmy's condition. His friend sent a message back that he would be on the next train out.

The next morning after breakfast, John and I headed for town. We had to know what was going on with Jimmy. In the night, John had wept and wept and thanked me over and over for keeping Jimmy here.

"I couldn't have stood it if he had taken off alone and I would never know what became of him," John said.

When we arrived at the clinic, Dr. Joe and Jennie Lu were already working on Jimmy. As soon as we arrived, Amy turned the care of the children over to us and headed into the clinic to help. John took all the older children for a ride in our wagon while I kept the young ones. It was quite a handful. I was glad to see Grandpa and Grandma Jones. They had talked to John and came to help. While we were taking care of the babies, I talked to Grandpa Jones about my desire to finance the building of a hospital. He suggested that we start a trust fund that the whole community could invest in and no one would need to know that I was the primary source or that I had a gold mine. He also suggested that if we were going to have a hospital, we would also need a hotel for family and friends. I agreed. We even began to draw up rough plans for developing that road between our two towns. We would widen the road and build the hotel across the road from the hospital.

"People could invest in this project and actually make money in the long run," he explained.

I had never thought of it like that, so I decided to turn the financial part over to Grandpa Jones. He was the banker and knew what he was doing. He was obviously getting excited about the possibilities.

"This is going to contribute to this town much more and in a better way than a gold rush," he exclaimed. "I'm glad you decided to do this while I'm still here to participate."

When John came back, Grandpa Jones explained it all to him and he started to get excited, too.

"This will create a lot of jobs in this area. And we will have a lot of people moving here. So we will have to expand the schools also. We will also need a lot more housing."

"Dr. Joe and Amy are interested in starting a nursing school," I added.

"I'd better call a town meeting for both towns so we can get the people's approval," John added. "You prepare a financial explanation," he said to Grandpa Jones.

"I'll invest most of the gold I have now," I said. "That way you'll have something to start with. Then when Jimmy's able to work in the mine, I'll add more."

"I will also invest in this," Grandpa Jones said. "I want to be in on the ground floor."

Just then, Amy came over to check on her children.

"You can go over to see Jimmy now," she said. "They've got him wrapped up like a mummy, but he's conscious."

Sure enough, he did look like a mummy, but his eyes were not covered. Jennie Lu was standing by his side with a pad that she kept pressing against his right eye.

"His eyelid is working now, but it's still bleeding a little bit," she explained. "Dr. Joe cut the scar tissue away and a lot of the dead skin from his face."

Jimmy was trying to talk, so I leaned closer.

"I'm kind of drunk," he said.

"We gave him whiskey so he couldn't feel the pain," Jennie Lu explained.

Just then, Dr. Joe came in from visiting other patients. He checked Jimmy's pulse and smiled.

"He's doing just fine!" he assured us. "When my friend gets here, we'll work on him some more. I just did the preliminaries. My friend has much more experience with this than I do, so I'm excited that he's coming. He'll probably be here tomorrow or the next day."

"That train and now the telegraph sure have changed our lives," John commented.

"If it wasn't for them, I probably would never have met you folks or Amy," the doctor agreed.

"By the way," he continued, "what happened to Little John?"

"He got his horse out of my barn and headed on out to the Indian Territory," John explained. "He said he'd be back."

"Probably with a Cherokee bride," Joe chuckled. "He doesn't want to produce anymore half breeds like us," he said as he glanced at me.

I just laughed, but there was a little ache inside as I remembered my mother. I remembered the Cherokee clothes I had found hidden away in her dress shop. She had said they belonged to someone she used to know. But now I knew that someone was her.

"Well, I'd better go back to help Amy with the children," I said as I turned to go. "It looks like Jimmy needs to sleep."

When we got out of the clinic, John asked if I'd mind if he started working on the town meeting he needed to organize. I told him to go ahead. I could handle the children by myself if need be, but Grandpa and Grandma were still there, so we had a great time together.

CHAPTER 47
His View

When I saw that Jimmy was in good hands and My Lady had everything under control with the children, I felt like a huge weight had been taken off of me and my mind turned toward that town meeting. I knew I had to make it a joint meeting for both towns because we wanted to build the hospital right in the middle between the two. So I started my politicking in Titustown. We would go home through Tateville and talk to Mr. Tate and let him handle that town.

Soon, Grandpa Jones caught up with me. "Those ladies can handle those children without me," he said. "I'm going to help you."

Everyone we talked to was anxious to have the meeting as soon as possible. Several men who were experienced in construction were already offering their services. But I didn't feel confident that any of them were experienced in the kind of construction we needed for that hospital. I shared my doubts with Grandpa Jones.

"I'm visualizing a huge brick building like I've seen in the East," I confided to him. "But none of these men has ever done that."

Mr. Jones was silent for a while.

"Don't you think we should build the hotel first, so there will be lodging for the workers when they come?" he suggested. "That would give you time to go back East and find the right man to build the hospital and teach our men that kind of construction."

"What a good idea!" I exclaimed. "I am so glad I've got you around! They can build the hotel like a big house—or several big houses. It will be wood construction like they do all the time!"

Everyone in Titustown was anxious to get on with it, but I told them we couldn't set a date for the meeting until I had been to Tateville and got their input. I asked for suggestions and they all said anytime was good for them.

"Another problem we're going to have is who to put in charge of the construction," I shared with Mr. Jones.

He was silent for a while again.

"I think it's going to have to be you, John," he finally shared. "Anyone else is going to cause conflict and division. And you've just built one of the most beautiful buildings around here with an amazing water system."

I thought about that for a while, then finally agreed. "I suppose you're right again," I said with a sigh. "I was hoping I could turn it over to someone else but I can see that what you're saying is true."

"How did you get the idea for a flush toilet anyway?"

"I saw one in all my wanderings around the country. So I decided to perfect it for My Lady. She deserved the best I could do."

"Absolutely!"

"So now, I guess I'll have to put one on every floor of that hotel. I think I can also put hot running water in there. I'm thinking about it, anyway."

"It'll be an amazing place, I'm sure," Mr. Jones said.

When we got back to the clinic, Caroline was ready to go. She told me that Jennie Lu was going to stay with Amy until Jimmy was able to travel, so we didn't need to wait for her.

"Good," I said. Then I told her about my need to talk with Mr. Tate about a joint town meeting.

"If we leave now, I can probably get it done today," I said.

We found Mr. Tate still in his store. After I'd explained everything to him, he agreed to organize this side for me.

"Remember," Caroline reminded, "there is to be no mention of that gold mine. That will be kept as quiet as possible. My investment will be totally secret."

"I understand. And realize now why I was never meant to have that gold. I would have used it totally to build myself and my business and it would have caused all kinds of trouble in this community.

But you're using it to build this whole area. I respect you two people above what I can put into words."

"Thank you! And we appreciate so much your encouragement."

When the day of the town meeting arrived, Jimmy was still at the clinic, but his looks were tremendously improved. The doctor from the East had come and gone and My Lady had paid him generously. The rest of her gold, except a few coins, she had given to Mr. Jones to set up an account for the expansion of our two towns.

When the meeting was called to order, I was surprised by Mr. Tate. He proposed that we combine the two towns. When that was approved, he proposed that the name be changed to McLane. I was stunned!

He explained that he and his brother had decided to start two separate towns because they couldn't get along very well, but they wanted to be close enough to help each other if the need arose.

"As you all know," he continued, "my brother died young, leaving no heirs. And I messed up so bad in the Stone affair that I don't want my name on this town. I'll start a historical society at my store just to keep the records straight, but the people who have done the most for this whole area are the McLanes, so let's name this new beginning after them."

There began to be applause that turned into a standing ovation. The proposal was passed without one dissenting vote. I was amazed. I'd never even imagined such a thing!

When it was my turn to speak, I felt a little flustered, but I thanked the people for their confidence and promised to try my best to live up to their expectations. Then I began to explain our plans for expansion. I never mentioned Caroline's part in this project, because that's the way she wanted it. I explained the need for a hospital and a hotel and all the ways that this project would impact our community. There would be an influx of new people and that would create a need for a lot of new construction. But new people would mean different cultures and different ideas along with new business opportunities. The good and the bad were discussed for a couple of hours. In the end, everyone voted in favor. Then I asked Mr. Jones to explain the financial situation. He explained where our fund now stood and how everyone could invest and if it was a success, everyone would profit—if not, their investment would be a donation. Anyone who was interested in helping could come to the bank and talk to him more.

"We have enough money right now to start on widening the road and building the hotel," I explained. "And I believe we have enough people right now to get that accomplished."

After the meeting, I signed up several men to start widening the road. They would start next week. Several of them were boys who had just finished school and had no jobs. So they were excited to be working and getting paid for it.

I could tell Caroline was very pleased with the way things had turned out and we both were anxious to share it all with Jimmy and Jennie Lu. We found them both sitting in Amy's house, watching the children. Jimmy was still covered with bandages, but he was already more recognizable.

"You didn't say anything about me, did you?" he asked immediately.

"No, we didn't," I responded, then I explained what happened as best I could. Caroline helped out and filled in the spaces.

"So this town is now called McLane?" Jennie Lu asked, incredulously.

"That's right," I responded, "and I had nothing to do with it."

Just then, Dr. and Mrs. Joe Slape came in the door.

"Congratulations!" they exclaimed.

"Congratulations to you," I said. "You're going to get a hospital to run."

"And we are so excited about it!" Amy exclaimed.

"That reminds me. I need to get some names from you, Joe, if you know who I could contact about building that hospital. We need someone experienced in that type of construction. I want a big brick building like I've seen in the East."

"The man who built our hospital is retired, I believe, but I'm sure he can recommend someone," Joe responded. "He built some of those big mills up in New England, then came down South and built our hospital."

"He sounds like the man we need."

"I'll send a telegram to Dr. Bitterly who was just here and see if he can contact him for us."

"Thank you!"

CHAPTER 48
Her View

When Jimmy returned to the Stone Place, he looked like he had patches on his face and neck. He showed us that he even had some on his right arm.

"But at least my arm works again," he said.

"You look much better," I said. "You're very recognizable now."

"Well, I'd like to take a cot out to the cave and start working on that gold mine," he said. "There's a lot of work to do there before I can get it up and running."

"You're welcome to take a cot out there, but we don't want you to live there, Jimmy. We want you here with us," I protested.

"I'll be going back and forth, but I need to spend a lot of time out there. That gold mine is the only reason I'm staying here," he said as he glanced at Jennie Lu.

When he was gone, Jennie went to her room and I didn't see her the rest of the day. The next day, she left for town without eating any breakfast. She said she wasn't hungry. This went on for a week. So the next time I was in town and visited Amy, I asked her if Jennie Lu was eating there or in the clinic.

"No," she answered. "I haven't seen her eating. Maybe she's going over to the restaurant to eat. She's been turning down my offers."

I finally confronted Jennie Lu.

"Are you fasting?" I asked.

"I guess you might call it that," she answered.

"How long do you plan to fast?"

"Until something happens."

"Until what happens?"

"I don't want to talk about it," she said. "It's between me and God."

So another week went by and I was getting worried. Jennie Lu was looking pale and spent a lot of time in her room. I kept trying to draw her out, but she refused to talk. She kept going to work, but I could see it was getting harder for her. Amy was getting worried, too.

By the end of the third week, she called for me and asked me to let Amy know that she wouldn't be able to work next week.

"You're not planning to fast another week, are you?" I asked in amazement.

"Yes," was all she said.

I grabbed a chair and sat down by her bed.

"Now, Jennie Lu, you're going to have to talk to me. I'm your mother and I'm not going to stand silently by and watch you commit suicide. If you're trying to make God do something by your fasting, it won't work. That's not the purpose of fasting. We fast so we can hear from God and do what He wants us to do. Not make Him do what we want Him to do."

"I don't know if I'm really fasting or just trying to lose weight," Jennie Lu responded.

I was stunned.

"Lose weight?" I exclaimed. "You have no weight to lose. You're skin and bones."

"I have to get small enough to fit into that dress," she said, glancing up at an old dress she had hanging on the wall. "I was wearing that dress when Jimmy left. He loved me when I was that small. He doesn't love me now that I'm so much bigger."

"Jennie Lu! You know better than this. You're not thinking straight. If Jimmy loved you for your size, then he's not the man for you. You know very good and well that no woman can maintain the same size for life. How small do you think you'll be when you get pregnant? I know for sure you'll never be that small again," I said, pointing at the dress. "You weren't even grown yet when you wore that dress. Then you were a child, now you are a woman! So start acting like a woman, not a child!"

"You're right, of course," Jennie Lu whispered as she tried to get up, but held her head and fell back into the bed.

"Wait! Don't try to get up yet. I'll get you something to drink from the kitchen. I'll be right back. Just wait for me. Don't try to get up."

"Okay," was Jennie's weak response.

I ran down to the kitchen and made a cup of tea, using the water I had cooked the potatoes in. I put some milk and sugar in it and hurried back to Jennie Lu.

After she had drunk half of it, she stopped and looked at me in amazement.

"What did you put in that tea?" she asked. "I can feel it going all through my body."

"I made it with the potato water," I laughed.

"I can tell it's full of nutrition. Think how much good food we're pouring down the drain."

"That's why I try to cook it down till there's just a little water left before I mash them," I responded.

"Do you have any more?" Jennie Lu asked. "I think I could get up after another cup of that."

"I think I can manage another one," I said as I hurried out the door. I was so happy to have my old rational Jennie back again.

After the second cup of potato tea, she got slowly up and began to dress.

"Thanks for waking me up," she said as we walked down the stairs together. "I don't know what came over me. Jimmy either loves me the way I am or he doesn't. I can't change who I am and I sure can't go back in time, can I?"

"Absolutely not! None of us can. I can't go back to being the tough woman I was when John first saw me."

"Heavens! I hope not!" Jennie laughed.

We were having breakfast when Jimmy came in from the mine. He usually came back every weekend to get cleaned up. We couldn't talk him into going to church with us, but he never refused a good meal. So he sat down at the table to eat breakfast. He kept glancing at Jennie Lu, who was sitting in the rocking chair, sipping another cup of tea.

"Jennie Lu, are you sick?" he finally asked. "You look so pale and thin."

She didn't answer for a long time, so he stopped eating and sat back in his chair and stared at her.

"I'm not sick now," she finally answered.

"Have you been sick?" he pressed her further.

Again there was a long pause.

"I guess you might say that," she answered.

"There's no maybe about being sick. Either you're sick or you aren't sick," Jimmy insisted.

I turned my back and smiled as I washed dishes. It sounded like the old Jimmy back again. He always wanted everything to be either black or white with no gray areas.

"Well, it all depends on how you define sickness," Jennie Lu responded.

Now I had to chuckle. Jennie Lu was being herself. She wouldn't allow herself to be put in a box.

Now Jimmy was getting exasperated.

"Jennie Lu!" he exclaimed. "Will you just tell me if you've been sick."

"I've been fasting," she responded. "But now I'm coming off my fast."

"Fasting! Why in the world have you been fasting?"

"Because I was a little sick in my head," Jennie laughed. "But my mother straightened me out and I'm fine now."

"How long have you been fasting?" Jimmy asked in a quiet voice.

"Three weeks."

He let out a low whistle.

"I couldn't do that if my life depended on it. Not with food all around me, especially your mother's cooking.

"I'm glad your fast is over. I don't like seeing you so thin and pale. It makes me nervous. I don't want you to be sick," he continued.

This time, I choked on the piece of toast I was eating while I worked. Then I started to laugh.

"Why don't you try a piece of toast, Jennie Lu?" I asked.

"Why, so I can choke on it the way you just did?" she teased.

"No, so you can get some strength."

"Speaking of strength, do you think you have enough to ride out to the mine and see what I'm doing?" Jimmy asked Jenny Lu.

"I think I can do it," she said as she accepted the piece of toast from my hand. "I'm feeling much stronger," she assured me.

So Jenny Lu and Jimmy began to gradually rebuild their relationship. And Jimmy began to rebuild his self-confidence. He even began to go into town once in a while. He was relieved that no one made too much of his appearance. John had made sure that everyone knew what had happened to Jimmy so they wouldn't be shocked when they saw him.

By the time Jenny Lu's seventeenth birthday came around, they were sweethearts again and planning their marriage. Jimmy gave her a beautiful ring for a birthday present.

John and I agreed to give them the Stone Place for a wedding present. Jimmy had to be there to work that mine and I was actually excited about returning to the McLane house. It felt like coming home to me. I had missed it ever since we left there. I missed seeing Jerry and all the guys coming in at night from the fields. And I guess my bad memories from the Stone Place would never go away. When I explained all this to Jennie Lu, she was at peace about taking over the Stone Place.

So we began moving back again. We didn't need to move much furniture because the McLane house was well furnished. John kept promising me that he would update the water system so it would be as convenient as the Stone Place. I kept assuring him I was fine with it the way it was. The whole place felt so homey to me. I kept remembering the relief of coming there the first time and I felt it all over again.

Jerry was elated that we were coming back.

"It's been so lonely around here without you," he exclaimed.

"You've sure kept that garden up in fine shape, Jerry. I really appreciate that."

"I couldn't let it go after all the work you put into it. I kept remembering you working in that garden when you were 'great with child' and it kept me going."

I gave Jerry a hug because I was choked up and couldn't speak.

Jennie Lu moved back into her room until her wedding. I put the babies in the room next to ours. When we were all moved over there, Jimmy moved into the Stone Place. He had to start helping the runaway slaves, besides working the mine. John kept overseeing both ranches.

I wanted to have a big wedding for Jennie, but I didn't know if Jimmy would agree to it. When I talked to him about it, he said, "I will do whatever Jennie Lu wants. I told her I'm her man if she wants me and she said she wants me. So it doesn't matter what anyone else thinks. I'm so overwhelmed by her love for me that nothing else matters to me."

Then I told him about the fasting incident.

"You mean she did that because she thought I didn't love her anymore?"

"Yes."

"I was so caught up in my own pain that I didn't see how I was hurting her," Jimmy whispered. "I thought I was setting her free, but I was deserting her. I hope I never do that again."

It made me a little uneasy to hear him say that word 'hope.' It didn't sound definite enough to me, but I put it out of my mind.

We had the wedding at the McLane ranch because that's the only place we could accommodate the crowd. It was a beautiful wedding with a delicious meal afterward, thanks to Jerry. Jimmy and Jennie rode away in our carriage heading for the Stone Place. They didn't want to go anywhere for a honeymoon. I watched them go with a strange feeling inside that I couldn't understand or explain. It had started when I gave Jennie Lu that necklace as a gift from her father. I guess old memories came rushing back. I kept remembering riding away with her father in exactly the same direction. The whole scene was too familiar. It made me very uneasy. Was something going to happen to Jimmy? Was this what they called a premonition?

CHAPTER 49
His View

We started construction on the hotel while the road was being widened. We soon had men from other communities applying for work. We put as many to work as we could. We soon had a tent community springing up where they were staying. But it wasn't long before I heard rumbles of discontent. So I got Zed Black to go in there as my spy. I wanted to get the troublemakers out of there as soon as possible. I'd learned my lesson in Tateville.

Zed told me about a man named Frank who kept complaining that we ought to have slave labor to do the pick and shovel work. He was trying to convince everyone that white men were never intended for such hard work.

When Frank received his paycheck on Friday, he was informed that his services would no longer be needed. After he and a few other trouble makers were fired, things settled down and the work progressed speedily. We soon had the road finished and the outer structure of the hotel completed. After I perfected the plumbing of my flush toilets, I turned the interior over to the men that I knew were excellent carpenters. I picked three and put one in charge of each floor. I figured they would compete with each other to see who could do the best work.

As soon as I was sure things were running smoothly, I headed back East to see if I could find the man Dr. Joe had told me about. It didn't take me long to find him and he was very interested in what we were doing. He was retired, but he wanted to come. We talked to his son, who was also interested. We discussed many things, including the possibility of making bricks right there in McLane. The son said his present job would be finished within the month and then he could come out and look things over. The father said he would come back with me. He knew all about making bricks because that's what he had done as a young man before he started using them in construction.

I was in a hurry to get home to My Lady and our babies. I kept remembering every confrontation we'd been through. I didn't want her to be alone for long. I didn't want her to ever use that shotgun again. I was also worried about Jennie Lu and Jimmy out there at the Stone Place with that gold mine operating. No matter how hard we tried to keep it quiet, someone was bound to figure it out. I knew we had made some enemies who would be looking for ways to get back at us. I finally had to explain some of this to Mr. Stone so he would hurry a little. He caught on right away and had himself ready to go the next day. When we got back to McLane, I headed right for the McLane house. I was relieved to find Caroline and our babies doing fine.

When I told Caroline about my uneasiness, she told me she had the same feelings about Jennie Lu and Jimmy. So I decided to head that direction the next day. Mr. Stone was very curious about the Stone Place. He began to question Caroline about her first husband who had the same last name as his. After talking for about an hour, he said he was relatively sure that Caroline's first husband was his nephew. He had a brother who had headed west and they never heard from him again. His name was Jedediah Stone, the same name as Caroline's first husband who was probably named after his father.

"My understanding was that his father died from a sickness that passed through the area and took quite a few lives. Then his mother died giving birth to him. The people of the community raised him," Caroline explained. "We can look for their graves when we go tomorrow if you desire. The Tates probably know more about it than I do."

"I would really appreciate that," Mr. Stone replied. "The loss of Jed has been a great grief in our family for years. The worst thing was not knowing what had happened to him. My mother went to an early grave grieving for him."

So when we were sure everything was all right at the Stone Place, we headed for Tate's Store. Jennie Lu came along because she wanted to know more about her heritage.

"I never really knew where Jed came from. I just knew he was an orphan who was raised by the people of this community and he loved and trusted them all, which led to his death," Caroline said.

Mr. Stone just gave Caroline a thoughtful look and said nothing.

When we introduced Mr. Stone to Mr. Tate and explained why he was here, Mr. Tate was excited. But when we told him about Mr. Stone's desire to find information about his brother, Jedediah Stone, Mr. Tate got very quiet.

"Did you know him?" Mr. Stone finally asked.

"Yes," was the quiet reply.

"Can you show me his grave?"

There was another long pause.

"Not exactly," Mr. Tate finally responded. "He was buried in a mass grave with at least twenty-five other people. We were never sure how many people we buried. But I can show you a list of the names that we knew were in that grave. I have it in my safe." He spoke as he headed for his safe. He came back with some papers and a few other things.

"These are his personal possessions that he gave to me to keep for him," he said.

As Mr. Stone looked through the things that Mr. Tate gave him, he began to sob.

"Oh God. Why didn't I come looking for him sooner? Here is a letter to our mother that would have meant so much to her."

"I didn't know where to look," Mr. Tate explained.

"He said he chose to stay with the sick people even though it would probably kill him," Mr. Stone choked out between sobs.

"Yes, he stayed and I ran. He asked me to take his pregnant wife with me. She was my cousin. I got my family out of here. I deserted all the sick people. There was no one to help them but Jed Stone. He was kind of like a lay preacher for us. He wouldn't leave the people to die alone. He nursed them and prayed for them and then he died himself. When I finally got the nerve to return, I found the church full of dead bodies. Some were half rotted away. I don't know if those children died of the sickness or they starved to death or died of thirst because there was no one to care for them." By this time, Mr. Tate was sobbing also. "We burned the church building, then we took their bones and buried them outside of town. I was a coward. Jed Stone was a hero. So we named his son after him and made a hero out of him. But when he discovered gold on the land I sold to him, I began to resent him. Why should he have the gold instead of my own son? So I ended up contributing to the death of Jed Stone Jr., just like I had to his father!"

"How so?" Mr. Stone asked.

"Well, it's a long story," Mr. Tate said with a sigh. "But I guess you've got a right to know the whole thing." He looked at me for confirmation and I gave him a nod.

The final outcome was that the hospital would be called "The Stone Memorial Hospital". Mr. Tate would start the brick plant on his land and let it be a cover for the gold mine on the Stone Place. And he would finally put the past behind him and go on. I was glad the whole thing had finally come out. We all assured him that we may have done what he did during the plague. None of us had ever been through it so we couldn't judge. I could tell it had done him good to confess the whole thing to us. He showed us where the mass grave was and where the church had stood that he burnt down. He had buried his niece near the mass grave. I suggested that he make markers for the graves and turn the whole area into a cemetery.

Mr. Stone mentioned again that he wished his mother had known these things before she died.

"She's with him now and knows all about it," Jennie said. It was the first time she had spoken during this whole amazing story.

"You're right, of course," Mr. Stone exclaimed. "That makes me feel a lot better."

"Now I know why I've never been willing to give up the Stone name," Jennie continued. "I have a destiny placed upon me by my grandfather. I must carry on for him."

"So you're my brother's granddaughter?" Mr. Stone asked.

"Yes."

“Then you will be my granddaughter,” Mr. Stone exclaimed, holding out his arms to Jennie, who came to him and accepted his hug. “I will take my brother’s place in your life.”

“I’m a nurse. I care for the sick,” Jennie said, “and I pray for them, too, just like my grandfather.”

Jennie invited Mr. Stone to stay at the Stone Place while he worked with Mr. Tate, developing a brick factory. There was no hotel on this side of town. And the factory would be right on the edge of the Stone ranch.

“I won’t always be here to fix meals for you,” Jennie explained, “because I’m working in town. You’ll have to take care of yourself most of the time. You can buy food at Tate’s store.”

It took Mr. Stone about a month to get the brick production going. He kept visiting our hotel construction and reserved the first finished room for himself and his wife.

“Save a room for my son, also,” he said. “He’ll probably bring his wife along, too, when I tell them what an amazing place this is going to be. We’ll be here by the time you’re ready to start the hospital if not before.”

“Well, remember we are a free state. I saw you had a negro woman working in your house when I was there,” John responded. “We’re anxious to have you come, but we don’t want any conflicts over slavery. We’ve had enough of that.”

“We’ll work something out,” Mr. Stone assured us.

CHAPTER 50
Her View

I managed to speak privately to Mr. Stone before he left. I asked him to see if he could get me something called a lawn mower that I had heard about. It was invented in Europe but I hoped he could get one in the East for me so I could give it to John for our anniversary and his birthday. He assured me that he could. He had seen a few in the East. They made beautiful lawns. So I gave him one of my gold coins.

"This will be far more than enough!" he exclaimed.

"Well, you could get one for each place," I said. "Then use the rest for the expenses for your trip out here."

"Mr. Jones has already paid my expenses. So I'll bring back what I don't use, or could buy extra lawn mowers and you could sell them? I'm sure everyone will want one when they see what they can do."

"What a good idea!" I exclaimed. "Let's try that. Get as many as this gold will buy."

After that, I kept wondering what I would do with the extra lawn mowers. Where could I put them and how much should I sell them for and how would I have the time to do that?

"Should I just give them away?" I asked the Lord one day. It was then that an idea started to develop in my mind. I could help one of our young men start a business. My mind went immediately to Zed Black's younger brother Jeremiah. John had told me what a hard worker he was and how he wanted to help him get started in life. He'd been working on the road and the hotel construction. So I tucked that away in my memory for future reference.

Just then, Little John appeared at the McLane ranch with a whole caravan of wagons. There were eight wagons full of people. They wanted to build a Cherokee community in our area. And just as Joe had predicted, Little John had brought his bride and wanted us to have a wedding for them. He said they would live in their wagons until they could build homes for themselves. So John helped them set up camp in the area between our two ranches. Then he called an emergency town meeting. He wanted to get the town to grant them the land behind the new hotel. So Little John could have an art studio near the hotel and they would have closer access to jobs in the community. This was approved by the community, but a few of the Cherokee people asked to stay where they were and work on our ranches. John said he could use their help, so their request was granted for that land also.

When we were making plans for Little John's wedding, I kept remembering the Cherokee clothes that were hidden in my mother's dress shop. So I finally got them out and showed them to the beautiful young bride. I asked her if she wanted me to wear them for her wedding. She was very much in favor. She showed me what she planned to wear that would blend well with my mother's dress. So I tried the dress on and it fit me perfectly. It gave me a strange feeling inside. It felt like something that had been asleep was waking up. When I heard the people singing hymns in Cherokee, I had flashbacks of my mother singing to me as a child. I was soon able to sing along.

The wedding went well. John and I and Dr. Joe and family acted as family for Little John. I could tell the people were shocked to see me acting like an Indian. But it felt wonderful to have my identity out in the open. I shed a few tears for my mother who was never able to do this.

We had another big dinner at the McLane ranch. Some of the Indian women made bread and other food for everyone to try. It ended up being a time of good fellowship and the breaking down of the walls of separation. I was relieved to hear John invite the ones who would be working on our ranch to bring their wagons over near us so they would have better access to water.

"When you've dug some wells and built some houses, you can move back over here," he said. I was nodding my agreement.

Little John and his wife moved into the hotel while he was building a log cabin for them. Several of the men were helping him. It ended up being a nice home with a special room for his art studio. He copied John's ideas for the water system. When the house was built, he came to get his picture of his mother. When I handed it to him, he held my hand and looked into my eyes.

"Thank you," was all he said.

"Keeping that picture for you was no trouble at all," I responded.

"I mean thank you for identifying with us and acknowledging us as family."

"That probably did more for me than it did for you," I responded as a tear spilled over and ran down my cheek. "I wish my mother could have known this freedom."

"She did the best she could for the time in which she lived."

"Yes, she did. And I know she's in Heaven where everyone is free and equal."

"Yes, right along with my mother."

"Yes, they'll be waiting for us over there."

CHAPTER 51
His View

By the time Fall came upon us, we had the hotel finished except for cleaning up the outside and designing the yard. So I started on the foundation for the hospital and asked My Lady to design the yard for the hospital. Actually, I had some of the men start the digging for the foundation way back in August. But now I was really going after it in earnest. I had a real sense of urgency about that hospital.

True to their word, the Stones from back East showed up the second week in September. They had an amazing amount of boxes to unload from that train. I couldn't imagine the purpose of all that stuff. But I got some men to help unload it. They left most of it there at the depot, covered with a tarp.

"We'll deal with all this later," Mr. Stone said with a smile. "Right now, we need to get settled into that new hotel of yours and get a good night's sleep."

So we loaded their trunks into my wagon and I got Grandpa Jones to use his carriage to carry the people to the new hotel. I mentioned to Mr. Jones that we would soon need someone to start a business to carry people back and forth from the train to the hotel and hospital. He nodded his agreement.

"I know just the person to do it!" he exclaimed. "I'll start training him right away."

I knew he was thinking of the oldest Slater boy. He was getting old enough to do something like that. It could end up being a good business for him. He might be able to employ his brother later on. It sure looked like Micah was going to end up being a preacher, but he might work with his brother for a while.

We soon had every one of those Indians working on the hospital, plus every man who could possibly get free from the land. It was harvest time and they had to bring in the hay. Soon, men started coming from other towns looking for work. We hired them all because I realized that we needed a barn and a carriage house for that hotel as well as the hospital. One man brought a wagon and set up a little restaurant right by the construction site. He had a booming business right away. The lady who had the restaurant in town didn't even mind because she was overwhelmed. We had planned to have a restaurant in the hotel, so we invited the man with the food wagon to help us get it up and running.

When we went home at night, My Lady and I would fall into each other's arms, exhausted but happy. But underneath our happiness there was always that sense of dread of what we knew was coming.

Jimmy was doing a great job with the gold mine. We all kept praying that there would be enough to finish all our buildings and get the hospital operating. Dr. Joe was buying the supplies that we needed back East. It seemed that every train brought either more supplies or new people to our town. We had insufficient housing, so people were living in wagons and tents. I had to get a crew of men started building houses as fast as possible. Winter was coming soon.

I was so busy that I forgot about my birthday and our anniversary until one day, Grandpa Jones came to the building site and said I was needed at home. I got really concerned.

"What's wrong?" I asked.

"I don't know," he answered. "Your wife asked me to bring you out to the ranch."

When we arrived, I saw a crowd, so I hurried into the dining room to see what was going on. I was greeted by a crowd singing "Happy Birthday". I was confused for a minute. Caroline came over and gave me a hug.

"Did you forget it was your birthday?" she asked.

"Yes," I said. "And worse than that, I forgot our anniversary."

"Well, I didn't forget and I have a surprise for you."

She showed me an amazing machine called a lawn mower. I had to go try it out. It made the grass beautiful and it was much easier than using a scythe.

"This will be a great addition to the hotel!"

"No, I bought this for you," my wife insisted, "to make your work easier. But I do happen to have a few extra ones."

"You do?"

Mr. Stone started to laugh.

"Remember all those boxes you helped me unload at the train station?" he asked. "Most of those are lawn mowers that need to be assembled. I brought them here for your wife. I guess she's going to start someone in business."

I was staring at my wife in amazement. Just then, Zed Black's younger brother walked up.

"This is the young man who assembled that lawn mower for you," my wife said as she put a hand on his arm.

"Well, thank you," I said as I shook his hand.

"He's going to start a business here in town. His sister is going to be the bookkeeper and I am the first investor," my wife explained with a smile. "Mr. Jones has agreed to teach them how to do it."

"We're going to call it 'The Lawn Mower Shop,' but we'll sell other things, too. Mr. Jones is going to take me on my first trip back East to buy supplies. Then I'll be on my own."

"Well, you'd better stock up while you can before a war puts an end to our trips back East," I said.

"Good advice," Mr. Jones muttered.

My comment put a damper on our spirits for a little while, but it wasn't long before we all shook it off and were back to our jovial mood. Every man there had to try out my lawn mower. Before the day was over, we had doubled the size of our lawn.

CHAPTER 52

Her View

Well, we did finish the hospital and the hotel and all the other buildings up on Hospital Road. We even built a place for the Blacks to have their hardware store. And we helped Dr. Joe and Amy get their nursing school built and operating right beside the hospital. It took the better part of two years to get it all done. When it was finished, John and I were hoping to be able to relax and enjoy our home and family. Jennie had a newborn baby girl named Flora Mae McLane and my two weren't babies anymore. I didn't want John to be so busy that he missed their childhood.

The Stones had moved in and became a part of our community. They emancipated their housekeeper and she also became a part of our community. She rented a small house and members of her family began to appear. We didn't know how they knew or where they came from and we asked no questions. She told me that they were her children who had been sold at the same time she was sold to the Stones. I saw their joy mingled with fear, and determined to defend their right to be free. John found jobs for them and squelched any complaints that arose.

"We have plenty of work here for everyone," was his constant reply, and it was true.

Our two towns were soon one town just as I had predicted. We were growing by leaps and bounds and everyone was busy. John and I were constantly trying to give our jobs to others so we could stay at home more. But invariably new needs would arise that kept us busy. But we finally did manage to stay home more and I really enjoyed living on the McLane ranch. John even found time to ride with his men and supervise his ranch. But he continued to insist that everyone was armed at all times.

The negro lady who was helping slaves to escape still came through once in a while. I was pretty sure that she was the one who was bringing Millie's children back to her, but I never asked any questions.

Then one day, John came back from the state legislature and just stood in the kitchen and stared at me.

"What is it, John?" I finally asked.

"We are at war!"

His words shook me and I had to take hold of the sink to steady myself.

"I've got to go warn the whole town," he continued.

"Can't you send the young men?" I asked.

"No, I've got to go myself and I want you and the children to go with me."

So we all went to town and most of our men came with us. We ended up sending them out and calling everyone to the church. It was a sad meeting and we did a lot of praying and encouraging each other. The hospital was well supplied and ready but we didn't want to think about what was coming.

After about a month, Jimmy and Jennie Lu appeared at our door. That wasn't unusual, but Jennie Lu had obviously been crying. Her eyes were red and swollen.

"What's wrong?" I asked immediately.

She couldn't answer.

"Is the baby all right?" I asked as I looked inside the blanket Jennie was holding.

"The baby is fine!" Jimmy answered. "The problem is me. Let's all sit down together so I can explain."

Jimmy told us that he felt he had to go fight in this war. He felt it was his calling. We were all stunned into silence.

"And I don't think I will come back," he continued, "so I want you, John, to promise me that you will care for my daughter as though she were your own. I've been praying about this and I feel I have to lay down my life to save the rest of the family. And I want my wife and daughter to move back over here until the war is over. Then she can do as she pleases."

Then he turned to me and said that the gold mine was just about finished.

"That was my other calling that I have fulfilled," he said. "Now I have to go on to the next and last chapter of my life."

By this time, we were all in tears. I put my arms around Jennie Lu and cried with her. John put his arms around Jimmy and sobbed.

Before it was over, several other young men from our community had joined Jimmy. One being Zed Black. We had a dinner for them at the church and a time of prayer before they left. Two of Lillie's sons were among them. Jennie Lu was barely holding herself together. She followed Jimmy right to his horse before he left. He held her and the baby one more time. Then he looked at John and me for help. We both went over and steered Jennie Lu away. He jumped on his horse and began to gallop away. Jennie Lu kept looking back until he was out of sight. We got her into our carriage and started for home. She was trembling and crying all the way home. She sat in my rocking chair and fed her baby when we got home. I had her old room ready for her.

The next morning when she came down for breakfast, she seemed to be her old self again.

"Well, here I am again," she said, "right back where I started. It seems like history is repeating itself. But it isn't as bad for me as it was for you. So maybe it will be even better for my daughter."

"Let's hope and believe that," I said. "Let's pray and ask God to lift this curse off of our descendants."

Jennie Lu managed to keep working at the clinic because she could leave her baby in Amy's house and not be far away. Amy spent more time at the hospital. They were both training other girls constantly. Dr. Joe had managed to bring several young medical students our way when they graduated back East so they were helping him in both the hospital and the clinic.

When Jennie Lu was ready, we took a wagon over to the Stone Place and helped her move back over to the McLane House. It actually took two wagons even though she didn't move much furniture. Just a few things she couldn't part with, like the cute little bed Jimmy had made for Flora Mae. He also had made her a high chair to sit up to the table when she is older. He had carved his name on the bottom of the seat with the words "I love you".

"It's a relief to get out of that house," Jennie said on the way back. "I hope I never have to go back there."

"It's strange, but I felt the same way when we left there," I said. "I thought it was just because of my bad memories there. It's such a beautiful house! I don't know why I feel so uneasy there."

"I guess I wasted a lot of time and effort on that place," John added. "No one wants to live there. Maybe it's haunted or something."

We all laughed but not very heartily because we weren't sure that it wasn't true.

CHAPTER 53
His View

When I heard that a large group of soldiers were headed our way, my heart just about stopped. I rode out to get a good look from a distance. I wanted to make sure they were from the North, not the South. It was obvious that they were wearing northern uniforms but I kept watching because something didn't seem right. As they got closer, I realized what it was. They were all Negros. When they came where I was, I was shocked to see that Zach was their leader. When he saw me, he dismounted and came toward me with his hand extended. I gave him a bear hug.

"Man, it is so good to see you!" I exclaimed. "How have you been? Did you ever find your mother?"

"Yes, I found her and spent some time with her before she died. Now I'm planning to invade the South before I die."

"Well, if you need a place to stay, the Stone Place is empty right now and you're welcome to take your whole company there."

"Thank you, Mr. McLane. I will do that, but I want to greet your wife and thank her once more for all she did for me."

"Well, come right this way. She's in that house you can see in the distance."

"Yes, I remember the McLane house."

My Lady was so happy to see Zach that she cried. He shed a few tears himself. They hugged and cried and talked for about an hour. Then he said he had to get back to his company. They would head for the Stone Place tonight.

"We plan to invade the South and I don't know if I'll ever see you again. But thanks to you, I know I'm ready for Heaven and so are all the men in my company. We pray and sing and read the Bible every night."

My Lady couldn't say a word. She just nodded.

I rode back with Zach and promised that if we heard guns at the Stone Place, we would come to back him up. He thanked me.

It was the next day that I began to hear gunfire. I called all our hands in and told them we were heading over to help. I told My Lady to head for town with the children and stay at Amy's house until she heard from me.

"We will defend this town to the last man," I promised. She put a few things in the carriage and started toward town.

By the time we got there, the battle was in full swing. It was obvious that a company had come up from the South, intending to wipe us out at the Stone Place and were surprised to find a company of Union soldiers there to defend it. When we arrived, the barn had been burnt down and the battle was raging around the house. There were dead bodies lying everywhere. When we joined the battle, we began to turn the tide in favor of the North. We used my stone walls as cover as we closed in on the house. Then a bunch of men rode over the hill with Mr. Tate as their leader. The South was now beginning to retreat. They were being blasted from three sides and their escape would soon be cut off. Some small groups had already surrendered. Many of them were wounded but others were still fighting as they moved out. They had the few men left in Zach's company right on their heels. It was a bloody mess. While I could still hear gunfire in the distance, I began to load up our wagons with the wounded and send them off to the hospital. I made no distinction between the North or the South.

"Once they're wounded, it makes no difference," I told the drivers. "They're all human beings for whom Christ died. Just get them to the hospital and see if we can save some lives."

We started stacking the dead bodies over behind where the barn had been.

"We can make a cemetery here," I said.

Among the dead, I found our friend Zacharias. I wept for him as I continued to work. Then I found his father's body also. Mr. Tate was wounded, but I thought he would survive. He told me to get his wagons and use them to carry the wounded so I did. His place was the closest to us. I asked him to tell my wife that I was unharmed when he got to the hospital. He had to have a bullet removed from his leg.

Two of my crew were missing and presumed dead. The rest were busy driving wagons filled with the wounded to the hospital. The inside of the Stone Place was a bloody mess. Most of the windows were broken and a lot of my stone work was severely damaged. The men who weren't driving wagons got busy digging graves. I told them to search each body for some identification that we could give to their family. I put the ones from the South in one box and those from the North in another. I kept all those from Zach's company separate.

After we had worked for two days trying to clean up the mess and bury the dead, some ladies from town brought us some food. That was a welcome relief.

CHAPTER 54
Her View

The war was a terrible time. I had to spend a lot of time in town because John didn't want us alone at the ranch. He was afraid of another attack like the one on the Stone Place. I almost lived in my mother's dress shop. Amy wanted us to stay with her and I did visit her a lot but I wanted my own place and the dress shop worked well.

Whenever there was a new wave of patients coming into the hospital, I would take care of Flora Mae and Amy's children right along with my own. Soon some of the other nurses began to bring me their children also. Then Grandma Jones would come and help me. It kept me busy so I couldn't worry or feel sorry for myself. While I cared for the children, I was constantly praying. Some nights, John would come and take me home. When that happened, Grandma Jones would care for any children whose mothers were working and had no one to care for their children. I soon began to realize that there would always be a need for childcare even when the war was over. So I began to look for the right person to train for that job. Finally one of the girls who came from the school to work in the dress shop asked if she could help with the children after school and on the weekends. She did so well that I was sure she was the one. So I began to train her. I also talked John into fencing the yard behind the dress shop so the children could play outside.

But then one of the new houses up by the hospital became available and I bought it so we could use it for our childcare program. When Hilda finished school, I started turning more of the work over to her and I started charging so she would have an income. Her mother was helping her so I could get away and spend time in the dress shop. Hilda's father had gone to fight in the war so her mother was alone.

I supervised the childcare program and I taught some of the students to sew in my dress shop and I went over to the other side of town every week for our ladies meeting. We prayed for the war to end. We all had someone we loved out there somewhere. So we tried to encourage and comfort each other.

I stayed very busy but I still missed my home. John had to spend time at the state legislature and I missed him when he was gone. I looked forward to the times he would come for me and we would spend a few days at the McLane House.

When news from the war came to us or new patients were brought into the hospital, I would get so upset I would walk the floor and pray for hours. I felt like I should be doing something but I didn't know what to do. One day, I left my children with Hilda and went to the hospital looking for Jennie Lu. As I walked through the halls, I saw people in beds lining the halls because there were no rooms available. Many of them were obviously in terrible pain. I couldn't help myself. I had to pray for them. When I put my hand on them, many of them would take hold of my hand and hang on with all their strength. Some kissed my hand and whispered, "Thank you". It seemed they were getting some relief, so I went through the halls praying for everyone. Then I started visiting the rooms and praying for them also. By the time I had finished the ground floor, I felt like I was floating, I was so happy. I had forgotten completely about looking for my daughter. But when I attempted to go up to the second floor, I was arrested by the guard. He took me to a small room in the cellar and locked me in there. I told him to find Jennie Lucinda Stone or Dr. Joe Slape. They would vouch for me.

When several hours had passed, I began to get concerned. I began to pray that God would send someone into the cellar. Finally, I heard a noise like someone was getting supplies, so I began to pound on the door and yell "Help!" at the top of my voice. I heard the person running up the stairs.

"I guess I scared that one away," I muttered.

But soon I heard more footsteps. I banged on the door again. This time I heard a key being put in the lock. The door was opened by a guard. This one was a young man from the school who recognized me.

"Mrs. McLane!" he exclaimed. "What are you doing down here?"

When I told him my story, he was shocked.

"He just left you down here? Let's go see my boss and tell him about this."

So I went with him, but I was anxious to go see my children and take them home with me. I felt uneasy.

When I walked into that office, the man behind the desk jumped to his feet and offered me his chair.

"Mrs. McLane!" he exclaimed. "What brings you to my office?"

When I told him the whole story, he turned pale.

"I heard that some of the patients were asking for the Angel Lady," he mused. "They must have been talking about you. But I can't imagine who would have dared to arrest you."

"I didn't know him," I responded. "But now I need to go get my children and make sure they're all right. This whole thing has made me very uneasy."

"I can understand that, Mrs. McLane. I will personally escort you to your children and make sure they're safe. And I will get to the bottom of this. I will call all the guards in tomorrow if you will come back and identify the one who did this to you."

"I will come if John will come with me."

As Mr. Wright was escorting me out the door of the hospital, John came striding up.

"Caroline! Where have you been?" he exclaimed. "Your daughter and I have been looking all over this town for you!"

I burst into tears when I saw John. I ran to him and couldn't even talk for several minutes. Mr. Wright had to tell my story for me.

"I'm going to kill somebody!" John exploded as he held me closer. "I'm going to kill somebody! I thought you would be safer in town, and this happened right in the hospital that you built!"

"You know, John, a few hours ago, one of our guards came to me and resigned. He said he was going home. He was the only one that wasn't a local boy. And he did a strange thing. He brought me a box of ammunition from that basement room where we store it. He said he wanted to save me a trip down there. I just realized that room is where your wife was imprisoned."

"That was him," I exclaimed. "He picked up that box and just looked at me for a few minutes. Then he turned and went out and locked the door."

"John, it could have been a long time before anyone found her. I don't know why that girl went down there. There's nothing down there but ammunition that we stored up in case of an emergency."

"Give me a young man and we'll go after him before he gets too far away," John said. "You go stay in your townhouse with Jennie Lu until I get back," he said, turning to me.

"If she feels the need to pray for the patients, will you supply her an escort?" he asked Mr. Wright.

"Of course. They've been asking for the 'Angel Lady.' I thought maybe an angel had come down and then disappeared."

CHAPTER 55
His View

Robert Wright showed me the direction that young man traveled as he left. He had watched him from his office window. So it didn't take us long to pick up his trail. He wasn't making any effort to hide it.

"He's very sure of himself," I said to the young man who was helping me. I had brought him along to make a positive identification when I caught up with our suspect.

By nightfall we had caught up with the young man. He had stopped early which was really strange. He didn't act like he was running.

"Are you sure?" I asked my young helper when he had identified the boy.

He was sure but I was puzzled by this young man's behavior. He was sitting by his fire, holding his head in his hands and rocking back and forth. So we moved close enough to hear him after we'd tied our horses at a distance.

"Oh God! Oh God!" he was moaning over and over again. "I'll go back in the morning and tell them where she is," he finally said. "I know she's a good woman. I saw her praying for all those wounded people. She didn't care if they were from the North or the South."

Then he went back to rocking and moaning. And I was left in a quandary. Should I go in and arrest him or wait and see if he'd actually do what he was saying? I decided to wait and see. We went back to where our horses were and spent the night.

At dawn, we heard him begin to move and sure enough, he was headed back the way he came. So we followed at a distance.

He headed straight for the hospital. When he entered Mr. Wright's office, I was waiting in a side room. Robert just looked at him and didn't say a word.

"I came back to tell you that Mrs. McLane is locked in the ammo room in the cellar," he blurted out.

"Why did you do that?" Robert asked in a calm voice.

"I thought I had to avenge my father. He said she made a fool out of him and he came to pay her back and died here."

"What changed your mind?" Robert asked again.

"I saw her praying for all those wounded soldiers and I knew she was a good woman and my father was a wicked man. I had such a guilty conscience that I thought I would go crazy last night. I guess God was after me."

"Well, James, I'm glad you have repented," Robert said.

"Aren't you going to go get her out?" he asked. Just then, I came through the door.

"She's already out, and you are lucky to be alive. I followed you yesterday, intending to kill you, but I heard you praying, so I followed you back here to see if you were sincere. My Lady is back in the hospital praying for people. I'll take you to jail now. You are charged with attempted murder."

"Yes, I am guilty," was all he said.

So I took him to jail and went looking for My Lady. I found her walking from the hospital to her town house where the children were. When she got into the carriage, she leaned against me. I could tell she was very tired.

"Let's get the children and go out to the McLane House," I suggested. She just nodded.

When we were resting in front of the fireplace that evening, I told her the whole story of the young man who had tried to kill her. She listened without saying a word. As we watched our children playing on the floor before us, we were overcome by a tremendous gratitude for our blessings. People were dying all around us and we didn't know what the next day would bring, but we were so grateful for this time right now.

CHAPTER 56
Her View

It felt like Heaven to be back at the McLane House. I rested a lot. Jerry insisted we have our suppers with him and the hands. I didn't argue because I was very tired. But I couldn't help but think about the people at the hospital. I prayed for them but I knew they needed to hear my voice and feel my touch. But I also knew that it was too much for me. I was neglecting my own children. It brought tears to my eyes to see how excited they were to have my undivided attention for these few days. Every few minutes, they would call me to come see what they were doing. We went for long walks all over the ranch. Sometimes John was with us. In the evenings when we were alone, I shared my feelings with John.

"Why don't you ask the women in your Bible Study to help you pray for the people in the hospital?" he suggested. "Once they get comfortable with it, they can do it on their own and free you up some."

"Of course!" I exclaimed. "Why didn't I think of that? I've been trying to do too much on my own. There are lots of other good Christians. God hears their prayers as much as mine."

"And," John continued, "if you would have had another person with you, that young man couldn't have locked you in the cellar so easily."

I thought about that for a while and didn't say anything. Something was stirring in me about that young man. I knew I had to visit him when I went back to town. But for right now, I just wanted to relax and enjoy my family.

When we went to church on Sunday, I was prepared to stay in town because John had a meeting on Monday, then he was heading off for the legislature. I knew he also was very tired. This war was exhausting. We never talked about it, but we were all constantly concerned about Jimmy. We hadn't heard one word since he left us.

On Monday, I went to visit the young man named James. He was shocked to see me and began to apologize for what he'd done. I told him I forgave him and began to ask questions about his life. I learned that he was the only son of his mother who was now alone on a huge plantation south of us. I could tell he was very concerned about her.

"I don't know what she will do when this war is over. I know the South is going to lose and all the slaves will be set free and then what? How will they live? And how will she live? She can't run that plantation by herself, and she can't pay all those slaves to work for her. I know she would like to get away from there, but she has nowhere to go and now I've got myself in a mess and I can't help her."

I listened to him talk for a while and then before I left, I suggested that we pray together for his mother. After we finished praying, I left and went to my ladies' meeting at the Tateville Church. We still called it that because it was on Tateville Ave. All the ladies agreed to help me with the visitation in the hospital. We agreed to go in teams of at least two people since the Bible says that two are more powerful than one. I took them all over to the hospital and started training them. They all stayed with me that first day. So we only got one floor done.

"Do you want to come back tomorrow and try to work in teams of two and do the second floor?" I asked. They all agreed. That would mean another day out of the dress shop but I thought it was important to move on before the ladies lost their nerve. So I stopped by the school to tell the teacher I wouldn't be in the dress shop tomorrow but I planned to be there Wednesday and Thursday for the students who were working with me.

It turned out that with the ladies' help, I got out of the hospital early enough that I could have done the dress shop. But since I had already canceled it, I collected a few things and headed for the jail. I took that young man a Bible and some paper and a pen and ink as well as some extra food.

"Why are you so kind to me?" he asked in amazement.

"I don't know," I responded. "Why don't you write your mother a letter and I'll try to get it delivered. She must be very worried about you!"

He just nodded.

When I left the jail, I headed back to the hospital. I knew there was a man who would be leaving soon and he planned to head South. After I'd talked to him, he agreed to deliver the letter to James's mother. So I felt relieved and free to go get my children and take them to the dress shop. I took them to the restaurant for supper and then we had a quiet evening together. The next two days, I was busy in the shop. I was giving sewing lessons as well as teaching the girls how to run a business.

"How would you like to start making hats?" I asked.

They were all excited to learn something new. I had found a trunk in the attic full of my mother's supplies for making hats. Since we couldn't get anything from the East because of the war, I knew these hats would be in great demand. I would like a new hat myself.

Friday morning, I took the children to the townhouse and headed for the hospital. Sure enough, that man was ready to leave. He followed me to the jail to get the letter. He had a long talk with James. I stayed in my carriage. When he came out, he said he would have no trouble delivering that letter. He knew exactly where the place was and would go right by it on his way home.

"Tell his mother that his trial will be at the end of this month and I'm going to do my best to get him released. Ask her to pray."

"I'll tell her," he said as he tipped his hat. "And thank you so much for all you've done for me."

"You're welcome. I pray you find your family all doing well."

I watched him as he walked with a limp to his wagon. He would never be the man he used to be but at least he was alive and able to function.

When I got back to my children, John was there waiting for me.

"Let's go home," he said.

I didn't dare tell John what I was thinking about James. I knew it would cause a big fight. John wanted that boy to suffer for what he'd done. But I felt that a month in our jail was enough. I wanted to send him home to his mother.

Things were beginning to calm down in our hospital because most of the war was in the East. Some of our doctors wanted to go help the troops in the battle areas, so we outfitted their wagons with supplies and sent them off with our blessings. It was an emotional send off to say the least. Jennie Lu couldn't even force herself to be present. We never talked about Jimmy but he was never far from all of our minds.

Since the hospital wasn't so crowded anymore, they decided to move the childcare program into the ground floor of the hospital. Most of the children belonged to the nurses so it would be more convenient for them to be able to visit their children during the day. And the young woman who was in charge of childcare would be able to get some nurses' training. Her mother was helping with the children. So that left my townhouse empty. While I was deciding what to do with it, I got a visit from Jennie Lu.

"Mother," she said, "I'd like to rent your townhouse. I'd like to stay in town more so I would be closer to my work. It's not that I don't like being out in the country. I'll come out to visit, but I want to live in town."

I just looked at her for a while. I realized that my daughter was all grown up and had her own life to live. It could be a lot worse. She could be getting in a wagon and heading West where I would never see her again.

"You can have it," I finally said. "You don't have to pay rent."

"No, I want to start making it on my own."

"Well, would you like to buy it?"

"Yes!"

So we went to the bank and got it all written up properly. Jennie was very excited to own her own home. She had never felt that the Stone Place was truly hers. I didn't say it but I could tell that Jennie was believing that Jimmy was not coming back. She was starting to move forward on her own.

"Now I won't have to spend so much time at Amy's place!" Jennie said. "Her children are growing and she needs all her space."

We moved Jennie's clothes from the McLane House to town. Then when John came back, we made a trip to the Stone Place to see what furniture could be salvaged from there. We ended up furnishing her house pretty well. Then Amy had a housewarming for her and she received gifts from all the nurses and many other friends as well.

"I can tell you're very loved in this town," I said to her when it was over.

She hugged me and cried a little.

"We've come a long ways," she said. "By God's Grace, we've come a long ways."

When Jennie was settled in town, John and I discussed the Stone Place.

"I don't want it to just sit there and be wasted, but I don't want to live there. You did a beautiful job on that house but I can't feel at home there. And now with blood stains on the kitchen floor, I'm really uncomfortable. Especially since I know that Zacharias and his father died right there."

"How do you know that?"

"Those soldiers that fought there told me the whole story."

"Well, tell it to me. I haven't heard it."

James told me that his father was using the war as an excuse to get even with me for making a fool out of him over Zacharias. So he got a whole bunch of men together to come and kill us at the Stone House. But when he got there and burnt our barn down, he was surprised to find a whole company of Negro soldiers there. During a lull in the fighting, he marched right up to the house, calling Zacharias's name. So they let him in the house. Zach lowered his gun out of respect for his father and when he did, his father shot him and yelled at him, "You ain't nothin' but a nigger."

Then he turned to the other men and told them to put their guns down. But they all shot him. They said he acted surprised like he actually thought those men would obey him. He thought they still had a slave mentality, I guess. So Zacharias and his father died right beside each other on my kitchen floor. But the other men said that

Zach died with a smile on his face and his father looked terrified and was saying, "Fire, fire, I see the fire!"

"Well, I can see why you don't want to live there," John said. "Why don't we make it into a Civil War Memorial. Old Man Tate could move his historical records over there. We could have someone write the history of every one of the original families and put it all in there. Then we could clean up the fire damage and make a park there with picnic tables and a playground for the children."

"That sounds like an excellent idea to me, especially since we already have that big cemetery there. Everyone in town could help and it would help us all get over this war."

"You're talking like the war is over."

"I feel like it's over. Maybe because all the fighting is in the East now. But it's been five long years and we've suffered long enough. Lord, let it be over!" I exclaimed.

"Amen," John echoed my heart's cry.

The next day, we saw a rider coming from town, waving a paper in the air. He rode into our yard shouting "General Lee has surrendered! General Lee has surrendered! It's over! It's over! It's over! Big celebration in town tonight. Meet at the church!"

I began to laugh and cry at the same time. John grabbed me and we danced all over our yard just like we did after our wedding. He sent Jerry out to call all the hands in from the fields. They left the wagons sitting out in the fields and headed in to get cleaned up.

"No more work today," John announced. "We're all headed for town to celebrate."

We all got dressed in our Sunday best and Jerry loaded all the food he was fixing for supper into the wagon and added lots of extras.

John and I took the carriage. Most of the hands just rode their horses.

When we got to the church, everyone was there. Jennie came running to greet us. She had got Big Guy and Baby Girl out of school so they were with her. We all went into the church and fell on our knees to thank God. You could hear sobbing everywhere. Finally the pastor asked us all to stand up and sing the Doxology. Then he led us in prayer for the families who had lost their loved ones in the war. He also asked God to heal our country. There was more sobbing.

"Now it's time to start rejoicing," he said. "No more crying. Let's rejoice that it's over."

So we did, even though we didn't know who had died and who was coming home. We had a big community supper and I insisted that we take food to the jail. John went with me but he stayed in the carriage. We also made a Welcome Home banner to fly whenever our boys would be coming home. We asked the man who ran the depot to let us know if any of our boys were coming home.

John talked to the whole community about the Stone Place. Everyone was excited to make a historical Museum there and especially to make a memorial to the Civil War.

We soon received notice that a wounded soldier was coming home. So we took our banner to the train station and waited. We saw a man slowly getting off the train. He was using a cane but still had trouble walking. I couldn't recognize him at first but when he came near, I realized it was Zed Black. His mother ran to meet him. She was trying to be brave. So were we all.

He finally silenced us all and spoke very slowly.

"I'm sorry to tell you all that Jimmy McLane and my younger brother both died at Gettysburg. They are buried there. This wounded leg is the only reason I'm alive. There are a few others coming back on horseback. I couldn't do that. I'm afraid my days of riding horses are over forever," he said, turning toward John. John put his arms around him and wept.

"I'm so glad you're here," he said between sobs.

Dr. Joe came forward then and led Zed to his carriage.

"I want to have a look at that leg," he said. "The sooner the better."

Zed stopped and looked around.

"Where's my mother?" he said.

She came out of the crowd, softly weeping. Zed put his arms around her. The rest of her children stood at a distance. He motioned them to come near.

"We'll go on together now," he said. "We lost one but we can go on together. We'll never forget him, but we'll go on. We'll run that store together. It'll be a family store. We'll see him again. He was praying when he died. Now I have to let this doctor see if he can help my leg, but I'll be home soon and I won't be leaving again. I'm going to take care of you," he said, turning to his mother, "for the rest of your life."

He had to have help getting into the doctor's carriage, but he was soon giving everyone a big smile and a wave. After he was gone, we all tried to comfort his family.

"I'm so grateful to have him back with us," his mother kept repeating as she wept.

Dr. Joe told us later that Zed had a broken leg that had never been set properly. He was able to fix it so that Zed would have less of a limp once it healed, but it would take a while to heal. He put a cast on it so he could walk once the pain subsided. But he had to stay in the hospital for a while. Dr. Joe had removed bone fragments and had to re-break the bone to straighten it out.

"He'll be better eventually but right now, he's in a lot of pain," Dr. Joe explained. "His mother is staying right by his side to keep him from trying to get up too soon. So I think he'll be all right."

"Shall we visit him?" I asked.

"I'd wait for at least a week, maybe two. He's nearly out of his mind right now. Sometimes he thinks he's back in the war and wants to go fight. The only thing that calms him down is the sight of his mother and the sound of her voice. I'm sure glad she's staying right with him. Of course, it doesn't help that we keep giving him whiskey to dull his pain. It dulls the pain but doesn't help his mental condition."

"Well, I hope you don't make a drunk out of him."

"We'll stop the whiskey in a few days. So don't worry. Fortunately, I still had some anesthetic in the hospital that I could use for the surgery. It's been impossible to replenish my supplies because of the war."

I was surprised at how calmly Jennie received the news about Jimmy. When I mentioned it to her, she just sighed.

"I guess I've done all my grieving already. I knew he wasn't coming back. He said so—remember?"

"Yes, I remember. Do you think we should go pray for Zed Black? Dr. Joe said to wait a week or two but I'm wondering if his mother needs our help."

"I'll drop by their room when I'm at work and I'll let you know what I think."

The next day, Jennie let me know that Zed's mother would really appreciate our help. So we set a time to go there together. We prayed for an hour and when we left. Zed was completely sober and his pain was diminished. Dr. Joe had him tied to the foot and the head of the bed so he couldn't move that leg. He said there was a whole segment of the bone missing and he was hoping that it would fill in some if they kept it stretched out.

"They wanted to amputate my leg," Zed explained to us, "but I fought them. I said, 'No, let me go home. Dr. Joe will save my leg.' But I've suffered so much, I'm wondering if I should have let them cut it off."

So I kept busy visiting the hospital and the jail until the day of the trial finally arrived. When James plead guilty to the charge of attempted murder, the judge turned to me and asked what sentence I felt should be imposed. When I started to ask for a pardon, John was indignant. He kept interrupting me and insisting on justice.

"John, am I going to have to charge you with contempt of court?" the judge finally asked. "Let the Lady speak!"

SO I told the reason that I believed that James had repented and would be a solid citizen. I also explained that he was needed by his mother. Then the judge asked John to give his arguments.

The judge surprised us both by coming up with a compromise.

"James Richards, you will work for John McLane for one year with no pay but room and board. If you do well, you will be pardoned and free. If you run away or give him any trouble, you will face a five year sentence in prison. Do you understand?"

"Yes, sir. Thank you very much," James said, but he looked at John with questioning eyes.

John just stared at the judge for a full minute.

"Do you accept this responsibility?"

John glanced at me and I saw him softening.

"I guess I can handle it," he finally responded. "But I'm not excited about taking a murderer onto my ranch."

"If in the future you feel that he is a danger in any way, you may return him to jail," the judge replied.

John just nodded.

I was already thinking of a way to get another letter off to his mother. My heart was stirred for her.

CHAPTER 57
His View

I had resigned from all my political activities so it wasn't hard for me to keep an eye on James. It didn't even take him a month to win me over. He was a hard worker and got along well with the other hands. I could see that his experience on his father's plantation was very valuable. I was soon thinking of ways to keep him around. The more we talked, the more I shared his concern for his mother. I suggested that we go get her and bring her back to McLane.

"That would be the best thing for her!" James exclaimed. "But what about all those slaves? She won't want to just walk away and leave them with no help. She really cares about them."

"Could you turn that plantation into a town?" I asked. "They could elect their own leaders and every family could have a small piece of land."

James started to get excited.

"Would you be willing to go there and teach them how to run a town?" he asked.

"I'll have to think about that," I responded. "How long would it take to get there?"

"About four days on horseback."

So I talked that over with My Lady that night. I said I'd probably be gone most of a month. We both hated to be apart that long. I had given up my political activities so I could be at home with my family. My children were growing up and I wanted to be there for them. But we kept coming back to the desperate situation of James's mother and finally agreed that we had to do what was in our power to do.

"We can't rescue everyone, but we can do something for this one woman and the people on her plantation," Caroline said. "We have to do what is set before us."

So we agreed to do it and I started making plans with James. I could tell he was very excited and very anxious to get on with it. He was very concerned for his mother. On the way, I learned many details of his life with his father. He confided to me that many of the slaves on his plantation were his half brothers and sisters.

"I guess they have as much right to that land as I do," he said as we traveled. I didn't say too much. I just let him talk and I listened. I realized that he had issues to deal with that I had never even thought about. One thing I knew for sure, his father's death had set him free to become his own man. And I was amazed that he was becoming such a good man. I said as much to him.

"Your wife changed the direction of my life and set me free from my father's influence. I saw the difference between a fake Christian and a real Christian. I decided I wanted to be real and I started to pray with her and God changed my heart. Now I want to see everyone at home set free also."

When we arrived at his home, I was astounded at what I saw. There was a huge mansion surrounded by miles and miles of fields. In the distance I could see rows of little cottages. Some could better be described as shacks. James was terrified when he discovered that the mansion was empty. There was no sign of his mother. He checked all the outbuildings. There was still no sign of her. We headed for the little shacks. People began to come out of them and stand in little clusters as we approached. The men in the fields left their work and began to head our direction. Everyone was very quiet and serious. They all gathered around us and blocked our way.

"Where is my mother?" James finally asked.

"Jimmy! Jimmy! Is it really you?" a quiet feminine voice sounded from one of the shacks. The crowd parted as a blur of blue flew by me and into the arms of James.

"I got a letter saying you had to wait a year," she sobbed.

James explained the whole situation to his mother and everyone else. Then his mother fell right at my feet, sobbing out her thanks. I raised her up and gave her a hug before returning her to her son.

"I'd like to meet with everyone tonight at the big house right after supper," James announced. "Then I will explain everything."

When we got back to the mansion, James asked his mother why she was hiding in the slave shacks.

"I'm hiding from Jack Suit," she explained. "When he heard that your father was dead and you had left to avenge his death, he came here to take over this plantation. He said if I didn't agree, he would take me by force and make me his slave, just like the rest of the slaves. He gave me a month to make up my mind. Our people were hiding me."

"Jack Suit owns a smaller plantation next to ours," James explained. "He's always been jealous of what we had."

"Haven't you heard that the South lost the war?" I asked Mrs. Richards.

"I've heard rumors, but Mr. Suit says it doesn't make any difference. If he has to pay his slaves, he'll get it back by charging them for their food."

"Well, we have a different plan than that," James said, and he explained it all to his mother. She listened intently to the whole plan before she spoke.

"So in the end, you and I would leave here and start a new life in McLane," she summarized.

"Yes, if you're willing to give up this plantation."

"I'm more than willing if I can feel that the people are well cared for. I don't want to leave and let Jack Suit take advantage of them."

We discussed the issue of individual versus community ownership of the land.

"I think we'd better subdivide the land," James finally concluded. "If it's community owned, the people in government will have too much power and they will end up right back where they started, in slavery. If everyone owns their own land, this place won't be so beautiful, but the people will be free."

"What's more important—the land or the people?" I asked.

At the meeting that evening, I got a clearer picture of what James was trying to do and how difficult it was going to be. There was no way he could accomplish it in one month. These people could not even comprehend what we were talking about. They had no concept of freedom. They didn't want to be slaves, but they were afraid to be free. They wanted James to make all decisions for them.

The next morning, I had a talk with James. I suggested that I teach him how to run a town, then he could appoint all the people that he felt were the most capable and slowly teach them how to do their jobs until he could slowly work himself out.

"It will probably take at least a year," I said.

"But the judge said I had to work for you for a year."

"You'll be working for me here. And when you finally make it back to McLane, I'll have a job for you—a paying job."

James gave a big sigh.

"I guess you're right," he said. "The only thing we accomplished in that meeting was agreeing on a name for the town."

"What name did they agree on?" his mother asked. "I never did hear what it was. I was too busy in the kitchen."

"Richards Plantation!" James said.

"I think the first thing you need to do is establish a police force. Things could get very dangerous around here," I said. "Do you have any guns?"

"My father had an arsenal in the cellar of this house," James responded. "I shouldn't have any trouble unless they've been stolen."

We went immediately to the cellar and found the guns and ammunition still there. James chose ten young men that he felt were reliable and I began to train them in the use of firearms. Mrs. Richards was given the job of producing some kind of uniforms for them. She enlisted the help of several of the women. I worked with the police during the day and in the evenings, I taught James about town government. He wrote everything down.

Mrs. Richards got inspired and started a school for the children and was training a young woman to take her place. They were using the old church building for the school and they were moving the church into the plantation house. I told them it was important that no one moved into that house when they left. It should become a community building. So they started using it that way right away. We made a small apartment for James and his mother in the back of the mansion. The huge living room was made into a meeting room for town meetings and church services. The people were shy at first, but they adjusted very quickly. James was training the spiritual leader of the people to be the first mayor.

At the end of two weeks, I had a good little police force in place and I could see the beginnings of a functioning town. James had a list of all the families and was beginning to divide the land between them. The change in the people was nothing short of miraculous. They were planning to build log cabins for themselves on their own land. James explained to the people that the money from the harvest this year would go into a fund to pay the policemen and get the town running, but next year they would all be harvesting their own fields and they would have to pay a tax into the town fund to pay the town expenses.

The day before I planned to leave, Mr. Suit appeared with five men. He was very arrogant and demanding, until he saw James and his police force.

"You are never to set foot on this property again," James said. "If you do, you will be shot."

Mr. Suit never said another word. He just turned his horse toward home.

The people began to laugh and sing and dance. It reminded me of the church service I'd been in on Sunday. The singing and dancing and rejoicing brought tears to my eyes. I kept thinking of Zach and wishing he could be here to see the liberation of his people. When I was asked to speak, I told them his story and the faith he had developed at our house. When I told about his death, there was a song of mourning sung for him. Then the pastor led the whole congregation in the salvation prayer he had prayed with my wife.

The people insisted that I stay for a farewell dinner. So I was delayed another day. The lady who had been Mrs. Richards's cook served the meal in the summer kitchen. She was planning to start a restaurant there. Her daughters helped her and they did an excellent job.

It was so exciting to see what was happening in Richards Plantation that I hated to leave. But I had to get home to my family.

"I'll be expecting to see you both in a year," I said to James and his mother. "May God bless you and keep you safe until then."

As soon as I got away from Richards Plantation, the pull of home was very strong. I kept prodding the horse to a faster pace and made it home in three days. I stopped in town to see Jennie Lu.

"Mother is at the McLane House," she said. "She hasn't been back in town since you left. One of the hands brings the children in for school. They say that Jerry is cooking for them. I'm glad you're back because I'm getting worried."

When I got home, My Lady was sitting on the couch in front of the fireplace.

"Come and sit by me, John," she said. "I've been waiting for you. Come tell me everything that happened."

I told her the whole story from beginning to end. She laid her head against my shoulder and laughed and cried through the whole thing.

"You're so good at rescuing women in distress, John. I'm so glad you let James stay there for a year with his mother. Together they'll accomplish great things."

"You're the one who did it. If I'd had my way, James would be in prison and his mother would be enslaved to that maniac neighbor of theirs."

"We've made a great team, haven't we, John?"

"Don't talk like it's in the past. You're scaring me."

"Well, John, I have something to tell you now."

She moved and showed me the pad she was sitting on. It was blood soaked.

"I've been bleeding for a while now and I think I don't have long for this world. I'm very sorry to leave you and our children, but I'm looking forward to Heaven."

"Let's get you into the hospital right now!" I exclaimed, jumping up and heading for the door.

"No, John, just sit here and hold me in your arms and tell me how much you love me. Then if I'm still here in the morning, I'll go to the hospital. But I don't think Joe can do anything about this."

"How long have you been bleeding?" I asked as I sat back down.

"It was starting a little bit before you left with James. I didn't tell you because I knew you wouldn't go and his mother would have no help. I feel like, sending you when I needed you was my last gift to the Lord."

I fell to my knees and started to pray. I was in an agony. I argued with God and begged Him to have mercy on me all at the same time. Soon the children came down from their rooms to see what was going on.

"Your mother is very sick," I explained. They prayed with me for a while, then fell asleep on the floor. I carried them back to their beds.

Big Guy woke up and insisted on walking.

"I'm ten years old. I can walk on my own," he insisted.

When I got back to My Lady, I did what she asked me to do. I held her in my arms and told her how much I loved her. She was as pale as a sheet.

"Without you, I'll be worthless again," I moaned.

"No, you won't. You've got two children and this whole town depending on you."

When she finally fell asleep, I just held her in my arms all night long. I wasn't about to let her slip away from me. When the rooster crowed, I woke the children and told them to get ready for school.

"You can eat breakfast in town!" I explained as I carried their mother to the carriage.

"Joe, you drive the horses," I commanded, "and don't be slow about it."

Jerry ran over to the carriage with a question in his eyes.

"Pray," was all I said. He stepped back as the carriage lurched forward.

Dr. Joe was still at home, so I stopped by his house. He took one look out the window and grabbed his coat and jumped in our carriage.

"What's wrong?"

"Bleeding—for nearly the whole month I was gone."

"Oh God! Have mercy!"

"Amen!"

After the surgery, Dr. Joe did not give us encouraging words.

"I don't think she'll make it, John," he said. "There's hardly any blood left in her body. I tried to repair the damage, but I doubt that it will work. She's just too far gone. I think she was just hanging on by sheer willpower until you got here."

Jennie Lu began to cry and blame herself.

"I should have gone out to check on her when she didn't come into town for so long."

"Let's not waste time blaming ourselves. Let's pray and see if God will give her back to us," I said.

So Jennie and I hit the floor on our knees beside her bed. We were both in agony of soul and didn't try to hide it.

Dr. Joe just stood in the corner and wept. The room began to gradually fill with people. The news was spreading. Amy came and brought the children from school. Grandpa and Grandma Jones joined us and then the pastor came and joined our prayer team. Soon the room was too full so people began to line the hallway. Some were praying, some were just silent. All were lives that she had touched.

Then something like a holy hush entered that room and silenced all of us. I looked up quickly to see if she was gone and looked directly into the face of Jesus. I don't know how I got so bold, but I began to plead.

"Please, Lord, don't take her. We need her."

"John," the Lord spoke patiently like speaking to a distraught child. "I came to tell you that I'm giving you five more years."

"Oh Lord, I'm so grateful for five years, but don't be angry with me, Lord, if I seem too bold, but could I please have more years than that? Our children won't be grown yet in five years and I would like to not have to spend a long time alone. You know how much I need that woman, Lord. Please have mercy on me."

"I have granted your request, John. I appreciate what you just did for me at Richards Plantation. But remember, just a few more years. I have need of her on the other side also." Then Jesus smiled at me. He wasn't angry. "John," He said, "you remind me of Abraham. I love you very much." When He said that, I felt His love going all through me. I fell at His feet but when I reached for them, he was gone. I arose slowly and looked around. Everyone was looking at Caroline. She had opened her eyes and was looking around.

"Where's John?" she asked.

"I'm right here," I said as I arose from my knees.

"I've been in Heaven, John. But Jesus said I had to come back because you were praying."

"I have been praying because you were dying and I wasn't ready to give you up."

So I took My Lady home and told her to rest up from her ordeal. But she couldn't seem to rest. She wanted to get on with her life again. She seemed to be in a hurry.

CHAPTER 58
Her View

When I got home from the hospital, I did a lot of thinking about how I should spend the time I had been given. I decided my first priority was the two children I had at home. I felt that they had been neglected during those terrible war years. I talked it over with John and he agreed. We had been depending on the school to educate our children and we hadn't done our part. So I started sewing lessons with Josie. And John started to take Big Guy with him and teach him how to run the ranch. They were both thrilled.

In two months' time, Josie was making her own doll clothes. She would work on them alone when I was busy elsewhere.

"Look, Mother, look what I made," she would say when she had found me in the garden.

After about six months, I began to encourage her to design her own clothes. She didn't hesitate and I was amazed at her skill.

"This is the one who will take over my mother's dress shop," I said to myself.

John said Joe was doing just as well on the ranch. He had a natural ability with animals. One day, he surprised us all by saying he wanted to be a veterinarian.

When a year had gone by, James Richards and his mother, Michelle appeared at our door. They had brought two wagons.

They stayed with us one night, then we put them up in the hotel. I was able to get Michelle a job in the childcare program at the hospital. James started working for John again so he was only with his mother on weekends.

I thought Zed Black and Jennie would end up getting married, but I was wrong. He married one of my Cherokee cousins. After a year, he was getting along with just a cane and he was glad that he went through all the suffering it took to save his leg. I had been taking my children out to visit our Cherokee relatives every week and that's when I saw him and visited with him. Zed was running the lawnmower shop and turning it into a hardware store. His sister was doing very well. I was glad to hear all the good news.

Then I noticed that James was going into town in the evenings once or twice a week besides on the weekends. I asked John if his mother was having problems.

"I think he's visiting Jennie Lu," he responded. "I think his mother is playing matchmaker. She met Jennie through the childcare program."

"Do you think he's really interested in her or just trying to get the property?" I asked.

"I don't think he knows who she is. He was telling me he'd met a nice young woman named Jennie Stone that he really liked and he was going to see her. I didn't let on that I had any connection."

"I'm going to go see her tomorrow and ask her to keep it quiet for a while. Someone will spill the beans eventually but I'd like to test him out for as long as we can," I said. John agreed.

I found Jennie in town on her lunch break and had an intense conversation for a few minutes. She agreed to keep her identity a secret for as long as she could. She also wanted to know if he was interested in her or her connection to us and all the property.

"I'll speak to the women in the childcare program to see if they've said anything to either of them and if not, I'll ask them to keep it quiet for a while. It's going to be hard though. We can't go anywhere that I'm not known."

"I know, but at least you have a different last name. That's a help."

Jennie told me later that the word must have spread through town like wildfire. Everywhere she went with James, everyone acted like they hardly knew her. She could hardly keep from laughing.

So for six months, I could only visit Jennie when I would sneak into town on her noon hour. Then she would let me know how things were going between her and James.

"He still hasn't figured out who I am," she laughed. "He thinks I came out here from the East to work in this hospital."

"Well, John just made him the foreman of the ranches and increased his pay."

"He told me that. He keeps asking me to go horseback riding with him out there and I keep making excuses. I'm not quite ready to let him know who I am."

Just then the waitress came to check on us.

"How long can we keep this game going?" she asked.

"I don't know," Jennie began to laugh. "Just a little longer. I really appreciate everyone's help."

When I got home, John informed me that we needed someone to manage the hotel. He wanted to know what I thought of hiring Michelle Richards. He was impressed with the way she had managed that plantation. So we headed back to town to talk to her.

She was excited about it when she found out she would have a nice apartment in the back of the hotel and her salary would be enough to live comfortably without help from James. He had been helping her from his salary at the ranch.

"I think James would like to get married, but he couldn't support a family and me at the same time," she explained.

We both just smiled and nodded.

John spent a week showing Michelle how to run the hotel. He said she was a fast learner and had already made some improvements. She related well to all the employees and John felt good about giving her the job. I just wondered if Michelle would be the one to take my place when I was gone. I knew I had a short time left down here.

The day finally came when Jennie let James know who she was. She asked him if he wanted to see where his father was buried. He did, so they rode horseback out to the Stone Place. Mr. and Mrs. Stone were living there and taking care of the museum. So they greeted Jennie very warmly and James was looking puzzled. Then Jennie showed him the mass grave that his father was in and the one Zacharias was in. Then she walked back toward the house and stopped at that grave stone.

"And this is my father's grave," she said.

"Your father?"

"Yes, my father."

"I thought you came here from the East?"

"I went to school in the East, but I was born and raised right here. I lived in that house at one time. Come inside and I'll show you more of it."

"Wait," he pleaded, "give me time to assimilate all this. Come and walk around with me and let me hold your hand while you explain things to me. I thought you were an outsider that I could bring in. But now I'm feeling like an outsider."

So Jenny patiently explained it all to him again. She even took him up to see her father's gold mine that he had died for.

"My mother buried him right here. I was sitting in the wagon, terrified."

"Who is your mother?"

"Caroline McLane."

James slapped his forehead and fell right to his knees.

"To think I've had the gall to be courting the daughter of the woman I tried to kill!" He got up and looked at Jennie. "If I had known I would never have dared to speak to you. Why didn't you tell me before this?"

"I wanted to test your motives."

So Jennie told him more of our story before bringing him back to the McLane House. There they announced their engagement. Jenny and I planned a quiet wedding this time, with only family and close friends present.

After the wedding, John and I agreed to make a will. We agreed that Jennie Lu would inherit the Stone Ranch and Joe and Josie would inherit the McLane Ranch equally with Jennie's oldest child, who John promised to treat like his own. All of the wealth from the gold mine would go to Jennie Lu at my death. We went to the bank and got Grandpa Jones to help us write it all up legally. I left my mother's dress shop, which I had bought from Grandpa Jones, to Josie.

By the time Josie was sixteen years old, she was quite a little business woman. Jack Slape, the young banker, was acting as her adviser. She had started dress shops in two other towns along the railroad line. She sent students from our school that she and I had trained to run them. When James saw what she was doing, he made a trip back to Richards Plantation and brought two of his half-sisters to be trained by us so they could start a shop. After a year, we sent them back with a wagon load of supplies.

"This is a startup gift," Josie explained, "but you'll have to send someone back to buy supplies. I've included a price list so you'll know how much it will cost. I won't have time to go to your place by wagon. I'll be busy on the railroad line."

When my children's eighteenth birthday approached, we planned a huge celebration. It was also a farewell for Joe. He was going away to school to become a veterinarian. It was at that party that Jack asked to speak to me in private.

"I just want to tell you how much I love Josie," he began. "I know you said we are cousins and I know I'm quite a bit older than she is. I don't want to do anything wrong but I can't help it. I want to ask her to marry me but not without your permission."

"Jack, you're not blood cousins. As far as I know, you're not related at all. And I don't know of anyone who would take better care of her than you. You've made a great team already."

"Does that mean I can ask her?"

"Yes, as far as I'm concerned, but we'd better ask for John's opinion."

John agreed with me and our party was expanded to include an engagement celebration. I was very happy to know that my daughter's future was secure.

That night as I sat with John in front of the fireplace, feeling very contented, I began to remember my trip to the other side.

"What are you thinking about?" John asked.

"I'm remembering my time on the other side."

"You mean Heaven?"

"Well, I'm not sure if it was Heaven or some other place. I didn't see any streets of gold."

"What did you see?"

"It was a place a lot like the earth. I was walking down a walkway on the side of a street. The walkway was hard and smooth, not like our boardwalks. The street was smooth like that, too. I didn't see any wagons or horses or carriages. On the side of the street where I was walking, there were some very nice houses—not mansions—but very nice. I thought they were made from bricks. On the other side, there was a very large park. I couldn't see the end of the park. There were many children running and playing in the park. Their laughter sounded like music. Then I noticed that when I took a deep breath, I could feel it going all through my body and healing and restoring me. That's when I realized I was not on the earth. Then I noticed that a fairly large building was being constructed in the park just across from the houses. So I walked right over to look at it. I didn't feel any hesitancy. I just walked right in and started looking around. It was beautiful but I was puzzled by one wall—or I should say—the absence of one wall. One end of what was obviously a classroom was open to the outdoors and I could not figure out how it was done. The room just seemed to melt into the outdoors and it wasn't unfinished, it was meant to be that way. While I was studying it, a man walked in from the other side of the room. I knew immediately that it was my father. But I didn't know how I knew because I'd never seen my father so young—with a full head of hair.

"'How do you like my building?' he asked.

"I didn't answer because I was grinning bigger and bigger. I could feel my smile stretching my face.

"So he took a second look at me and recognized me.

"'It's my little Caroline'" he exclaimed. 'No wonder they wouldn't tell me who they were bringing up to run this school!'

"He started toward me with arms outstretched, but just before he got to me, I was snatched away."

"I guess I was the one who snatched you away," John said.

"I guess so."

"Do you mind?"

"No, I'm glad to be finishing up my work down here. I'm very grateful for the years I've had here. But I still think about all those children."

Neither of us said anything for a while.

"Remember, John, it's been eight years. He said just a few over five," I concluded.

"I remember very well," he said as he held me closer.

"I've asked the Lord to let me be here for Josie's wedding."

"I'll have to ask them to postpone the wedding," John laughed.

As it turned out, they did postpone the wedding because they couldn't find a place to live and they didn't want to move in with us. So Jack started building a house for them. I should say, he hired some men to build it. It went up pretty fast, but it still took six months. That gave me more time to plan the wedding. Jennie helped me and Jerry was there to cook as usual. But when it was all over, I was exhausted.

"Why don't you and I take a second honeymoon," John suggested. "The trains go clear out to California now. We could go see the Pacific Ocean. Our kids are all on their own now."

So we did. It was wonderful. But when we got back, I was still tired. It seemed I was tired all the time. I spent a lot of time sitting in front of the fireplace. Sometimes, John would come and sit with me and we would remember old times. Then we would laugh and cry together.

"God has been so good to us!" we both agreed.

Sometimes when I would do my housework, I would get an ache in my chest. So then I would sit down again.

John and I went for carriage rides on Sunday afternoons. We visited all our friends and relatives. We even visited the Stone Place a few times. It was wonderful to have the war over.

It was exactly ten years after my near death experience that I was awakened in the middle of the night with a terrible pain in my chest. It was the worst pain I had ever felt, but I couldn't make a sound or move. I finally mustered all my willpower and managed to put my hand on John's arm, but I couldn't squeeze it and wake him up.

"Oh no," I thought. "When my hand is cold, it will wake him up and he'll know I tried to wake him and he'll feel bad." But I couldn't move it. Then I began to see people in the distance, waving at me. I recognized my parents and John's parents. Zach was there and many others.

Then I left my body and began to be pulled upward as if by a magnet. I hovered for a while, looking down at my body lying beside my husband. It seemed that I had to make a decision. I was hanging between two worlds. I compared the two. It seemed my work was done down there. I remembered all the children on the other side and decided to go on.

CHAPTER 59

His View

I'm growing old now. I walk the streets of this town that bears my name and most of the people don't even know who I am. Sometimes in the night, I feel that cold hand on my arm and I'm jerked awake again to find it was only a dream. But most of the time, I'm very happy. This town has grown so fast that I hardly recognize it. I stop in at My Lady's dress shop to see if Josie would happen to be there.

"Daddy!" she calls. "Come see my new addition."

She has set aside a room for Cherokee-style clothing. My Lady's Cherokee dress is hanging on the wall. Several of the Indian girls are working there, creating clothes. I walk over and touch that dress and then turn quickly and leave the room.

"Dad! Come see what else I'm doing."

The front part of the shop looks just the same, but the back has been expanded clear to the next street. They've made a parking area and Jack bought the land across that street and built a big two-story factory for Josie. But now they are building another big building which is to be apartments for the girls that are coming to work in the factory.

"They are taking up all the rooms in the hotel," Josie explained, "and the hospital was complaining. It's going to be called the Caroline Apartments."

I blink back the tears and give Josie a hug. Then I turn up Hospital Drive and head toward the Stone Memorial Hospital. I cross the street and go in the hotel to see if Michelle is busy. She and I have become good friends. I told her right from the beginning that

I never intend to marry again, but we could be friends, since we share the same grandchildren.

"John, so glad to see you. Do you know that we're invited to the McLane house for supper tonight?"

"Yes, I know. I was coming to see if you knew."

"Well, come in for a cup of coffee."

"You've sure done a great job with this hotel. This restaurant was a great idea. You've doubled the income."

"And you've doubled my salary."

When I left Michelle, I walked through the hospital on my way to my house behind the hospital. A few people waved at me, but most didn't know who I was. I walked up to the house that used to be My Lady's townhouse. Memories rushed through my mind and brought a few tears. In the last ten years, Jennie Lu had so many children that she gave up her nursing career to raise them. She and her family moved out to the McLane house and I moved into town. It's been a good trade off for all of us.

That evening at supper, I was surprised to see so many people.

"What's the occasion?" I asked.

"Today is the anniversary of the day that John McLane stopped at the Stone Place and changed our world and the future of this whole community."

Everyone broke into applause.

"Really?" I said. "Are you sure?"

"I have it right here in my journal," Jennie responded. "I was going through my mother's things that were left in this house and I found it. In those terrible days, I wrote something every day. It was like a school lesson for me. I would write and Mother would correct it. She was always trying to educate me, even though our situation seemed hopeless. You can see her marks in my journal," she said as she handed it to me.

I took the little book and read it through my tears.

"Did you know that your mother is teaching children somewhere on the other side?" I asked. Then I told them all the story she had told me.

I watched Jennie serving the food and controlling her family and I marveled.

"Jennie," I finally said. "Do you realize that you have become just like your mother? I thought you were going your own way and would be totally different, but you have gone around and come right back to your roots."

"I know," Jennie laughed. "Isn't it amazing? Do you suppose she can see down here?"

"I know they can sometimes," I responded. "Do you remember how I nearly lost my mind at her graveside?"

She remembered, but some of the others didn't know what I was talking about, so I told them.

"They brought her body out to bury it beside my parents. I went crazy when they threw the first shovel of dirt on that casket. I jumped into the grave and shouted, 'NO! NO! Don't throw dirt on her!.' I guess I thought I needed to rescue her again. I threw myself on her casket and started to cry my eyes out and I wasn't quiet about it. Everyone was embarrassed and didn't know what to do. Then I heard a voice calling me.

"'John! John!' He said and I knew it was Jesus who had appeared to me the first time she died.

"'Look up, John!' He said.

"So I slowly raised my head and looked into the sky. There I saw Caroline with her parents and my parents and her cousin and Jimmy was there and many others.

"'I'm up here, John,' she called. 'I'm not in that grave. I'm happy up here. We all are. You'll be with us in a little while.'

"I watched until they faded from sight and then I climbed out of the grave.

"'Go ahead!' I said. 'She's not in that box. That's just a discarded shell.'"

Mrs. Stone was writing as fast as she could.

"I want to record all of your story for your descendants," she explained.

"Since that time, we've sent a lot of people up there. Grandpa and Mrs. Jones, Jerry, Mrs. Tate, Zed Black's mother, and I'm just waiting for my turn."

"Well, as long as you're with us, we're going to celebrate this day," Jennie said. "But I don't think your work down here is over yet."

"What else is there for me?"

"Well, Dr. Joe is concerned about Mr. Tate. He's been in the hospital, you know."

"Yes."

"He could go home now, but not to live alone."

"His son never came back?"

"No, so Dr. Joe asked me about turning my house into a home for the elderly since it's so near the hospital. They could send someone there as often as needed."

"Well, I sure can't turn Ol' Tate away. Can he bathe himself?"

"He can as long as someone is there in case he falls. He has a chair with wheels and he can walk short distances."

"I know he's had the shakes pretty bad for a while."

"I told Dr. Joe that you were living there now so it would be up to you," Jennie concluded.

"Well, here I am with another job. Even my old age has been redeemed!

"Now, there is something I need to explain to all of you," I said. "My wife and I made a will before she died. In that will, Jenny Lu's daughter Flora Mae has equal standing with our children. Because of the marriage covenant I made with Jennie Lu's mother, all of her children are my grandchildren. But Flora Mae McLane is also connected to me by bloodline relationship because her father Jimmy McLane was my brother. Therefore, I am her uncle by blood. When Jimmy went away to war, he said that he was laying down his life so that the rest of us could live. We were all guilty before God for the sin of slavery even though we didn't participate. We looked the other way and let it go on for many years. He said that God would accept his sacrifice and let the rest of us go free. And it was by God's grace that none of us were at the Stone Place when the attack came. Before he left, he asked me to be a father to his daughter, and I promised that

I would. So because of that promise, she is my daughter. So I am connected to her by three strong cords that cannot be broken. One is a covenant, one is a bloodline, and one is a promise.

"I just want the other grandchildren to know why she has a special place. I love you all equally. But I must honor her position."

By the end of that speech, Flora Mae was standing by my side. There were tears in her eyes.

"My grandfather, my uncle, and my father," she said. "I have not always appreciated you. Sometimes I was angry and blamed you for letting my father go off to that war and die alone, but you have been so faithful to me and I intend to be faithful to you in your old age."

Then James came forward.

"I also want to express my gratitude and loyalty to you," he said. "I come from a family committed to be your enemies, but you forgave me and have made me your son-in-law. You have even made me the overseer of all your property and I intend to see that all your descendants inherit a rich reward."

"I have to give my wife credit for that," I said. "I was ready to let you reap what you had sown, but she interceded for you and turned my heart toward you. She sent me to rescue you and your mother even though it almost cost her life. And now you both are a great blessing to me."

Then Little John came forward.

"I want to thank you for honoring the Cherokee blood that you brought into your family. Though we were outcasts, you brought us in and have made us an honored part of this community. You have encouraged your children to honor their heritage and that has blessed all of us."

"I wish my wife could hear all of this," I said. "I couldn't have accomplished anything without her. It was because of her that I did all these things."

"I have made a painting of you and her together," Little John said as he brought it out and presented it to me. "This is how I will always remember you."

It was so real that I began to weep. I still missed her so much.

"We will put this in a prominent place in town to help us all remember," he continued.

The rest of that evening we spent remembering and thanking God for His blessings upon us. Sometimes I thought Caroline was there, but when I looked around, I was always disappointed. But I know it won't be long until we're together again.

ABOUT THE AUTHOR

My husband and I have been missionaries and church planters for the last fifty years.